WHISPERS OF RUIN

THE SHADOW REALMS
BOOK 10

BRENDA K DAVIES

Brenda K Davies

CHAPTER ONE

KAYLIA'S HAIR stuck to her cheeks as she used her small sword to hack through the endless jungle of Doomed Valley. She'd known coming to this place of lore, where few survived, would be difficult, but she hadn't considered that she'd be constantly surrounded by dense, green foliage shrouding her like a warm blanket.

The thickness of the jungle also blocked her view of nearly everything more than a foot away from her... including her allies on this trip. Even worse, it prevented her from seeing the countless enemies lurking in the vegetation.

And though she couldn't see them, she felt eyes following her every move. Somewhere in this land of green, humidity, and bugs, something was salivating over the idea of eating her; she was sure of it.

Glancing nervously at the trees overhead, she expected to see some beast crouched there, waiting to pounce, but the limbs remained barren of anything more than leaves and vines. Kaylia slapped at a bug buzzing around her ear before using her sword to cut through more vines.

Brokk, who was somewhere ahead of her, had already

slashed through this area, but the jungle had closed around him after he passed to block the way for the rest of them. Brokk's sword thwacked against the plants as he hacked at them.

Only a few feet separated them, but she couldn't see him. If something happened to him, she wouldn't know until either the noise stopped or she encountered his remains. She shuddered at the possibility and swallowed to get some moisture into her parched throat.

She'd never suffered from claustrophobia before, but as the vegetation crowded her, it felt like the jungle was determined to bury her in its verdant tomb… just as it had so many before her. Kaylia swatted at another bug before tugging at the collar of the green tunic cleaving to her.

She could be walking through her graveyard right now. She tugged a little more at her collar.

This is not the time. Get it together, or you really will die here.

That was so true, and since she had no intention of dying in this place, she wouldn't let her imagination run away with her… no matter how many monsters it conjured. There were plenty of real monsters to be concerned about in this place.

She would give anything for some armor, but after the first hour here, she'd learned wearing her lightweight protection and not dropping from dehydration were two things that could never go together here. She'd peeled it off and left it behind. Packing it into her bag wasn't an option; the last thing she needed was more weight slowing her down.

Kaylia lifted her tired arm to cut through more vines and leaves but froze when she spotted the symbol carved into a tree trunk at least fifteen feet in diameter. She lowered her sword and stepped closer to the tree.

Her fingers traced over the symbol of a circular snake eating its tail. She recognized the ouroboros and had seen it before entering this realm, but she'd seen it far more since entering here than elsewhere.

The symbol didn't feel anywhere near as innocuous in Doomed Valley as it did in other realms. She didn't know why someone or something had put it here, but nothing was *ever* innocent in this realm.

But it didn't matter; she couldn't stand here and stare at the thing. She had to get moving, or the lycan behind her would cut her in two before realizing she was here.

CHAPTER TWO

WIPING the sweat from her forehead, she lifted her sword and carved through the vines blocking her way. Every part of her ached, and she was as wet as if she'd jumped into a lake with all her clothes on, but stopping wasn't an option.

As she worked through the jungle, she tried listening for anything hunting them, but it was impossible to hear much beyond the thwacks of those surrounding her. Anything could be tracking them through the foliage, and they would never know until it pounced.

Just like they'd never known about the beast who stole the dwarf from their campsite shortly after arriving here. That creature came in and dragged the dwarf into the night before they ever saw their foe.

She didn't have a chance to put up a protection spell before the beast attacked. The dwarf's fingers had left deep gouges in the earth as it tried to keep from being torn away, but none of them had seen it happen.

The reminder caused the hair on her nape to rise, and she glanced nervously overhead again. Nothing was perched there, but it could happen so fast that she might never know a creature was there until it landed on her back and tore out her spine.

Stop it!

Her mother used to say her big imagination, with all its fantastic ideas and stories, was a blessing. It felt like a curse in this place.

Kaylia absently rubbed her neck before scratching a bug bite and continuing. Not only did they have to worry about the unseen beasts at night, but also the whispers.

Those incessant mutterings had etched onto her brain, where they haunted her days even though they only came when the sun set. She couldn't make out what the whispers said other than their names on occasion, but deep in her soul, she knew they spelled ruin.

Kaylia wiped the endless sweat from her brow and resisted the urge to sit down as she continued through the jungle. It would be easy to open a portal and leave this place, but they were here for crudue vine to save Lexi.

They couldn't turn back without it, but they could send someone back to Dragonia to see if anyone else had found the vine. It would have to happen eventually, but no one had mentioned it yet.

Probably because leaving here and returning to the exact spot would be difficult. Not only did everything here look the same, but she swore the jungle changed around them.

This place was a living, breathing entity hell-bent on destroying all who came here. Returning to the same location in this place of endless green, trees, and humidity could prove impossible if they left. She hadn't seen anything to differentiate one spot from another.

Without a clear marker, they could open a portal and return anywhere in this place. They could search land they'd already explored or start somewhere new and have no idea they were doing such a thing, which would be a colossal waste of time.

They could leave a portal open, which could prove extremely dangerous for anyone who happened upon it. Or, worse, they could let something free into the realms that was *never* supposed to leave this one.

It was a problem they'd have to figure out when the time came. For now, she had to remain focused on getting through this coffin of green.

A rustle to her left had her turning her head in that direction. Tensing, her fingers tightened on her sword as she braced for an attack.

CHAPTER THREE

THE LEAVES beside her rustled and swayed before parting. A head popped through them.

Kaylia froze, uncertain of what to do about the adorable creature. Her sword remained raised as she stared into a pair of big, brown eyes fringed with thick black lashes. A long, furry gray snout protruded beneath those deerlike, soulful eyes.

The creature blinked at her before stretching its head closer. Kaylia braced herself to slice through the creature's slender neck.

It may look all cute and cuddly, and she *hated* the idea of killing any living thing, but if this animal was like everything else in this realm, it was about to take a bite out of her arm or spit poison in her face. Instead of trying to eat her, the creature sniffed and pulled its mouth into something resembling a smile before vanishing into the jungle.

Despite not having been eaten, Kaylia didn't relax. For all she knew, it had decided she smelled delicious and left to gather a horde of big-eyed creatures, all eager to devour her.

She wasn't in the mood to be someone's lunch today, and she doubted it would be any cooler for her in the bowels of some fluffy beast. She waited a few more seconds, but when a group of those animals didn't return to pounce on her, she started carving through the jungle again.

After another hundred feet, she stopped when she spotted another ouroboros carved into the thick brown trunk of a towering tree. Her head tilted to the side as she examined it.

The symbol was almost identical to the last one, but there were small differences. The circle wasn't as perfect, and the snake wasn't as detailed. Different hands had carved them.

She didn't understand *why* someone bothered to carve the circle of a snake eating its tail into the various trees and rocks they'd found since arriving here.

Running her fingers along the symbol, she felt no power from it, but that didn't mean anything. There could be an old, faded magic in it or one she couldn't penetrate. As a witch, she was very attuned to the world and anything enchanted, but there were powers even she couldn't penetrate or detect.

However, she didn't think this symbol was magical. It felt more like someone or something marking its territory.

And she didn't want to know what that something or someone was. She hoped never to encounter them as she had no idea what would happen if someone discovered them where they shouldn't be.

With a sigh, she lowered her hand and started through the dense foliage again. Trees brushed her face, and the vines clung to her arms as they tried to hold her back, capture her, or offer her up as some sacrifice to all the deadly things surrounding her.

Her skin itched from the pollen coating the leaves and trans-ferring to her. She slapped away more bugs before scratching at one of the many bites on her arm. Between the bugs, the heat, and the pollen, she felt half ready to crawl out of her skin.

While she worked tirelessly to carve her way through the jungle, she pondered everything she knew about the ouroboros. Many believed it symbolized rebirth, immortality, protection,

WHISPERS OF RUIN   11

self-reliance, unity, and nature's cycles. They saw it as a good thing.

Yet she'd heard others say it was a symbol of doom, a representation of those condemned to repeat the same mistakes over and over again, going in circles, chasing one's tail. And some saw it as a sign of evil.

She'd never given it much consideration before; she'd never had a reason to... until now. In this place, she could only see it as a symbol of doom, and she truly hoped they weren't going in circles in this forsaken land.

A shout up ahead jerked her from her reverie as another shout followed it. They didn't sound hurt or scared, but something about the tone spurred her into motion.

Kaylia forgot about the symbol as she hurried to catch up with the others.

CHAPTER FOUR

THOUGH BROKK WAS ONLY a few feet before her, the jungle had already moved in again to cover his trail. Some dismantled branches guided her onward as she carved her way toward the voices ahead.

Finally, after what felt like hours but was probably only a minute or two, the cloying foliage gave way to a small opening. She was about to step from the jungle when something buzzed in her ear before darting down to bite her neck.

Kaylia slapped the offending creature and pulled her hand away to discover blood and a flattened insect almost the size of her palm. Thankfully, she'd brought an ointment that cleared up the countless bug bites she'd received, but she couldn't put it on until they stopped for the night. Until then, she'd remain a bitten, itchy mess.

Wiping her palm on her pants, she stepped into the small clearing and took in her surroundings. Brokk stood to her left with his sword at his side and his aqua-blue eyes fixed on the trees.

The sweat dampening his hair had turned its dark blond shade almost brunet as it stood up in disheveled angles around his wide cheekbones. Light brown stubble lined his square jaw, giving him a more menacing air than she'd grown accustomed to before arriving here.

She'd only seen him clean-shaven, but shaving in a jungle wasn't easy. The black tunic with green piping he wore cleaved to his lean frame, and the hint of a black cipher showed at his neck, but more of the dark fae markings spread out beneath his short sleeves; they flowed down to his wrists.

Kaylia couldn't deny that he was a handsome man who radiated power. However, that didn't matter to her anymore; she'd given her heart to Fabian years ago, and he still possessed it. He always would.

When Kaylia shifted her attention to the valley below, she felt Brokk's eyes flick to her, but she didn't look at him again as she drank in the verdant splendor sprawled out before them. This must have been the reason for the shouts, a warning there was a break in the jungle, a place where they could rest and eat before plunging back into its suffocating depths.

The trees didn't appear as large down in the valley, but that was probably because she stood on this ledge, looking down on them. Once she was back amongst them, she was sure they would tower over her as they did now.

What remained of their group filed out of the jungle behind her to gather on the ledge. They still had seven lycans, two dwarves, and two, full-blooded dark fae on this journey with them.

Many powerful immortals remained with her, but they could have brought an army into this place, and it still wouldn't have felt like enough. This place was too vast and too deadly.

"We should rest here and eat before entering the valley," Brokk said.

When he spoke, the tips of his fangs were barely visible, though they weren't extended. A vampire could never completely hide their fangs. That sight used to make her stomach turn, but she didn't mind Brokk's fangs.

Kaylia shaded her eyes to study the sky. The sun was just past its zenith. It felt like days had passed since they'd continued their journey this morning, but they'd only been walking for five or six hours.

Afraid if she took a break she might not get up again, Kaylia slowly sank to the ground and bit back a moan as she eased her weight from her aching feet and legs. She'd often spent days outside, harvesting ingredients for spells, basking in nature, running naked through fields, and dancing beneath the moon, but this realm was a different level of exertion and exhaustion.

She'd sell her soul for a shower or a plunge into an icy stream where she could cool off and lay in the water, letting it soothe and strengthen her. They'd yet to find a water supply, but it had to be out there. This place was too lush and green not to have a water supply somewhere.

Still, no matter how bad or gross she felt, she had no intention of opening a portal and leaving this place. She would *never* leave Lexi trapped in the stone-like state Kaylia had frozen her in to save the young woman's life.

Not only had she come to consider the young arach queen family, but they'd all fought too hard and lost too much to put Lexi on the throne where she belonged. They couldn't lose it all now.

She wouldn't allow the Shadow Realms to tumble into chaos again, and they would if they lost the last living arach. Lexi was the only one who could harness the power of the throne and control the dragons without going mad.

Whoever else sat on that throne and controlled the dragons would go insane from its magic... as so many already had. After everything they'd been through, and all the lives lost, Kaylia wasn't about to let that happen.

Keeping her eyes on the valley, she tugged off her pack and

set it in front of her. She pulled at her tunic before opening her bag and pawing through it.

She would have preferred the cool comfort of one of her dresses to the pants hugging her legs, but trekking through the jungle in a dress would probably be the worst decision she'd ever made, and she'd made quite a few over her lengthy lifetime. It was impossible not to after all the years she'd lived.

She contemplated putting some salve on her bug bites now, but the little bloodsuckers would feast a lot more before this day was over. Originally, she cast a few spells to keep them away, but the determined insects always managed to find a way around it.

If she had the power, she'd eradicate every bug in this jungle, but that was beyond her abilities. She'd gotten more used to the insects, but still loathed them.

Removing some dried apple slices, cheese, and her canteen full of water, Kaylia munched on her lunch. It all looked so peaceful down there, but she knew more death awaited them among the trees.

CHAPTER FIVE

BROKK BIT into a piece of dried venison while he surveyed the land below. If it was anything like what they'd already traversed today, the journey ahead would be miserable, but they'd come this far. There was no turning back now.

He looked over what remained of their small contingent before his gaze settled on Kaylia. She'd pulled her knee-length, silvery blonde hair into a braid she'd encircled around her head and pinned into place. Strands of it had fallen free to frame her oval face, and exertion and heat had flushed her cheeks.

Her translucent, pewter gray eyes were wary as she bit into one of her apple slices and absently waved away a mosquito. The sun filtering through the thick canopy of leaves shimmered off her hair and emphasized her aquiline nose, rosebud lips, and the slight cleft in her stubborn chin.

Even with streaks of dirt marring her ivory skin and sweat beading her forehead to slide down her cheeks, she was still one of the most striking women he'd ever seen, and he'd seen many. At first, he'd really disliked her; she'd been cold, vicious, and had an unreasonable hatred of vampires that pissed him off.

Yes, all witches and vampires had been at war ever since a

vampire killed the last witch queen eight hundred years ago, but her loathing for vamps was over the top. He didn't know if she'd been good friends with that queen, and he hadn't cared at the time; he'd just wanted her to help them without throwing a tantrum and tossing him and Sahira out of her home.

It had taken some maneuvering, but they finally agreed to get her to give them the harrow stone and help in their fight against the Lord. She'd still been bitchy about him and Sahira for a while, but most of her attitude had faded with time.

Time and circumstances changed things like that. Fighting for one's life and the freedom of the realms had a way of creating bonds between immortals. He'd forged a few bonds he never would have seen coming while fighting to remove the Lord from the throne that belonged to Lexi.

One of those bonds was Kaylia.

And as they worked together more, Brokk went from barely tolerating the witch to gradually liking her more and more. She was strong, ferocious, and loyal. There wasn't anything she wouldn't do to ensure the Shadow Realms stayed safe and Lexi retained her throne, including coming to this forsaken hellhole.

Now, not only did he like her, but there were times when he couldn't take his eyes off her. He'd always wanted to fuck her and would have even when he borderline hated her—he was a man and a dark fae, after all, and she was gorgeous—but he also found himself oddly fascinated with her.

It was a strange sensation, and one he wasn't familiar with when it came to women, but he couldn't take his gaze off her when he should pay attention to his surroundings. With a concerted effort, he tore his attention away from Kaylia and focused on the deadly land again.

CHAPTER SIX

Around him, the others ate, too, but the food only sated some of a dark fae's hungers. Thankfully, the three lycan women were more than open to accommodating the needs of the dark fae with them.

If they stayed here long enough, Brokk would have to turn to one of the lycans as the other dark fae had, but because he was only half dark fae, he didn't have to feed as often. To satisfy his vampire thirst, he'd brought a couple of bags of blood with him, and he could hunt. He'd already hunted and fed from one of the many creatures here.

He wasn't exactly looking forward to screwing one of the lycans. Although they were usually a fantastic screw, wild and eager, they weren't what he truly desired. His gaze strayed to Kaylia again, but even with her improving attitude toward vamps, he doubted she'd let him feed from her.

If she would, he'd feast on her and enjoy every second of it. But since that wouldn't happen, he'd have to settle for one of the lycans.

As he contemplated it, his stomach did a strange, turning

sensation, but he ignored it. He'd do whatever it took to survive and not starve or become weakened by hunger. Any weakness in this place would result in death.

Hopefully, they'd find the crudue vine and be gone from here before that became necessary. *But it still won't be her.*

His gaze returned to Kaylia. The hunger that hadn't stirred for the lycans woke as he eyed her. He quickly shoved it aside. There was no point in contemplating things that could never be.

They'd forged a friendship through plotting, blood, and death, but it would never be anything more; she'd never allow it. She'd warmed toward him but retained some distance, and he'd never seen her show any interest in a man, which was strange as most immortals embraced their sexuality and relished in it—not as much as the dark fae, but they all still enjoyed fucking.

He didn't understand her indifference toward sex and was curious as to why she didn't embrace her sexuality more, but they hadn't become friendly enough for him to ask questions like that. Maybe one day, but he doubted it.

He bit off more of his dried meat as he focused on something other than her. He smacked away an annoying bug and chomped more angrily on his food.

As a kid, he'd dreamed of exploring Doomed Valley. He'd read every story he could find on it and been determined to enter the mysterious land as soon as he was old enough.

When he became a man, he'd realized he preferred women and luxury to jungles and monstrous creatures. The first time he had sex, his dreams of exploring Doomed Valley vanished, and he'd never regretted it.

Now, he was a brother seeking to save the only woman his brother had ever loved. He wouldn't let Cole down, which meant he wouldn't leave this jungle until he had the crudue vine in hand.

Everyone with him had come because they were looking to keep Lexi on the throne, and while he was here for that, too, he was also here to save his brother. He'd already lost five of his brothers during the war against the Lord; he wouldn't lose Cole as well.

He loved Lexi; she'd helped save his life after a dark fae ran him through with a sword, and her presence on the throne would save countless lives. He would do everything he could to save her, but the idea of losing Cole propelled him into Doomed Valley.

Also, if Lexi died, the Shadow Reaver would destroy them all, and he didn't feel like being torn apart by shadows unleashed by the brother he considered his best friend.

At the memory of what Cole could do with those shadows, and how close they'd already come to losing him once, the dried meat became more like sawdust in his mouth. He shoved it back into his pack, took a swig of water, and stored everything away again.

He started to rise, but vibrations in the earth stopped him. Brokk frowned as he placed his palm flat against the ground, but what he felt wasn't what unnerved him most; it was the slow way Kaylia's head came up and turned toward the jungle.

Witches were far more in tune with the earth than other immortals; whereas he could barely feel a rumble that made him curious, the color drained from her face. She started shoving her things into her pack.

"We have to go!" she shouted as she worked.

The others all turned to look at her with confusion, but Brokk threw his pack onto his shoulders. Sensing Kaylia's urgency, they all packed up and rose.

Kaylia was on her feet with her bag halfway on her shoulders when the ground started shaking enough to vibrate his legs. Deep within the jungle trees, branches snapped as something thundered through them.

Brokk turned to see what was barreling toward them, but the wall of green was so thick it was impossible to see whatever was rapidly approaching. The cracking of trees grew louder as some of the taller ones overhead vanished like they'd been ripped from the earth and thrown to the ground.

"Shit." Brokk had no idea what was coming for them, but it was coming fast. "Run!"

CHAPTER SEVEN

KAYLIA'S HEART clenched as she plunged over the ledge into the jungle below. The hill was so steep she couldn't run. Instead, she slid down as dirt and debris kicked out from under her feet.

This section of the jungle wasn't as thick as what they left behind, so she didn't have to slash her way through the dense foliage. Instead, she skidded, slipped, and nearly went down as the earth fell away beneath her.

Every rapid beat of her heart screamed at her to move faster, but it was impossible as branches, leaves, and vines slapped and stuck to her. It was as if they were trying to capture and hold her prisoner so that whatever followed could destroy her.

Frustration filled her as she yanked against a vine clinging to her forearm and threw herself forward. She barely managed to keep herself from plunging to the ground, and the only reason she succeeded in staying on her feet was because her shoulder slammed into a tree and jerked her backward and upright again.

She jumped over a fallen tree and skidded further down the hill as thunderous crashes followed her. The ground vibrated so violently it pitched her off her feet a few times while breaking trees screeched their protests and crashed to the earth.

Halfway down the hill, she encountered a thick wall of brambles spreading through the jungle. In front of her, Brokk elegantly darted to the side to avoid the thorns and sprinted down the hill.

Kaylia spun to the side to avoid plunging into them and successfully trapping herself for whatever hunted her. Thorns ripped at her arms, shredded her flesh, and spilled her blood as they tore across her.

A cry alerted her that one of the dwarfs wasn't fast enough to escape the brambles. She looked up in time to see the pained expression on the man's face before momentum carried her further down the hill and away from the dwarf.

There wasn't anything she could have done to save him as the vibrations closed in on them, but guilt tore at her as she left him behind. She could only hope he managed to get a portal open in time to flee or somehow managed to free himself.

She doubted the portal was an option as he'd have to free himself from the brambles enough to enter it. Kaylia almost looked back to see what happened but stopped herself; seeing the outcome wouldn't accomplish anything. All she could do was run.

But no matter how fast she ran, the vibrations grew closer, the earth shook more, and the trees around her swayed from the impact. She didn't dare look back to see what awaited them, but she practically felt it breathing down her neck.

She could open a portal but might never locate this spot in Doomed Valley again if she did. She might be leaving behind everyone who had come to rely on her, and worse, whatever chased them could follow her through the portal and into another realm.

She didn't have to see it to know she could never set the monster behind her free on the realms; it would only result in a lot of death if she did. Leaving the dwarf behind was bad enough; being the cause of the loss of numerous lives would be far worse.

Brokk jumped onto a log and leapt over it as he hurtled down the hill. She'd always considered herself graceful, but he moved with the speed and dexterity of the dark fae and the vampires; it was breathtaking to watch… if she had any breath left in her lungs.

Kaylia stopped skidding enough to leap onto the log and over it. When she landed, she stumbled a few feet before a tree branch caught in the back of her shirt. She jerked herself free and followed Brokk down the hill.

Somewhere behind her, someone shrieked. A few seconds later, one of the dark fae flew past her. She couldn't tell which one it was as it flashed past her in a tumult of black hair and streaks of red. It took her a few seconds to realize the red was blood.

When the dark fae crashed into a tree, a massive beast raced past her. With a snap of its hooked, bony snout, it bit down on the fae's legs and snatched him off the ground.

The man howled as he beat at the creature while it chomped down on him again. Kaylia inwardly screamed against the brutality of the attack and threw up her hands to… to… she had no idea what spell could free the man from this when she couldn't have freed the dwarf, but she hated the helpless feeling engulfing her.

Ahead of her, Brokk turned back like he was going to help the fae, but before he could do anything, another enormous creature surged out of the woods and clamped down on the top half of the fae. They tore at the man, each fighting over their half until they ripped him in two.

Before she could blink, they gulped down their prizes. Wrath crossed Brokk's face as he sprinted back toward her, but his movements slowed as he tried to scale the hill.

"Hurry!" he yelled at her.

He had given up trying to flee these beasts and would now stand his ground, but she didn't know how any of them could make a stance against these monstrosities. From what she'd glimpsed of them, they consisted of more bone than flesh, and that bone didn't reveal any weak spots.

They looked like armored dinosaurs with thick plates surrounding heads larger than a rhino's. *Oh, Hecate.*

They had to open a portal; it was their only chance of surviving this, but they'd lose so much if they did and risked hurting so many others. Every survival instinct she had screamed at her to flee this place, but she kept her hands by her side and didn't open a path to freedom.

Arriving at her side, Brokk gripped her arms and pulled her in front of him as a lycan soared over their head and smashed into a tree. The tall, powerful woman hung there briefly before sliding down to the ground.

Brokk nudged her forward. "Run!"

Only five feet separated them from the lycan, and Brokk ran toward the woman. Before he could get to her, a mouth fastened onto the woman.

CHAPTER EIGHT

BROKK STAGGERED BACK as the gigantic jaws closed inches away from him. Before he could do anything more than stare, it gulped the lycan down.

When the woman's feet vanished from view, the beast's head swiveled toward him. Knowing it would eat him even if it was full, Brokk unleashed a punch that shot the creature's head to the side. A crack accompanied the blow as his knuckles caved in, and agony exploded up his arm.

With the creature distracted, he sprinted back into the woods in pursuit of Kaylia and the others. He wasn't sure how many others were still out there or ahead of them.

He glimpsed some of them running through the woods, barreling toward an unknown future. They all could have fled through a portal, but they must have all come to the same conclusion as him... opening a portal now could end in disaster if these things were allowed free in the realms.

Most immortals could be selfish pricks, himself included sometimes, but everyone here had battled to make the realms safer; they weren't about to unleash a fresh hell on them. Maybe some had opened a portal and fled; he doubted it. They were in this to the end, even if that end was barreling toward them.

Ahead of him, a branch caught on Kaylia's bun. The stick worked through the thick strands as she ran and tore the bun free. Streamers of silvery blonde hair dangled from the branch while the braid whipped behind her like a banner.

He could teleport out of this mess, but he was the only one, and he wasn't going to leave the others behind to save his ass. He leapt over another log, skidded around a large rock, and jumped a small creature that screamed as it raced out of the way.

No matter how fast he moved, he couldn't get away as hot, fetid breath kissed his neck. It blew down his shirt and tickled his hair, but before the creature could spear him, Brokk threw himself onto the ground and rolled.

As he bounced down the hill, he saw the beast's horn thrusting forward into the space where he'd been. If he was still there, it would have speared him through.

Another agonized scream pierced the air; it started high before gurgling and cutting off. The ground heaved beneath the weight of the beast's feet, tossing Brokk off the ground and into a tree.

His breath exploded out of him, and while he struggled to get air into his lungs, he got his hands underneath him, pushed himself up, and ran. His chest burned, and his body protested movement as his cells screamed for oxygen.

He couldn't stop, though; stopping meant death. Finally, after a few feet, his chest muscles relaxed enough for him to suck in a wheezing breath as, all around him, trees toppled beneath the rampage of the beasts bearing down on them.

Kaylia was to his left now and further ahead. To his right, a female dwarf spun and slashed out with her battle-ax. It crashed against the beast's three-foot-long horn, driving it into the earth.

The dwarf started to lift her axe when another beast lunged forward and closed its beak on her head. It lifted her into the air, tossed her up, and opened its mouth to gulp her down whole like a pelican with a fish.

Fuck.

This time, while he ran, Brokk pulled the shadows around him and enveloped himself in their dark embrace. He vanished from view.

Pouring on the speed, he raced down the hill after Kaylia, the only one he could still see and knew for certain was alive. They could look for any other survivors afterward, but as another scream filled the air and the creatures all shifted their attention to them, Brokk doubted there were any other survivors.

Forcing himself to relax, he pictured reaching her and touching her and felt his body give way as he transported to within a few feet of her. He went to grab her to enshroud her in shadows too, but she released a cry and plummeted to the ground.

Her fall alerted him to the large branch sprawled across the ground. He jumped over it as she bounced down the hill, her hands over her head as she sought to protect herself.

Kaylia flew three feet into the air and crashed to the ground again before jumping to her feet and sprinting down the hill. Brokk's heart lodged in his throat as panic dug into his chest. He couldn't let anything happen to her.

I have to get to her! He didn't question the intensity of his need to do so; he pushed himself faster while weaving in and out of the creatures destroying everything in their path as they barreled down the hill.

The size of a tank, the monsters were as solidly built as the humans' war machines that had proven useless against the Lord and dragons. During his nightmares, Brokk could still see those lumbering machines burning beneath the dragon's fire as the mortal occupants screamed.

During his worst moments, the smell of their burning flesh would return to haunt him as if he were still there on that battlefield, questioning why anyone would unleash such torment on a species so much weaker than them. But then, the Lord had never been sane, reasonable, or filled with any mercy.

The sound of these things brought those memories back to him. For a second, they nearly buried him, and he had to fight to stay grounded in the here and now as he sought to escape this mess with Kaylia at his side… if he could.

CHAPTER NINE

STILL ENSHROUDED IN SHADOWS, Brokk ducked a horn and raced down the hill after Kaylia as all the beasts focused on her. They were determined to get one last snack in before the end of this shitty day, but he refused to let that happen.

He teleported close to her again, but her momentum kept her out of his reach; at least he was closer. He couldn't try getting in front of her; if she crashed into him and sent them flying before he got the shadows around her, it could prove disastrous.

Brokk was only five feet away and closing fast when she shoved back a grouping of large branches, ran forward, and vanished. Used to losing sight of the others in this place, Brokk didn't slow as he sprinted toward where he last saw Kaylia.

It wasn't until he was crashing into the thick branches that he realized the creatures had eased up in their chase. Their large hooves plowed up the earth as they skidded to a stop behind him.

A chill trickled down his spine a second before the ground gave way. Instinctively, he leapt for one of the vines dangling from a tree he'd just pushed through.

His broken hand protested the movement as his fingers locked around the vine, and he swung out over a sea of white. He closed his legs around the vine and gripped it with both hands as he swung back toward the shoreline, where the beasts huffed and puffed while pawing the ground.

He didn't get close enough for those things to grasp him, but it didn't matter as shadows still cloaked him, and they were gazing forlornly at Kaylia. Brokk frowned as he looked from the beasts to the sea.

He had no idea what it was, but it covered Kaylia up to her chest. She was easy pickings for those things, but they refused to go after her.

That can't be a good sign.

Kaylia held her hands over her head as the dozen or so creatures gave one last huffing breath and turned away. Their feet thudded against the ground and vibrated the white sea as they retreated up the hill and into the jungle.

Once they were gone, Kaylia's shoulders sagged a little, but she kept her hands over her head as she struggled to move through the thick, white goo. Releasing the shadows cloaking him, Brokk revealed himself as he swung back over her.

Kaylia squeaked and leaned away from him before righting herself. While doing so, she sank deeper into the muck.

"How long have you been there?" she demanded.

"Not long. Are you okay?"

"I'm alive; how about you?"

"Same."

"Where did those things go?"

"Back up the hill."

"Good. They were assholes."

Brokk chuckled as the vine slowed its swinging. "They were."

"What about the others?"

"I don't know. I haven't seen or heard any of them, and in the end, those creatures were all focused on you. One or two of them might have gotten away, but I think they're all dead. We can look after we get you out of there."

He scooted further down the vine and ensured his legs were latched securely around it before releasing it. He fell, so he was bent backward, and his arms dangled over his head.

His pack shifted so it pressed against the back of his head and shoulders but remained secured to him. Kaylia stretched her fingers toward him, but the second she moved, the substance tugged at her, pulling her further down.

A small whimper escaped before she suppressed it and stubbornly lifted her chin. Her fingers strained toward him, and he stretched further until he bent his back into an angle it did not appreciate.

Frustration filled him as their fingertips brushed a few times, but he couldn't connect more than that. Gritting his teeth, he strained further until something cracked in his back, but he refused to lose her.

CHAPTER TEN

THEIR FINGERS BRUSHED... *so close.* An electric thrill ran through him at the sensation of her skin. It was unexpected and unfamiliar, but it shot from his fingers to his toes.

He stretched a little further, pushing his body to the limit. *Almost there. Almost there.* Only centimeters away, he could almost feel her skin again and the reaction it incited in him.

Another skim of fingers, his muscles ached from being pushed to their limits, but just when he thought this would never work, they closed the distance enough for her fingers to grasp his broken hand.

Brokk didn't make a sound as his bones scraped together and shifted beneath her hand. If she knew she was hurting him, she might let go, and he'd never get his hands on her again.

The muscles in his arm strained as he managed to pull her up enough to reach her with his other hand. Finally getting a good grip, he clasped her arm in both of his and groaned as he worked to pull her from the mire. The more he pulled, the more it sucked at her until her arm slipped a little.

"It's not letting go," she whispered.

The fear in her pewter eyes did something strange to him. He *loathed* her distress and would do anything to ease it, but the more he pulled at her, the more the white sea tried to drag her into its thick depths.

Brokk's shoulder felt like it was about to rip free of its joint as he strained to pull her up while that shit tugged at her, nearly ripping her free of his hold.

He was half vampire and half dark fae; neither species possessed the strength of a lycan, but they were far from weak. He should have been able to free her but was failing.

Her fingers bit into his arm and raked through his skin, but he didn't feel it. Her lower lip trembled when she met his gaze, and the desperation in her eyes caused his fangs to lengthen as helpless fury filled him.

He understood why those monsters hadn't followed her into this. They knew better.

"What about a spell?" he inquired through his teeth.

"I already tried a levitation spell, but I couldn't pull free of it. I also tried a spell to part it; it didn't work."

The sea pulled at her again, jerking her down until he barely held her fingers. She was up to her neck in it now and sinking fast.

Her delicate chin tilted up as she tried to keep her face above the substance. *I will not lose her.*

"You're not in this alone," he told her.

But she was, as he remained safely on a vine while she sank further into oblivion. Pain shot through his broken hand when it tightened on her.

It did little good as, with another jerk, the mire ripped her free of his grasp. Before he could grab her again, the sea sucked her down so fast he didn't have a chance to touch her fingertips before they disappeared beneath the white sea.

His heart sank as his chest constricted and self-hatred filled him. He'd failed her. He'd promised not to let her go, and he'd lost her.

Beneath him, a sucking whirlpool rose to the surface. He gazed at the swirling depths as they spun faster; no wonder he couldn't pull her free. That was pulling her away from him the whole time.

Within the twisting eddy, he glimpsed her fingertips, still stretching toward him and the sky as she clung to the hope she could somehow break free of this. But there was no breaking free; he could see that now.

They'd come here on a mission and known there would be casualties. He should pull himself up and get out of here. He was the last one standing, the last hope for the crudue vine and Cole, but he'd never rid himself of the memory of the gut-wrenching terror in her eyes.

The feel of her hand and the electricity that passed between them lingered on his skin. He had no idea what lay below. She might be stuck in this sea for eternity, or it could go somewhere else, somewhere more dangerous, but as her fingers disappeared again, he knew he had no other option.

Whatever lay below, he'd find a way out of it and through the rest of this shithole. He'd find the crudue vine and return to his family, but he could never live with himself if he let her face this alone.

Brokk removed his sword from his sheath, untangled his legs from the vine, and dove into the vortex.

CHAPTER ELEVEN

KAYLIA'S CHEST constricted as the white substance crushed her within its embrace. It twisted her around, spinning her until the world became a blur of white.

She didn't want to shut out the world; she yearned to take it all in, but when the cloying substance tried working its way into her eyes, it forced them closed. She hated the blackness and the unknown but couldn't do anything to fight it as it pulled her further into the abyss.

At first, she held her breath, but the substance squeezed her chest until air burst out of her lungs. Wheezing, she tried not to inhale, but her body's instinctive need for oxygen compelled her to try to get air into her brutalized body.

The second she did, she regretted it. The thick substance coated her nostrils and adhered to her lips as it clogged her mouth and worked its way down her throat. The small grains of it were like sand, but it was thicker and stickier as it clung to every part of her.

Coughing, she tried to expel the substance, but she only succeeded in inhaling more of it. The terror clawing its way up her throat was like a vicious, wild beast seeking to break free, but it had nowhere to go.

The pressure against her chest was reaching a snapping point, and a new fear grew that it would eventually crush her. It would be a horrible way to go, but far preferable to spinning around in here throughout eternity while she became only a husk of a living creature.

She was sure that at any second, her rib cage would implode, smashing her heart and tearing it from her chest to end her. Kaylia couldn't inhale the sticky substance; her chest wouldn't rise as the weight bore down on her.

The spinning grew faster, whipping her around and battering her braid against her face. Despite the panic digging its claws deeper into her, that braid pissed her off. She wanted to tear it away from her face, but her hands were caught above her head, making them useless.

And then, like a tornado sucked back into the air, the vortex released her, and she fell. Her arms flailed as she sought something to grasp while tumbling through space.

Her stomach lurched, and bile surged up her throat; she blinked against the substance sticking to her lashes and eyes, but she couldn't register what she was seeing. She'd spun around so much it was impossible to know where she was, what was up, what was down, or anything beyond the falling.

When she was beginning to think she might fall forever, she crashed onto something. If she had any breath, the abrupt halt would have knocked it out. Instead, every bone in her body screamed in protest while she lay there, curled into a ball on her side.

The stop hadn't hurt as much as it should have after the fall, but though the ground was solid, it had a rubbery feel. Still, every part of her felt like a berserker had beaten her, and she couldn't get any air into her lungs, which were *screaming* for it.

Finally, her body started working again as coughs wracked

her until she was sure her spine would shatter. Air somehow managed to wheeze past the sticky substance coating the inside of her mouth.

It eased some of the burn in her lungs as she coughed and gagged until her throat was raw, and she was sure her ribs would crack. That sticky shit swelled up her throat, and she managed to lift herself a little before she vomited.

And once she started, she couldn't stop as more of that awful stuff spewed from her. The force of her purge made tears stream down her cheeks as spasms rocked her.

She was still trying to rid herself of the offending material when something thudded beside her. Despite her inability to get her body under control, her survival instincts screamed at her to face whatever new threat had arrived or run.

On hands and knees and still barely able to breathe, she got her feet under her as she prepared to flee; she'd open a portal out of whatever this place and back into Doomed Valley to get away. She wasn't in any condition to fight.

She was about to leap to her feet when Brokk rolled onto his side next to her and started coughing. His sword fell onto the ground next to him.

Relief flooded her, and she collapsed. Sitting with her shoulders hunched forward and hands in her lap, her head spun as starved brain cells filled with the oxygen denied them.

Her hand rose toward Brokk, but it blurred before falling weakly back to her side. She wasn't sure she could have run from him if he had been a threat.

What is he doing here?

Her throat was too raw to voice the question, and it wouldn't be fair to ask him now when he was in the same condition as her only a few minutes ago. Instead, she tried to touch him again and offer some comfort, but she was still too weak to move.

After a few minutes, she wiped the vomit from her mouth with the back of her hand and attempted to stand. When she did, her legs wobbled, and she almost went down again but managed to stay upright.

Kaylia stared at her feet as she willed them to be steady enough for her to move; while she did so, she registered the blue sky beneath them and the white, fluffy clouds floating past. Dizziness and delirium didn't fog her mind.

She wasn't hallucinating this; it was real. She was standing on the *sky*.

Her head tipped back, and she blinked at the thick canopy of trees surrounding a sea of white hell. The jungle was above them now, the tops of the trees facing them as they hung upside down over her head.

CHAPTER TWELVE

SHIT. Her stomach sank as she realized where they were and what happened, but she wasn't ready to process that information.

Instead, she went to Brokk's side and knelt next to him as he finished heaving up what he'd inhaled and swallowed of that awful substance. When she placed her hand on his back, his shudders shook her palm while he worked to expel what remained inside him.

She rubbed his back as he sat on his heels with his head bowed and his shoulders heaving. His powerful muscles bunched and flexed beneath her palm as a strange warmth crept through her. She couldn't quite put her finger on what it was or why, but she had to fight to stop herself from leaning against his side as she sought to comfort him.

Brokk retched one more time before using the back of his arm to wipe his mouth. His hand fell limply back to his side, but he finally lifted his head.

The corded muscles of his lean body went rigid as he took in their surroundings. "What is this?" he muttered in a raw, hoarse voice.

"It's a mirror realm." Her voice didn't sound any better than his, and it hurt to speak, but she did so anyway. "I've only encountered one other before. That one was small, but I don't think we'll be as fortunate with this one."

"A mirror realm. I've heard of them before but never been to one."

"They're not very common."

"But when you enter one, you're stuck in it."

"Yes. Until we find the way out. Sometimes there are many exits, and sometimes there's only one."

"Fuck."

Kaylia's hand fell away from his back when he moved away from his vomit, settled onto his ass, and shrugged off his pack. A strange sense of loss filled her, and she stared at her palm for a second before lowering it to her side.

Guilt over missing the connection between them filled her, and she scuttled a few feet away from him and where she'd thrown up before sitting again. She tried to shove the guilt aside, but it festered like an infected wound as her thoughts turned to Fabian… her dead fiancé.

She shouldn't enjoy touching any man when she'd lost the only one she could ever love. Still, she found the fingers of her other hand absently rubbing her palm as the memory of Brokk lingered there.

Using only one hand, he opened his pack as he spoke. "At least those things aren't here."

Kaylia shoved her hands into her lap and clasped them together. "There could be other things."

"I'm sure there are."

With his teeth, he uncorked a bottle and took a sip. He swished the contents around his mouth before turning his head and spitting it across the sky. It rolled across the surface, beading up as it went.

He scowled at the splash of green liquid marring the smooth surface. The scent of mint and herbs drifted to Kaylia from the mouthwash he'd used.

She removed her pack and searched out her teeth-cleaning potion. She had to get rid of the vile taste in her mouth as she focused on something other than the life she'd lost.

As she gargled some of the liquid, she watched Brokk re-stop his bottle with his teeth, place it on the sky that had become their ground, and shove it into place with the hand he'd used to hold it. He kept his other hand loosely turned up beside him.

Kaylia spit out her mouth rinse and recorked her bottle. "What happened to your hand?"

"I broke it when I punched that tank of a beast."

Kaylia recalled the cracking sound of his punch landing against that creature's head. Brokk hit it hard enough to knock it to the side, something she wouldn't have believed possible until she saw it happen.

Then she recalled his grip on her arm while stuck in that pit of misery and his determination not to let her go. He'd held her with *both* hands and never shown any sign he'd broken his hand while clinging to her.

Kaylia shoved the bottle back into her pack and, ignoring the guilt still plaguing her, crawled back to his side with her bag in hand. She sat next to him and waved at his broken hand. "May I?"

When he nodded, she tenderly lifted it into her lap and cradled it to examine the bones. His hand was so badly broken she couldn't see the knuckles; they'd bent downward, and the rest of his hand had swelled up around them.

"You held on to me," she said. "How did you do that with this hand?"

"I wasn't going to lose you."

Kaylia gulped when his eyes met hers, and something almost

tangible sizzled between them. Her fingers itched with the impulse to feel it, but there was nothing to touch... *or maybe it's him I want to feel.*

That was very true as she longed to learn the contours of his body. And those words... *"I wasn't going to lose you."* They did something to her insides, made them all warm and fuzzy while they melted her bones and turned her into mush.

If he kissed her right then, she wouldn't resist. In fact, she'd throw herself into his arms and kiss him back with every part of her being.

And he hadn't lost her; he'd followed her into this realm while not knowing what awaited him. He could have died, and it would have been for *her.*

Kaylia didn't understand the emotions battering every part of her; she couldn't quite put a finger on what those emotions were, but they made her head spin. *What is going on?*

Unable to answer that question, she tore her gaze away from him in the hopes of regaining some control. She ignored the small thrill running from him and into her as she delved back into her pack.

It had been centuries since she'd noticed a man, but it was impossible to ignore him as he leaned close enough for his breaths to tickle her cheeks. All she could smell was peppermint on his breath; the crisp, refreshing scent filled her nostrils as his body heat caused butterflies to erupt in her stomach.

She didn't think anything could feel good after what they'd endured, but he did. While working to gather her supplies, she couldn't stop studying him under her lashes.

His brow furrowed, and his lips pursed as he stared at their joined hands; she didn't know if his perplexed expression was because of his broken hand or because he felt this strange connection between them, too.

There is no connection. Your heart belongs to another.

It was true; her heart would always belong to Fabian, but she couldn't deny that something sizzled between them as her breaths became shallower and awareness of him crackled through her. Taking a deep breath, she tried to ignore the guilt rising to suppress her strange excitement as she focused on his shattered hand.

CHAPTER THIRTEEN

KAYLIA SEARCHED through her bag for something to help him. "How did you fall off the vine? You held on well when you were trying to help me."

"I didn't fall off it."

The hair on Kaylia's nape rose as an unsettling sensation descended over her. With hands that trembled slightly, she removed the medical kit she'd packed and set it on a cloud passing beneath the ground between them. The medical kit remained where it was while the cloud traveled on beneath the mirror's surface.

Hesitantly, she met his striking blue eyes. She didn't know what to say as she searched his face. His lopsided smile caused something more than guilt to tug at her heart.

He used his free hand to brush the loose strands of hair back from her face. "I wasn't going to let you face this alone."

Kaylia gulped at the realization she found him handsome, and not in the clinically assessing way she'd analyzed many other men over the past three centuries, but in the intriguing, captivating way she once found another man… the man she loved dearly.

The man who was so cruelly ripped away from her by a vampire… like Brokk.

At one time, the reminder of that would have caused her to fling Brokk's broken hand away and probably smash it into smaller pieces. Loathing, antipathy, and hate were all too kind words for the way she once felt about vampires.

If she could have, she would have hunted *every* vampire down and eradicated them from all the realms. She couldn't do that without unleashing a brutal war between vampires and witches, and such a war would leave far too many dead.

Even during her worst periods of rage and extreme suffering, she wouldn't allow herself to be the cause of so many deaths. She wasn't the Lord; she wasn't insane with power and without a conscience.

She was a simple woman who'd lost someone she loved dearly, and no matter how badly it hurt, Kaylia refused to be the cause of the suffering and death of other witches. Regret filled her for everything that could have been and never was with Fabian, and there was still grief; there would always be grief.

There was also guilt now, but not hatred, or at least not toward Brokk and *all* vampires. She'd learned that not all vampires were bad and worthy of death. Brokk and Sahira had helped show her that.

Sure, some vamps didn't deserve to walk the realms, but others, such as Brokk and Sahira, were different. She could almost convince herself it was because they were only half vamps, but Del was different too, and he was full-blooded.

Plus, countless other vampires had helped fight against the Lord. They'd stood by her side to take down the tyrannical man.

They'd died to help put Lexi in power and to end the slaughter the Lord had unleashed on the realms. She couldn't blanket hate an entire species of immortals anymore.

She still missed Fabian and would until the day she died, but she'd spent too many years being angry, bitter, and hiding from the world.

She should move on; it's what he'd want her to do, but not with other men. There would never be another man for her, but she could go into the realms and experience happiness again.

Kaylia removed the materials she required to splint his hand. He wouldn't have to wear it long, as he'd heal fast, but it would help ease his discomfort.

When she turned toward him with the supplies, he rested his hand on hers. "There's no need for that. It will heal soon."

"This can help alleviate the pain."

"It's not that bad."

He was lying; she could see it in his eyes, but she didn't argue. The stubborn man would never admit it.

With a sigh, she returned the supplies to her pack. Afterward, she unstrapped her dagger from her hip, lifted her braid, and sliced it off at the shoulder.

"Why did you do that?" Brokk inquired.

She dropped the four-foot braid on the ground. "It's only a danger here and might get me killed. I'd much prefer life to long hair."

Brokk undid what remained of her braid with his uninjured hand. "It looks good."

She was sure he was saying that to protect her feelings but didn't care. It had been years since she'd cut more than a few inches from it, and it felt weird, but she should have cut it before coming here.

"I guess it's time to find our way out," she said.

Brokk rose beside her. "I've never been in a mirror realm before. What should I know about it?"

"It's like we're inside a mirror," she said. "I'm sure there will be some surprises along the way, but there's always a way out."

"Good."

"Just not through a portal. If you open one, it will only bring you back here; we're trapped in a reflection of the realm above."

"You know I'm still going to have to try it."

"I know."

Brokk rose, opened a portal, and stepped into it. He reemerged through the same portal.

"Well, that's interesting," he murmured.

"And unnerving."

"That too."

"We should go."

Brokk studied the portal for a few more seconds before waving it closed with his hand. "We should."

With that, Brokk reclaimed his sword and sheathed it. They shrugged on their packs and walked across the pristine blue sky toward whatever lay ahead.

CHAPTER FOURTEEN

So far, the mirror realm was a lot easier to travel through. They didn't have to hack through a jungle or have anything in hiding looking to eat them or giant monsters hunting them down.

Traversing across the spongy sky and clouds was far faster, but he also didn't like being stuck here until they found the way out. According to Kaylia, there was a way out of this place, but he'd never been trapped anywhere like this before and didn't like it.

He'd always been free to come and go as he pleased; this place had changed that, and while it was less threatening than the Valley—so far—he'd far prefer to be back amid the vegetation and lethal beasts than stuck here.

And there was always the chance she was wrong about there being a way out; neither of them had ever encountered anything like Doomed Valley before. This place had a way of turning everything upside down... literally.

He glanced at the trees above his head and their thick, green vegetation pointing toward him. It was all so weird, but nothing had been normal since entering Doomed Valley.

And now, they were the only ones left on this journey... he

was fairly certain of that. Some of the other dark fae could have slipped into the shadows before they were trampled or eaten, but even as a half vampire, he was stronger than most dark fae.

Depending on their power level, he could sense or see most of them while they were enveloped in shadows. He hadn't done either while running from those things.

Of course, he'd also been focused on surviving and getting to Kaylia; he could have missed them, but he didn't think so. Maybe, once they were free of this place, he'd discover that some of the others had survived, but until then, he could only walk beside Kaylia across the sky.

He glanced at her as she walked with her chin high and steely determination etched across her face. Her short hair framed her face as it bounced against her shoulders.

He liked the shorter length on her; it somehow made her more approachable. But then, she could be bald, and he'd still find her beautiful; it was impossible not to.

Unable to resist, his gaze traveled leisurely over her. Dirt and blood covered her clothes, but he couldn't help admiring the way the pants hugged her taut ass, an ass he'd like to grab while she rode him.

When his cock stirred, Brokk shifted his gaze away. He doubted she'd appreciate the images running through his mind, but he couldn't help pondering what it would be like to peel those clothes off and feast on her naked body while it moved against his.

We have to get the fuck out of here. And they had to do it soon, as he'd awakened his dark fae appetite, and though it hadn't been an issue before, it was rearing its head now.

While they'd become friends since their first encounter, he doubted she'd ever shown any interest in him or any other man in that way. Still, he easily recalled her hand on his back and the concern in her eyes when she saw his hand.

He also recalled the way she looked at him. For one second,

he'd thought she might see him as a man and want something more from him, but it passed too fast for him to be sure, and she'd barely looked at him since they started walking.

When Brokk glanced at his feet, he experienced the same unsettling feeling he had since landing in this mirror realm. He kept expecting the solid ground beneath his feet to evaporate and to start freefalling.

"Is there any chance this could give way, and we'll start falling again?" he asked.

"No."

He lifted an eyebrow at her clipped response but didn't say anything. He wasn't exactly in the most conversational mood either; he'd far prefer to be doing something else with her.

Despite her assurance they wouldn't plummet into oblivion, he eyed the changing sky warily. Doomed Valley could change things into whatever this savage land wanted them to be. He didn't trust it.

Still, he couldn't help being awed by the place as brilliant colors streaked across the sky. Reds, pinks, and oranges spread beneath his feet, stretching as far as he could see and turning the clouds into rainbows.

They traveled a little further, but as the sun sank from view, he called an end to the day. Kaylia turned toward him and opened her mouth to say something but closed it again. She removed her pack, set it on the ground, and sank beside it.

Brokk did the same as he settled onto a passing cloud streaked with colors. He'd never touched a sunset before and couldn't stop his fingers from stroking the colors. It may only reflect what was happening on the other side of the mirror, but it was magical.

When the colors vanished with the sun, he removed food and water from his pack. Across from him, Kaylia munched on a carrot while watching the moon rise.

Bathed in the moon's radiance, her hair glowed more silver,

making her appear ethereal as her skin shimmered. She was a being of magic at home beneath the moon.

Brokk ate some of his dried jerky as he basked in the radiance she emitted. He wanted to touch her, but since she'd been so distant most of the day, he didn't think she'd appreciate him getting closer.

He decided to try to learn more about her instead. "How did you encounter a mirror realm before?"

CHAPTER FIFTEEN

HER ATTENTION WAS DRAWN away from the horizon; she smiled at some memory as she pulled a loaf of bread from her pack. She broke off a piece before shoving the rest inside.

"I was a child when it happened," she said. "My sister and I were exploring the woods not far from our home when I moved a log in search of some criten mushrooms we needed for a spell. Instead of finding the mushrooms, I fell down a hole. It turned out I'd fallen into a tunnel that led straight into a mirror realm.

"Mina jumped in after me, and we were trapped there for a couple of days before finding our way out. My mother was so worried about us. I thought she was going to break my ribs as she crushed us against her when we returned." She absently touched a cheek. "I can still feel her tears falling on my face. I was so happy to be home."

"What about your father?"

She shrugged. "He came around occasionally, but we barely knew him. They never married, but both wanted children. If I'd been a boy, I would have gone to live with him and the warlocks, the same with Mina. Instead, we stayed with our mother in Verdan. He didn't have much to do with us, but he was kind and always brought us sweets. They'd agreed to have two children together; unfortunately for him, we were both girls. We were happy about it, though."

"What became of your parents?"

"My father was killed by another warlock when I was barely more than a girl, and a wendigo killed my mother when I was two hundred. I still miss her terribly."

The small smile left her face as sadness settled over her features. He hated the melancholy enshrouding her and wished he could take back his question. He knew how painful the loss of family could be.

"I have no family left," Kaylia murmured. "Mina also died a thousand years ago."

"I'm sorry for your loss."

"Thank you. It was supposed to be the two of us until the end, but a troll changed that."

Brokk fisted his hands to keep from comforting her. She'd settled far enough away to make it clear that distance was what she wanted.

"I still miss my brothers and father," he said, "and I'm sure I will a thousand years from now, too. I sometimes think I still hear or see them from the corner of my eye, but they're never there when I look. And they never will be."

"That's the funny thing about loss; you never really lose it."

When Kaylia smiled at him, he saw she was trying to lighten the mood, but the sorrow in her eyes made it clear she didn't feel the humor she was trying to impart. And he didn't think all her grief was for her family, but then, Kaylia was older than him and had most likely endured a lot of losses over the years.

"No, you don't," Brokk agreed. "How old are you?"

He knew she was older than him, and he might have learned her age at some point, but he couldn't recall it now. Then again, so many things had happened since they first met that most of it had become a blur of fighting and death.

"I'm around fifteen hundred, but I don't know my exact age. I lost track years ago."

That meant she was at least nine hundred years older than him. "It is difficult to count that high."

Kaylia blinked at him before laughing, and Brokk grinned as her laughter filled the air. It warmed his heart in a way he'd never experienced before, and he knew he'd do everything he could to make her laugh more often. It would be difficult in this place, but not impossible.

At one point in time, he'd considered her a heartless bitch, but while she could be vicious —she'd thrown him and Sahira out of her home the first time they met—he'd learned she was also vibrant and beautiful. He'd come to understand the heart he once believed didn't exist was bigger than most.

"How old were you when you went to live in the crone realm?" he asked.

Her smile faded as her laughter died, and he once again regretted asking his question, but he was infinitely curious about this woman.

"Twelve hundred or somewhere around there, and I didn't go to live there, I created it. That outer realm was little more than rock when I arrived. I went there to be by myself, but with some magic and a lot of work to make the land more fertile, it started growing around me.

"After some time, other witches retreated from the realms to live there too. At first, I wasn't sure I wanted them there; I was content to spend the rest of my life living a solitary existence, but many of them needed somewhere to retreat to also, and I couldn't deny them that. The more witches arrived, the more the land grew around us as things have a way of doing. Eventually, more creatures and witches arrived until it became the realm you saw."

He frowned as he took another bite of his meal. He didn't understand why anyone as vibrant, powerful, and beautiful as her would prefer to lock herself away from others to live such a lonely life. It didn't make any sense.

"Fascinating," he murmured.

He studied her as he debated asking his next question. He'd caused her some sadness with his others, but she was answering them, and he enjoyed learning more about her. She intrigued him.

After a few more minutes of internal debate, he finally asked. "Why did you retreat to the crone realm?"

CHAPTER SIXTEEN

IMMEDIATELY, he regretted his decision as her face became cold and her gaze shifted away. He should have known better than to keep pushing.

"Because, sometimes, life has a way of making you prefer death," she whispered.

His eyebrows rose at this; he couldn't understand her statement. During his darkest days, when he was in the middle of a war, death surrounded him, his brothers were dying, and even after he lost his father, he'd never thought like that.

His heart was broken; Brokk was sure he'd be the next to fall and was terrified he'd lose more of his family, but he *never* would have welcomed death. Even now, haunted by memories of war and the love he'd lost, he far preferred life.

What did this vibrant, beautiful woman endure to make her say such a thing? How deep was her loss, and how many had it taken to break her?

She'd always been as strong as dark fae metal to him, but like those powerful weapons could do, something had cut her deeply.

He didn't point out that even if she would have preferred

death, she'd somehow survived whatever had propelled her into the crone realm. She hadn't chosen to die; instead, she locked herself away and created a vibrant, magical place out of a barren rock.

For someone who claimed she would have preferred death, she sure weaved a lot of life into the realms.

"You've lost some of your brothers and your father," she murmured.

"I have."

"What of your mother?"

"As you may have guessed, my mother is a vampire."

He wasn't sure if his words or teasing tone were the right approach. The reminder of his half-vamp bloodline might shut her down completely, but when a small smile tugged at the corner of her mouth, he knew he'd taken the right approach.

"Like your father, she sometimes came around when I was a child and often brought me presents when she did. She never really wanted to be a mother and didn't hide it, but she wasn't cruel. She was happy to leave me with my father while she lived a more childfree existence. That's what she preferred, and it worked for all of us."

"Did it ever bother you?"

Brokk pondered this. "Not that I can remember. It was simply always the way it was, and between my father and my brothers, I was surrounded by love, even when my brothers were being assholes."

"That must have been often."

He grinned at her. "It was, especially Orin."

"That's no surprise."

No, it wasn't. Brokk's smile faded at the reminder of his older brother. He'd missed Orin, and he loved him, but he was a big part of the reason their father was dead.

He still hadn't completely forgiven Orin or Varo for choosing to fight against their father, and he sometimes questioned if he ever would. Orin and Cole were the ones who bashed heads constantly, but Brokk would truly love to punch Orin in the face, far more so than Varo.

Hitting Varo would be like kicking a puppy. Hitting Orin would feel so fucking good.

"What became of your mom?" Kaylia asked.

"She's still alive, or at least I've received no word of her death. She sent condolences when my father died and told me she'd like to see me when I have time, but I haven't had much of that lately. I'm sure we'll meet up again at some point. We always do."

"I hope you get to see each other again."

They didn't speak again until she removed her blanket and a jar of cream from her pack. She smoothed the cream over her bug bites before offering him some. Brokk shook his head; he had an ointment he'd put on later.

Kaylia returned the cream to her bag and settled onto the starry sky. She used her pack as a pillow as she lay on her back with her hands on her belly while staring at the jungle above them.

After a little while, she whispered words he couldn't hear and lifted her hands to weave a protective spell around them. So far, they hadn't encountered anything else in the mirror realm, but he was glad she wasn't willing to take the chance of something sneaking up on them while they slept because he sure wasn't.

At least with the spell in place, he could get some sleep tonight, though he doubted it would be much. He could never let his guard down in this place.

"Good night," she said when she finished the spell.

With that, she rolled over so her back faced him. He watched her for a while as he ran his fingers over the stars. He pressed on different ones and made constellations out of the small, twinkling lights.

This was the only chance he'd ever have to touch a star;

while he wasn't actually touching them, he was fascinated by the magic of this realm. He flattened his palm against them before glancing at Kaylia's back. Her breathing was slow and steady, indicating she slept.

As time passed, a chill crept into the air. Unlike the humidity of the jungle, the sky in this place was wintry.

Removing his blanket from his pack, something he hadn't used since arriving here, he settled down near Kaylia and pulled the material over him.

CHAPTER SEVENTEEN

HE WASN'T sure what time it was when he woke to shaking beside him. At first, he bolted upright, certain those beasts had somehow found their way into the mirror realm and were thundering toward them, but the sky didn't quake with the same intensity the earth had when they were above... or below?

It didn't matter. What mattered was that something was coming at them.

He gripped the sword he'd placed beside his head before going to sleep and pulled it toward him. Confused, he searched the twinkling stars and moon before realizing the shaking came from his right.

He looked over to see Kaylia curled into a ball; she had a cloak and blanket pulled over her. The cold had never bothered him much, and he tended to tolerate lower temps than most, so he hadn't realized how much the temperature fell while he slept.

She shivered, and her teeth chattered, and judging by the tight squint of her eyes, she was awake but trying to make herself sleep. He stretched his hand toward her shoulder, seeking to comfort her, but pulled it back.

He wasn't sure how much she'd welcome his touch. Instead, he dug into his pack and removed a cloak.

He placed it over her before settling his head onto his pack again. Folding his hands on his stomach, he stared at the trees above them as all around him stars spread infinitely onward.

He half expected the vines and other things he knew existed in the jungle to float down toward them, but only the tips of those towering green trees remained above. The jungle would keep its secrets and monsters to itself... for now.

Kaylia's shivering eased, but when it didn't stop, he edged his pack and blanket a little closer. Lying beside her, with his arm against her back, he tried to provide more warmth for her as her teeth chattered.

When he couldn't take her suffering anymore, he rolled over and draped his arm around her as he edged closer. He half expected her to throw him off or elbow him, but she nestled a little closer.

Brokk gritted his teeth when her ass fit perfectly against his crotch. He had to will himself not to get hard as heat flooded every aspect of him and her supple body reawakened his dark fae hunger.

When her teeth continued to chatter as she snuggled a little closer, Brokk forgot about his baser instincts as the urge to protect and shelter her roared to the forefront. Everything in him eased, and a sense of rightness stole through him when he slipped his arm around her.

"Is this okay?" he asked.

"Ye... ye... yes," she chattered out her response as she settled against him.

She was about six inches shorter than his six-foot-three height, but her curvaceous body fit perfectly against his. Her natural, sweet scent was stronger than the blood and dirt still clinging to her. She smelled of earth and freshly sprung leaves. It was the aroma of life, yet she'd admitted there was a time when she would have preferred death.

The reminder of that caused his teeth to clamp together. He didn't understand why she'd felt that way and hated the reminder as he held her closer and settled his head on his pack.

He draped his leg over hers, drawing her closer and shutting out the cold as her shivering gradually eased and she relaxed against him. Her breathing slowed as she finally drifted asleep, but Brokk remained awake.

He was acutely aware of how right she felt in his arms and never wanted to let her go.

.

CHAPTER EIGHTEEN

When Kaylia woke, the sun was starting to rise. It peeked through the clouds about a hundred yards away from her, but its warmth still didn't touch them.

The cold air iced her cheeks and turned her breath to frost. Beneath Brokk's cloak, and with him wrapped securely around her, she barely felt the icy air that had woken her last night and made it impossible for her to return to sleep.

She recalled the chill wracking her bones, but nestled securely in his arms, it was a distant memory. He was far too warm for it to be anything more than that.

Brokk still slept soundly, unaware she was awake but still very aware of *her*—the rigid evidence of that pressed against her back.

When she realized he was aroused, her first instinct was to jump up and run as far as she could from him. She pictured sprinting across the open sky as she sought to run away…

No, not from him, but the emotions he stirred within her. Emotions and sensations she hadn't experienced in hundreds of years and had never expected to feel again.

But as she lay there, she became acutely aware of the

growing ache between her legs as she was comforted by the warmth and strength surrounding her. His build was lean, but the man was all chiseled muscle as he enveloped her.

What she wouldn't give to roll over and run her fingers over his chest, down his abdomen, and toward his erection. He'd be hot and thick in her hand, and he'd groan while she stroked him, arching into her touch, demanding more, until she couldn't take it anymore and she straddled him....

Kaylia broke the thought off as a rush of desire and guilt pummeled her. Her nipples rubbed her bra, her breath came quicker, and every part of her begged to turn into him.

He wouldn't turn her away; he was already aroused and part dark fae. He'd welcome her, he'd feast on her, and he'd fuck her until she begged for mercy.

She'd relish every second of it, too... even if she shouldn't. *Fabian.*

The reminder of her dead fiancé helped douse some of the longing being in Brokk's arms had awakened, but while it should have eradicated it completely, it didn't. She didn't understand why Fabian's memory didn't completely eliminate her desire for another man.

He was the one she loved, the one she'd vowed never to forsake, even if they were never officially bound by marriage. Yet, here she was, lusting after another man and one who was also part *vampire.*

The word sounded like it should be something gross in her head, and not too long ago, it would have been, but she didn't feel repulsed by it now. Yes, a vampire had killed Fabian, but that vamp wasn't Brokk.

Kaylia closed her eyes while a tumult of grief, yearning, self-loathing, and rightness bombarded her. She didn't understand how this could feel right, but it did.

Maybe it was because it had been centuries since anyone last held her and she'd felt any desire for a man, but there it was, low in her belly and growing with every minute they spent together. And it was so wrong.

She squeezed her eyes shut as memories of Fabian flooded her. He'd been so handsome with his light brown hair and warm brown eyes.

He had this special way of looking at her that radiated love and made her toes curl. When he touched her, she came alive beneath his fingers and the passion of his kisses.

It had taken her a while to fall for him, but once she did, she'd tumbled head over heels into it. He'd been her everything.

But as Fabian's face floated before her, the image of another man with dark blond hair and striking blue eyes replaced it. And once Brokk's face was there, her musings turned lustful again as she pictured grasping his pointed ears while he bent his head between her thighs.

She was a traitor, a betrayer, and awful for longing for another man, but she was also wet and alive in a way she hadn't been in too many years to count. She'd forgotten what it was like to feel this way, and as much as she hated the guilt bombarding her, she also welcomed how her nerve endings tingled and her heart raced.

She was supposed to marry Fabian; their lives were meant to be forever entwined and would have been, if that vampire hadn't ripped him away. It didn't matter if it had been centuries since Fabian died, she'd given her heart to him, and immortals didn't often do that.

Love was a bond for eternity; even the dark fae king, Tove, had known that....

But Tove also had sex with other women after he lost his wife.

That's because he was a dark fae and required sex to feed and live. You're a witch, so what's your excuse for wanting another?

She was a witch but also a woman with needs... even if those needs hadn't stirred in centuries. However, things had changed a *lot* in her life recently.

She'd stopped locking herself away in the crone realm, a realm she'd loved dearly, but it was her hiding spot from the world. It was a sanctuary she'd turned into a thriving, beautiful place and a prison for herself.

Looking back, she could see that now. She'd turned it into *her* prison. She'd kept herself away from any suffering that might come from living in the realms... but also any of the joy.

Sure, there was plenty of joy and life in the crone realm, but it was easy to have those when you knew there was little that could ever harm you there. And while no one wanted to experience pain, it was part of life. It was what made the good moments better.

And there had been no temptation in the crone realm. Sure, they had a few visitors from the other realms, some of whom had been men, but for the most part, she'd barely interacted with a man since losing Fabian.

It was no wonder that once locked in the embrace of a man again, she'd feel desire. She may not be a dark fae who thrived on sex, but she was a sexual being, even if she'd been celibate for the past three hundred or so years.

Still, though all of this made sense, it didn't do anything to dissolve the guilt churning inside her. She was a woman with needs, but wanting Brokk when her heart belonged to another was wrong.

Squeezing her eyes closed, she buried the yearning in her belly as she carefully wiggled her way out from under Brokk's arm and leg. It took some maneuvering, but she finally managed to free herself.

She instantly regretted it as the cold rushed in to embrace her, and she missed the strength of his arms around her, but she'd made the right choice. Glancing back, she was glad to see he remained sleeping soundly, which was convenient considering her bladder was far from empty, and there was nowhere to go discreetly around here.

She put on her cloak and walked back about a hundred feet the way they'd come. Once there, she did what she needed and returned as Brokk started to stir. When she was a few feet away, she stopped as she realized his twitches and mutters were more than a normal waking.

Distress etched his face when he rolled over. Since she'd left, he'd gone from sleeping peacefully to dreaming of something that upset him.

Unable to stand his suffering, Kaylia stepped toward him to wake him. She froze when his eyes flew open and a snarl twisted his lips. His fangs had extended and were visible, as was the vivid red of his eyes.

CHAPTER NINETEEN

NORMALLY, such a blatant reminder of the vampire part of him would have infuriated her, but she couldn't find any anger as he blinked at the sky, and his face gradually eased into something more relaxed. The red faded from his eyes as he draped an arm across his forehead and stared at the trees above.

She started to ask him if he was okay, but his words stopped her.

"Do you ever dream about the war?"

Kaylia clasped her hands before her as she shifted her gaze to the beautiful hues streaking the sky. "I do."

When he didn't say anything, she returned her attention to him. He remained staring at the trees, his lips shut, but the outline of his fangs remained visible behind them.

"You fought in the Lord's war, too," she stated.

"I did."

"It lasted much longer than the one we waged against the Lord."

"It did."

"You probably saw a lot of awful things, especially if you were in the human realm for any of it."

"I was."

His two-word answers revealed more about how the war had affected him than anything more elaborate he might have said. She could only guess at the horrors he'd witnessed while the Lord waged war against mortals, who'd lived in peaceful oblivion about the existence of immortals until he unleashed hell on them.

"How long were you there?" she asked.

"Too long."

She waited, uncertain of what else to say.

"I fought on the Lord's side during it," he said.

"I know."

"It's not what I wanted, or my father, or any of my brothers. We believed we were doing the right thing by plotting secretly against him instead of directly standing against him like Orin, Varo, and three of my other brothers did."

"You were."

"Were we? We didn't stop him."

"*No one* could have stopped him at that time. You were missing two vital pieces: the discovery of Lexi's true heritage and Cole becoming the dark fae king. Without Cole going through the trial, he never could have become the Shadow Reaver."

"My father had to die for that."

Kaylia's heart ached for him. She'd always seen Tove as a heartless bastard, but from everything she'd seen of his sons, there was a lot of love there, even when they wanted to kill each other. That had come from their father.

"I'm sorry," she whispered.

He didn't speak for a few seconds before sighing. "If he'd known how everything would have worked out with Cole, he would have chosen death. I know many think he was an asshole, but he loathed the Lord and everything he stood for. He would have done everything in his power to destroy him, including die."

It was strange to get this glimpse into a man she'd always considered heartless. There had been far more layers to Tove than she'd ever realized, but there were many layers to everyone. Peeling them away made life more fun and scarier, as there was never any way to know what lay beneath.

Lowering his arm, Brokk rolled to the side and pushed himself into a sitting position. He studied the sky before turning toward her. His eyes remained haunted, but he smiled.

With his tousled hair and sleepy grin, he was striking and boyish. The combination did funny things to her belly.

"Did you sleep okay?" he asked.

"Yes, thanks to you."

His smile widened. It wasn't smug or sly; it was simply a smile of genuine warmth from a man with a good heart... despite his heritage and the atrocities he'd witnessed.

She'd never been the biggest fan of vampires *or* dark fae. Vampires had been the witches' mortal enemies for over eight hundred years, and the dark fae were pompous, self-serving, borderline-sociopathic assholes.

But somehow, the combination of those two things became a good thing in Brokk. She never would have believed such a thing could happen until she met him. Somehow, the arrogant King Tove had raised a few good sons... excluding Orin.

"Good." Brokk sat up and stretched his arms over his head. "Let's have breakfast and see if we can get out of here today."

"I hope so."

Kaylia settled a few feet away from him and pulled her pack over to remove some food and water. She wanted out of this place. It was far too confusing here.

And she had to put some distance between herself and Brokk. It was the only way she could eliminate her festering guilt, and it was best for both of them.

CHAPTER TWENTY

THE SUN GLINTED all around them as the sky remained cloudless. The bright yellow orb was far off in the distance, but Brokk had to squint against its radiance as sweat dripped down his back.

While the nights cooled off far more than in the jungle, the days were almost as hot. It was strange, considering he felt far closer to the sun here, and he thought it should be warmer, but without the trees to trap in the heat and humidity, the temperature wasn't as oppressive.

While he appreciated being free of all the death traps, creatures, and bugs of Doomed Valley, Brokk was tired of the monotony of this place and frustrated by their inability to leave it. He kept reminding himself all mirror realms came to an end, but it did little good when he was ready to be free of it now.

They were never going to find the crudue vine while trapped here. And they were never going to get home.

Brokk shifted his pack on his back as he recalled they wouldn't find any food or water here either. Supplies weren't drastically low, but his appetites for blood and sex couldn't be satisfied with food and water.

It would become an issue soon... especially while trapped here with Kaylia. She was too much of a temptation, and it would be more difficult to keep those appetites under control if he went for much more time without.

They'd already stopped for lunch, and the sun was sinking lower in the sky as day progressed toward night. The endless sky was their ever-constant companion, but as their shadows started lengthening across the blue surface, something rippled in the distance.

Beside him, Kaylia's step faltered a little before her gaze lifted to his.

"Did you see something like that in the mirror realm you were in?" he asked.

"No."

Brokk studied the strange ripple in the distance. In Doomed Valley, and possibly here, that movement couldn't be good.

However, they didn't have a choice; they had to continue. Turning back wasn't an option, and maybe an exit lay ahead.

Plus, it was nice to see something other than the endless blue sky. He didn't know how long he'd think that was true.

As they drew closer to the ripple, it became a sea of moving green parts swarming over one another like bees in a hive. He couldn't distinguish one piece from another or what they were, but they were either all disjointed or a giant mass of... *something*.

He wasn't sure what he'd prefer, but he'd do anything not to smell the rank aroma drifting from them. His nose wrinkled as the putrid scent of rotting flesh and something musky and feral wafted on the air.

Kaylia's delicate brow furrowed as the small cleft in her chin became more noticeable when her lips pursed. He was glad he wasn't the only one completely confused and repulsed by whatever lay ahead.

As they edged closer, the green mass started taking shape and forming into something more coherent, yet he still couldn't understand what was happening. Arms and legs flailed as little green creatures crawled all over each other and scrambled to climb the stairway behind them.

Rising from the sky, the stairs were as blue as the ground beneath his feet and looked made of glass. He might not have noticed them if it hadn't been for the brawling creatures.

The monsters hissed, spit, and wrestled as their brethren ripped them backward, slammed them off the ground, and pounced on them. They bashed each other's heads off the stairs before climbing over their unconscious victims.

Now that they were closer, the hundreds of glistening white bones scattered around the base of the stairs and across the sky became clearer. Some of those bones still had chunks of meat hanging from them, and most were too big to belong to these creatures, but some did.

What are these things? And why are they here?

While walking here, Brokk was so focused on figuring out what the green mass and bones were that he hadn't noticed the steps until they were closer, but now his gaze fixated on the stairs stretching toward the trees. At the very top, the stairs ended at a door at the top of a tree.

The way out!

He was so excited to see it that he forgot about the vile little monsters and stepped toward the stairs. When Kaylia gripped his arm, her nails dug into his flesh as she looked from him to the creatures and back again.

"They're gremlins," she whispered.

Brokk's eyebrows shot up. He'd heard of the mischievous, often volatile and violent creatures before but never encountered them. Yet here they were, in a mirror realm, beating each other up and down the stairs while making awful, guttural, and animalistic sounds.

He studied the creatures blocking their way toward the door.

Right now, none of the little monsters had seen them as they remained focused on their lethal game, but that could change, and if it did, he suspected the gremlins' focus would shift to *them*.

CHAPTER TWENTY-ONE

"WHAT ARE THEY DOING HERE?" he whispered.

"I don't know, but it can't be good. They destroy everything they touch."

"They're blocking the exit."

"There will be another one."

But he didn't want to wait for another one. Brokk examined their shadows spreading out behind them as the sun sank lower.

They could use their swords to carve through the devilish creatures, but the gremlins far outnumbered them. While the gremlins were currently focused on killing each other, they'd turn on him and Kaylia the second they saw them.

"I can cloak us," he said. "Then we can get closer to see if we can get past them, but you'll have to get closer to me."

Brokk frowned at the flicker of unease that crossed her face before she bit her bottom lip, and her gaze darted away. Anger settled into the pit of his stomach; he'd believed she wasn't as annoyed or disgusted by him as she once was.

At least not after last night and *everything* they'd endured together in this Valley and Dragonia. They'd fought together, and he'd followed her into this fucking mirror realm to ensure she stayed safe, yet she *still* didn't like the idea of getting closer to him.

He was fine to keep her from freezing to death, but he was well aware of the distance she'd kept from him most of the day. They hadn't exactly walked side-by-side since entering Doomed Valley, but they'd always been within a few feet of each other.

Now, she'd stayed at least ten feet away from him all day and barely spoken a word. He didn't know what had changed between last night and today, but he was sick of this shit.

So what if he was a half vampire? He'd considered himself her friend, yet she didn't want to get close enough for him to cloak her too. Between him and a bunch of little green monsters who would most likely eat them, he considered himself the better option.

Kaylia didn't agree.

If she preferred to walk through them without any protection, that was fine; he sure wasn't going to try anything so stupid. "Or you can walk through them on your own."

Kaylia gave him a small smile that didn't reach her eyes. "I'd prefer not to."

When he stared expectantly at her, she took a deep breath and moved to within an arm's length of him. Brokk couldn't suppress his irritation as he scowled at her. *What is her problem?*

"I'm not going to bite you," he grated from between his teeth as he kept one eye on the creatures. "And it's only a matter of time before they notice us, so you'll have to get closer, or they'll come for us. Our shadows are the only ones I can use, and they're not enough to keep us cloaked unless we're closer together."

Their eyes clashed as she threw her shoulders back and lifted her chin before moving to stand beside him. When their arms brushed, she gulped.

Brokk's teeth ground back and forth as his hands fisted. While he hadn't expected her to jump in his bed after last night, he'd thought it brought them a little closer together and forged a new bond between them.

Apparently, it had made her determined to get further away from him. And since he had a conscience, he couldn't leave her there exposed, like a part of him wanted to do.

Even if she cast a protective spell around herself, those things would swarm her the second they saw her and bring her down. She was far better off being invisible to them, something she'd realized, but she still acted like it was a burden for her.

Fuck her.

That would be fun.

He shook his head to rid it of *that* idea; it would not happen. She was making that abundantly clear.

He drew the shadows around them, cloaking them in their embrace and making them invisible to the monsters still pummeling each other on the stairs. Moving silently forward, Brokk tried not to grimace at the horrible sounds the creatures made, but they sounded like a cross between squealing pigs and irate cats as they beat each other senseless.

He had no idea what they were trying to prove with their strange game, but more than a few of them lay broken and unmoving along the staircase and at the bottom of it.

Their big green ears flopped with their movements while their humanoid-like features twisted with wrath. They had big, red, bulbous noses that reminded him of the humans' clowns, and their razor-sharp teeth clacked as they screeched and bit into each other.

More than a few had the arm or leg of a fellow gremlin dangling from their mouths. They'd ripped the appendages from their fellow monsters, and some used them as weapons to pulverize the others as they gradually made their way up the staircase.

Their bodies were more human than monster. No taller than three feet, they had legs and arms, but the tips of their fingers ended in three-inch-long nails that looked more like knives as they rose high before flashing down to slice into flesh.

Beside him, Kaylia shuddered a little before going still again. The gremlins climbed higher while ripping each other down and throwing their brethren to the bottom. It was like they were playing some demented game.

Brokk had no idea what that game was, but he was certain they were all losing. And there was no way they would get past all their compact bodies to the top of those stairs. There was no room for them to go unnoticed while climbing.

Shit. They were so close to getting free, yet these repugnant little beings blocked their way.

CHAPTER TWENTY-TWO

MOST OF THE creatures were clustered near the bottom of the stairs. They were the ones who had been tossed aside, battered, and ripped apart, yet they still screeched and squawked while beating each other.

Leaning closer to Kaylia, Brokk whispered in her ear. "If we leave, will we find another way out?"

It was pointless to stand here when they had no chance of escaping. Kaylia looked longingly at the door before nodding. He understood her reluctance to leave behind the only exit they'd found so far, but staying here and trying to get through these things wasn't an option.

They started to edge their way away from the creatures and the carcasses littering the ground around the stairs when one of them finally made it to the top. Once there, it released an ear-piercing shriek, tipped its head back, and pounded its chest with fisted hands.

Its ears flopped back until they nearly touched the ground before the gremlin lifted its head, raised its arms, and jumped up and down while turning in a small circle. It had become the winner in their sick game.

The others all stopped to watch as the winner started down the steps. Its feet kicked out extra far, and it practically skipped as it bared its jagged teeth in an ear-splitting grin.

The other gremlins moved out of its way, gathering at the far edges of the stairs and risking falling over the edge as no banister or wall protected them from doing so. Those gremlins bowed so low their foreheads touched the ground, as did the tips of their ears.

What is going on now?

When the champion stepped off the last step and lifted his hands into the air while screaming again, the others all rose. Some clapped the winner on the back, but many retreated to settle on the pristine blue sky... except the sky was far from pristine in this area.

A lake of red was at the base of the stairs and spreading across the blue. Some of the blood was darker and crusted like it had been there for a while; other sections were a vibrant, scarlet shade that seeped across the sky.

Some of the creatures lifted bits of discarded meat and started eating. Most of those parts looked like they were from some of the animals who roamed Doomed Valley. They must have fallen into this mirror realm too, and some of the pieces looked like they belonged to immortals who had met the same fate.

The winner sauntered over to a larger, newer beast, ripped its leg off, and stuck it in his mouth. As it walked, the others scampered to get out of the gremlin's way; they revealed more remains as they did so... most of those remains were more gremlins.

Brokk's stomach churned with revulsion for these monstrous things. They might be the most repulsive creatures he'd ever encountered, which was saying a lot.

As the winner walked through the crowd, Brokk realized their strange stair-climbing game had made this one their king, leader, or whatever these creatures called whoever ruled over them.

The new head gremlin settled himself onto a rack of picked-dry ribs. He draped one arm over a glistening bone while happily chewing on the hairy leg he'd claimed as his.

Judging by the freshness of that leg, the gremlins must have had some other unfortunate victim come through here recently. When it did, the gremlins attacked and killed it, but not before it destroyed a few of them, too.

One of those they killed must have been their former leader. The stair game had been their insane way of crowning a new ruler.

Some of the tinier gremlins scampered forward, but when they went for the fresh meat, the leader lowered his leg to shriek at them. Bowing their heads, the smaller ones curled into themselves as some bigger gremlins hopped toward them.

The smaller creatures retreated. As they did so, they claimed some meat from the remains of their own kind and went to sit a few hundred feet away from the leader. Once there, they started cannibalizing their own.

Yep, they're the most revolting things I've ever seen.

Kaylia placed both hands over her mouth as she muffled a gagging noise. He almost went to comfort her before recalling she would most likely rebuke him.

He dug his fingers into his palms as the little green freaks settled in with their meals. They were lucky these things had been preoccupied with their stairclimbing contest when they first came upon them.

He and Kaylia wouldn't have known what they were, but the gremlins would have seen them coming and attacked. They wouldn't have been given much time to defend themselves before the gremlins swarmed over them.

But their competition was over, leaving the stairs unblocked. They'd have to make their way around the blood to avoid leaving footprints, but they could get to the steps, the door, and freedom from this place.

If they got to the door and opened it, these things would know they were there, but they could slip through before the gremlins ever got to the top. From there, he could pull more shadows around them and disappear easily into the jungle.

"We have to try for it," he whispered in her ear.

She glanced uneasily at the feasting gremlins before nodding. If they were careful, they could do this.

CHAPTER TWENTY-THREE

THEY CREPT toward the sea of blood. They edged around it to the staircase, carefully avoiding scattered bones and a small, sleeping gremlin under the steps.

Beside him, Kaylia winced as she stepped over dried remains, planted her hands on the stairs, and pulled herself onto them. Brokk followed swiftly after her; they couldn't get too far apart, or the shadows would fall away from her.

Brokk held his breath when he climbed onto the step. They looked made of glass, but he half expected them to creak beneath his weight.

Instead, their footsteps remained noiseless as Kaylia climbed to the top with Brokk beside her. When she reached the top, her hand rested on the knob, and she glanced back at the gremlins before looking at him.

Those things would come for them as soon as she opened that door, but they'd have a good head start. He had no idea what might await them in the jungle, but they could evade these beasts; he was sure of it.

He nodded at her to continue, and she twisted the knob. She

frowned when it didn't move beneath her hand. She tried again, but it remained unmoving. Her face becoming more frantic, she seized it with both hands and tried again.

Brokk watched the gremlins feasting below, but they'd soon tire of their meal and start moving around again. Would they return to the stairs?

For all he knew, the stair game was an hourly occurrence for these monsters and how they passed their time between kills. With a growing sense of urgency, he forgot about not touching Kaylia as he moved her hand away and grasped the knob.

He tried twisting it as he leaned his shoulder against the thick, wooden door and pushed all his weight into it. If he succeeded, the door would splinter apart when it came open, but he didn't give a shit as long as it opened.

He couldn't let these things know they were there if they couldn't escape. Below, some of the gremlins stirred, but it was only to retrieve more food before retreating again.

He now understood why they weren't running free through Doomed Valley. They hadn't been able to get through the door, but instead of moving on to another exit, they'd established a camp here, and judging by the number of bones, it was a successful one.

When the door refused to give way to him, he focused on Kaylia. "Can you cast a spell over it?"

"I'm not sure it would break it open, and if it doesn't...."

She didn't have to finish; they knew what would happen then. It would only draw the gremlins' attention to them.

"We can both control air," he murmured, keeping an eye out to ensure the gremlins' big ears didn't catch his words. "What if we gather enough to batter the door with it?"

"If it doesn't work, those creatures will know we're here."

And they'd both be trapped. He eyed the door as he considered their options. He hated the idea of being this close to getting away from this place and being unable to do so. Freedom was *right there*, at his fingertips, and still so far away.

He resisted kicking the door and attempting to batter it down, but it would only make things worse. Taking a deep breath, he tried to calm the ire festering inside him as he came to the only conclusion he could.

"We can go back down and see if there's another way out."

Kaylia looked as disappointed as him while eyeing the door. "There will be."

It took everything Brokk had to turn away from the door. Below, some of the monsters finished eating and rose.

They waddled back and forth as their full, bloated bellies weighed them down. Brokk sneered at the disgusting creatures, but now that they were on the move again, they had to do something.

"We should go," Kaylia whispered.

"What if the next exit is locked too?"

"If there's nothing else there, we can do more to get through it." Kaylia glanced nervously at the door. "If this is protected by magic...."

Her words trailed off, but Brokk understood what she was trying to say. They'd likely fail to batter it down with air if magic protected it.

They were at an exit and no closer to escaping than last night.

"Come on," he murmured.

When Brokk clasped Kaylia's elbow, the warmth of her skin burned into his hand, and an overwhelming protective urge assailed him. It was the last thing she wanted, but every part of him was ready to do whatever it took to get her safely out of this.

He gritted his teeth against his impulses as they silently descended the steps while the waddling gremlins settled into separate piles of bones and flesh. There, they lay down and fell asleep.

Their awful snores filled the air, but thankfully, their noise covered any sound he and Kaylia might have made as they crept through the carcasses and creatures. He hoped never to see the foul-smelling monsters again, but Doomed Valley never kept its monsters leashed.

CHAPTER TWENTY-FOUR

KAYLIA SPENT much of the day dreading the night when they would stop. The memory of being locked in Brokk's embrace—secure, warm, and aware of sensations she'd believed dead for hundreds of years—haunted her.

But with it came the guilt. And that guilt had spent a fair portion of the day chewing at her like a rat on wires.

Not only was she exhausted from their endless walking, the monotonous scenery, and their encounter with the gremlins, but she was also emotionally battered. That was the worst of it, as every step was an effort while sleep beckoned her.

The sun had set, and colors flooded the sky when Brokk suggested they stop for the day. She was both happy to stop and dreading what the night would bring.

Eventually, it would get as cold as last night, and she had no idea how to battle that. She couldn't fall asleep in Brokk's arms again. It would only make everything worse if she did.

But as she told herself that, the memory of his hand on her elbow and the warmth it created inside her returned. Her skin still tingled from his touch, and she easily recalled the desire he awakened in her this morning.

Closing her eyes, she tried to shut out the memory of the way her body came alive in his arms. She couldn't take the chance of that happening again.

Yes, she was a woman with needs, and she supposed she had a right to fill them, but giving in to her desire would be a betrayal to Fabian and a knife through her heart. Still, she couldn't stop surreptitiously watching him as he settled in for the night.

She found his inherent grace fascinating to watch. Neither of them had bothered to change; they didn't have many options for clothes, and if he was like her, she saw no point in putting her clean clothes on a dirty body, but even with grime on him, he was still handsome and alluring.

No one should look that good while covered in dirt and blood, but he did. She wanted to hate him for it; instead, she fought to keep from crawling into his arms.

He'd be a good kisser; she was sure of it. And once she started kissing him, she'd never stop. Kaylia gulped before tearing her attention away from him. She tried to focus on something… *anything* else as she tried not to think about *him*.

Above, the jungle was already dark, while down here, the fading sun still sent streaks of pink and red across the sky. It truly was beautiful, even if she was tired of being here.

Her attention returned to Brokk as he leaned back on an elbow, stretched out his legs, and studied the jungle while munching on some dried meat. She couldn't help admiring how the colors played across his handsome face and danced in his eyes.

Few men were as attractive as him, but he wasn't arrogant. He was simply just… *him*.

That only made him more appealing. Stifling a sound of disgust, Kaylia dropped her pack on the ground and settled in beside it.

She pulled out some bread and cheese. Chomping on a piece

of increasingly stale bread, she scowled at the trees above while cursing herself and this doomed realm.

They had to get out of here so they could return to Dragonia. For all they knew, Cole or Orin could have already found some crudue vine, and Lexi was awake again. She could be stuck in this realm and far too close to him for no reason.

The sooner they were free of this place and she was away from Brokk, the better. But as she thought it, disappointment filled her.

She didn't want to be free of him.

And with that realization came more guilt. Kaylia threw her bread into her pack. Hecate, she hated this.

As the sun sank lower, the chill crept into the air again, and she dug into her bag to remove more of her clothes. Putting clean clothes over dirty ones was a waste, but she'd do whatever it took to stay warm without Brokk's aid.

She tugged on another layer of clothes and her cloak, but they didn't keep the wind from howling across the land and finding every crevice in her wardrobe. As the colors faded from the sky, ice filled her veins.

It hadn't been this windy last night, but this place was determined to make her miserable. She hated it here for many reasons, but this cold was number one.

It didn't bother Brokk as much as he pulled out a blanket, folded it in half, and laid it on the ground. He didn't pull it open to crawl into it and didn't layer himself with clothes.

Resentful of his resilience to the cold, Kaylia scowled at him as she set her blanket on the ground. She cast a protective air bubble around them, which helped shut out the wind but not the cold.

She'd give anything for a fire, but that wouldn't happen in this land of endless sky. Instead of settling beside burning wood, she pulled back her blanket and crawled into the sandwich she'd created.

Nestling into it, she drew her knees up to her chest and tried to shut out the cold as she put her head on her lumpy pack. It wasn't the best pillow in the world, but it was far better than nothing as she clamped her teeth together to keep them from chattering.

Beside her, Brokk remained sitting on his blanket with his knees drawn up and his arms draped over them. He looked peaceful, but she sensed a wealth of tension running beneath his surface as his gaze constantly roamed over the night.

She didn't know how, but eventually, sleep claimed her.

CHAPTER TWENTY-FIVE

WHEN KAYLIA WOKE the next morning, Brokk was wrapped around her again. She vaguely recalled shivering herself awake before warmth enveloped her and she settled back into sleep.

This time, she didn't feel the evidence of his erection against her back, but that didn't stop her from experiencing a sharp longing for this man and everything that could never be. She closed her eyes and tried to breathe through her mouth to avoid inhaling his enticing scent of man and fresh rain, but his aroma had ingrained itself on her.

Why was he so warm, and why did he affect her like this when *no* others had for centuries? And *why* did she have to be trapped in this place with him?

She knew the answer to that last question, though it did her no good. And neither did inwardly whining about this unexpected twist her life had taken.

Her life had taken many other unexpected and *far* worse twists over her many years, and not only had she dealt with them all, but they'd made her stronger. This one would, too... eventually... somehow.

She should pull away from him as she had yesterday. Her

cheeks and lips were icy, but she could handle the cold; she just had to *move*.

Instead, she remained nestled against him as an image of Fabian, lying on a beach with his hands propped behind his head as he grinned up at her, filled her mind. He'd been tall and all lean muscle while watching her dance naked in the sand.

She could still feel the pulse of energy flowing up through her feet and spreading through her body. The ocean and sand had teemed with life, strengthening her as she threw her arms wide and basked in the sun's rays.

When she collapsed, exhausted and laughing beside him on the blanket, he'd pulled her into his arms—

Kaylia quickly shut the memory down. It was bad enough she was lying in the arms of another man, but she shouldn't recall that while doing so. Her eyes fluttered open, and she gazed at the colors spreading across the sky as the sun rose.

Brokk didn't say anything, and his hold on her never changed, but he was awake. She was certain of it.

"You know," she whispered, "I was engaged once."

Brokk stopped breathing at her revelation, and then his breath tickled her nape as he expelled it. She had no idea why she'd told him that; maybe it was to remind herself of why she shouldn't be enjoying lying beside him so much.

Maybe it was to make him pull away, to make *her* move, or perhaps she wanted to tell him. He was easy to talk to, and until it became so complicated for her, she'd enjoyed being around him and considered him a friend.

"His name was Fabian, and he was a warlock." Now that she'd opened this can, it kept coming out. "I met him at a friend's Samhain party. At first, we were just friends, but over time, our relationship became something more… something amazing, rare, and precious. We were planning our wedding when a vampire killed him."

Brokk's arms constricted around her. "I'm sorry."

"It's why I created the crone realm and went to live there. I didn't know what else to do with myself, where else to go, where else to..."

Hide. But she didn't say that part out loud. She was a little ashamed of herself for having run away. She hadn't considered it so before, but now it felt cowardly.

She should have stayed and faced life without Fabian instead of running away. At the time, retreating from the world had been a balm to her battered soul, but she could never do it again. No matter what future hurts she endured, she would never run from the world; it was far too beautiful, and there was too much good she could do in it for her to hide again.

"Nothing was ever the same after he died. I intended to stay in the crone realm until I died too, but then you and Sahira arrived, and those plans changed."

"What happened to the vampire?"

"Fabian's brother killed him. He was there when it happened and was the one who told me about Fabian's death."

Brokk was silent for a little while before speaking again. "Would you go back to the crone realm?"

"No. I'll miss Fabian until the day I die, but I'm not meant to remain in only one realm. I see that now. Besides, he would want me to live and enjoy things again. I needed to go to the crone realm and build something beautiful there to help me heal, but that time in my life is over. There are many new, beautiful things to build in the realms... if we can save Lexi."

His arms squeezed her again. "We'll save her, and if not us, then someone else will. I have faith in that. Cole won't rest until he finds the crudue vine."

Brokk was right about that. Cole would do everything in his power to save Lexi, but... "I hope he doesn't destroy the realms to do so."

Brokk didn't protest her words or say that his brother would never do such a thing; they both knew he could. If Lexi died, nothing would stop the Shadow Reaver from taking over and leveling everything in his way.

They had to get out of here, but she didn't move as she allowed Brokk's presence to soothe the ragged edges of her tattered heart. If things had been different, if there had never been a Fabian, she might have fallen in love with this kind, powerful, ruthless man who held her so tenderly.

But things could never be different.

CHAPTER TWENTY-SIX

WHEN THE SUN was fully up, Brokk knew it was time to let go of Kaylia but was reluctant to do so. She fit so perfectly against him and felt so right in his arms that it felt like he was releasing a piece of himself.

But she didn't belong in his arms... or at least, she didn't think so. The conversation of her dead fiancé wasn't brought up on a whim.

This Fabian was why she'd been so distant and cold yesterday. She didn't have to tell him that; he could read between the lines. She felt guilty for sleeping beside him because she'd enjoyed it; that was why she remained in his arms now.

She was warm and lush, and he'd give anything to caress the silken skin beneath her clothes and hear her moan his name, but she'd brought up her fiancé to drive a wedge between them. He didn't give a shit about ghosts, though.

They were both very much alive, and there was no reason for them not to enjoy each other, but he couldn't bring himself to push it further. She told him about her fiancé to place a mental barrier between them, and he would respect that.

While he understood her reasons for trying to keep her

distance from him, he couldn't bury his disappointment. He wanted her, and she was still in love with a dead man.

He was trapped in a special kind of hell.

"I hope you don't mind me sleeping beside you again," he said. "You were shivering pretty bad again last night."

"I don't mind. Thank you."

Reluctantly, Brokk unraveled his arms from around her and pushed himself to his feet. He stretched as he surveyed the endless, empty landscape while trying to keep his focus on anything but her.

They had to get out of this mirror realm; at least in Doomed Valley, there were plenty of lethal distractions. Killing something trying to eat them would make him feel better.

"Hopefully, we can find a way out of here today," he said.

"That would be good."

They retreated to separate sections of the sky and relieved themselves before returning to their packs. Once there, they brushed their teeth, ate a quick breakfast, and set out across a much cloudier sky.

The gray clouds rolling in darkened the horizon as they blocked out the sun. He wondered what would happen if it started raining. Would it fall from the ground or down from the trees?

It would be interesting to see, but no raindrops dampened them as they continued their trek across the sky. They wandered for hours before coming across another set of stairs.

At first, Brokk wasn't sure what was ahead of them as, like the last one, the stairs mirrored the sky, but he spotted a difference in the landscape before it solidified into a possible escape.

Thankfully, this set of steps didn't have hideous monsters racing up and down them, and bones didn't surround them. That didn't mean the door would open; like the last one, it could be sealed by some magical barrier. At least they could try to do more to this door if it didn't open.

As they ascended the stairs, Brokk prepared himself to discover the door locked, but when he rested his hand on the knob, it twisted beneath his palm. He glanced at Kaylia before pulling his sword from its sheath; she did the same.

"I'll cloak us in shadows," he said.

"Okay."

Brokk drew their meager shadows around them before bracing himself for what lay beyond and pushing open the door. He was prepared for almost anything… except stepping from the mirror realm and into a war.

CHAPTER TWENTY-SEVEN

SCREAMS AND SHOUTS rebounded around them as steel crashed against steel, bowstrings twanged, and arrows whistled as they flew past their heads and into the trees. Kaylia staggered back when a man with a mouth full of bloody teeth screamed while racing toward her.

His arms waved over his head like a demented monkey. It took her a second to process he didn't mean any harm as he fled the chaos surrounding them.

She stood, waiting for the man to run around her, but she'd forgotten that shadows still enshrouded her until Brokk jerked her out of the way. For now, they remained hidden from whatever was causing this insanity.

Brokk pulled her forward and wrapped his arms around her as he secured her back to his chest. His sword remained in hand, pointed toward the ground as he moved, while hers remained trapped before her. Retreating hastily, he pulled her away from the chaos.

When Kaylia glanced back at the doorway they'd emerged from, she spotted the gaping, black hole in the center of a tree big enough to drive a truck through. The hole was a dark, shadowy place about as inviting as the bowels of Hell.

The man, more afraid of what lay behind him, ran straight into the tree and on toward an unknown fate in the mirror realm. Kaylia questioned if they should do the same and return as well.

If they avoided the gremlins and had no other surprises ahead, they could safely travel through it until the next staircase led them to…?

Who knew what it would lead them to? It could be something far worse than this, considering how badly everything had gone so far in this realm.

Arrows thudded into the trees around them. Brokk pulled her down as he folded himself protectively over her and led her through the jungle while trying to evade the missiles flying around them.

At first, she couldn't tell who was fighting or what immortals were out there; it could be some survivors from their group. If it was, they had to help them.

Then she spotted a group of snakelike creatures with a serpent tail in place of feet and clawed, scaled hands that clasped their weapons. While their lower bodies were snakes, their upper half was a man or woman. Some paused to rise on their tails, making them nearly ten feet tall.

None of them wore clothes, not even the women whose breasts swayed with their rapid, slithering movements. Many had hair flowing to their waists; some had it longer, while others wore it a little shorter.

Helmets adorned their heads, but it was the only protection they wore as they fired arrows and moved with the speed of a striking viper through the trees. They were so fast they nearly blurred while darting in and out to avoid the arrows flying their way from a group of immortals who had surrounded themselves with a circle of fire.

And she and Brokk were trapped in the middle of their fight.

Kaylia gulped as Brokk pulled her against the trunk of another tree. The thickness of the foliage in the jungle often blocked the sun from reaching the ground, but the black clouds choking the sky turned the day to night.

Thankfully, the fire created some shadows, allowing Brokk to keep them hidden. Kaylia's heart hammered as screams of rage and agony emanated around them.

An arrow hit the tree only inches from Brokk's head, but he didn't flinch or try to move again. Beside his head, the arrow quivered as fear churned in Kaylia's stomach.

It had come so close to him…. *I can't lose him.*

The thought blazed across her mind with an intensity that rattled her more than the battle waging around them. Taking a tremulous breath, Kaylia adjusted her grip on her sword before flattening herself against him as more of the serpentlike immortals raced to surround the fire.

They should open a portal out of here, but returning would be almost impossible, and they'd made it this far. Still, failure was better than death, and they could always try again.

She liked the idea of returning here about as much as playing hide-and-seek with an ogre, but she'd do whatever was necessary to save Lexi. They couldn't help if they were dead.

Before she could voice her opinion, a clap of thunder reverberated across the sky. It was so loud that Kaylia almost threw her hands over her ears as the earth quaked beneath her feet.

The thunder still boomed as a jagged tear zigzagged across the earth, cutting a path through the center of the snakes. They screamed and tried to flee but didn't all get out of the way in time to avoid the pit.

Kaylia's eyes widened as the earth devoured those snakelike beings, and the thunder rolled away. Just as the creatures were filling the gaps the death of their brethren had created, lightning shot down from the sky.

The rapid fire of electricity pierced the treetops, but a few jagged bolts made it through to take out the snakes. The impact of the lightning gouged craters in the earth as sparks flew into the air. The hair on Kaylia's nape stood up as the air pulsated and crackled with electricity.

Despite her every intention to keep a wall between her and Brokk, her fingers encircled the corded muscles of his forearms, and she squeezed. She needed this connection between them, this assurance he was okay as anarchy reigned around them.

"We have to get out of here," Brokk whispered in her ear.

Kaylia nodded, but before she could suggest escaping through a portal, more lightning hammered the earth around them, making it almost impossible to move. Brokk flattened his back against a tree as he held her closer, sheltering her from the worst of the storm.

The whistle of another barrage of arrows peppered the air. Brokk shifted her so she stood behind him, caught between him and the tree as he used his body to shield her from the worst of it.

"I can cast a protection spell!" she shouted.

Another round of thunder drowned out her words as more lightning sizzled across the sky and crashed into the earth. She kept expecting a deluge of rain to start pounding the ground, but it remained dry.

In front of her, Brokk moved his head a little to the side a second before an arrow hit the tree. His instincts had told him it was coming, and he'd moved out of the way in time to avoid it, but it had been so close.

Too close. And what if he's not fast enough next time?

CHAPTER TWENTY-EIGHT

HER FINGERS BIT into his back before reluctantly releasing him to sheath her sword. After she finished, she lifted her hands to cast a protection spell. She'd just started it when Brokk reached behind him, grasped her wrist, and pulled her before him again. He returned his sword to its holster.

"Wait!" she shouted, but the storm swallowed her voice.

Brokk hunched protectively around her again as his arms cinched around her waist. Kaylia turned her head to shout into his ear that she could cast a protection spell, but before the words left her, a passing snakelike immortal whipped out its tail.

The immortal had no idea they were there, but it struck a lucky blow as its tail whipped across her legs and knocked her feet out from under her. She would have hit the ground if Brokk's arms weren't locked securely around her.

Unfortunately, the blow happened simultaneously with a lull in the thunder, and her cry drew their attention. The creature's head swiveled toward her, and its yellow eyes with their elliptical pupils locked on her.

The snakelike man couldn't see her, but he knew she was there. She could tell by the flare of his nostrils and the flicker of his forked tongue as his lips skimmed back to reveal his hooked fangs. Her skin crawled at this serpent characteristic in the face of a handsome man.

Before she could blink, that tongue lashed out and slapped her in the face. Kaylia recoiled as a low growl rumbled up Brokk's chest. He pulled her back a few steps as the scent of her blood permeated the air, and a warm trickle ran down her cheek.

When the man eagerly scented the air, Kaylia placed a hand over her face, hoping to stifle the blood he smelled. Brokk swung her around and stepped before her as the man detoured from his attack on the immortals behind the fire and came toward them.

With panic fueling her magic, Kaylia lowered her hand from her face and started weaving her fingers through the air as she recited the words that would protect them. They could either flee this area or open a portal and leave Doomed Valley once they were sure none of these monsters would follow them through.

Thanks to the mirror realm, they no longer knew where they were in Doomed Valley. For all she knew, they were back near where they first started and heading back into land they'd already traversed.

Or you could be within feet of it.

That was the worst thing about this place; it hid *everything* while fucking with their heads and unleashing countless nightmares on them.

Before she could finish her spell, lightning slammed into the top of a tree to her right. A zigzagging pattern cut through the tree's center as another bolt hit the ground only inches away from her.

The impact lifted them off their feet and flung them backward. They hit the ground and bounced across it before Brokk crashed into a tree. He came to an abrupt stop while her momentum caused her to tumble head over heels.

His fingers clawed at her, seeking to draw her back as she

was torn from his embrace and into one of those awful creatures. Kaylia's weight knocked the woman off her path and almost toppled her over, but she managed to return her balance as she swung a sword down.

The monster would have cleaved her in two if Kaylia hadn't gathered her hands against her chest and pushed up with them both while shouting the words, "Wall of air, protect me. Wall of air, shelter me. Wall of air, belong to me!"

She shoved upward to knock the woman's sword aside. A blast of air hit the woman in the face, lifting and pushing her back. Kaylia dodged the tip of the tail streaking toward her face as another crash of thunder rocked the earth.

Twisting, Kaylia watched in horror as another jagged crack raced across the ground... straight toward her and the woman rising onto her tail. Fury etched the woman's features as she searched for Kaylia, but before she could start forward again, the earth opened below her, and the woman screamed as she tumbled into oblivion.

Turning onto her belly, Kaylia clawed at the dirt as she got to her feet and started sprinting. She only made it two steps before the ground gave way beneath her feet.

Her scream was cut off by her heart lurching into her throat as her body fell toward certain death. Desperate to keep herself from tumbling into oblivion, her nails broke as she clawed at the earth, but gravity kept dragging her down... down... down.

She was starting to tip backward, starting to freefall into nothing, when her flailing hand caught a dangling tree root while something snagged her ankle and jerked down. Kaylia gasped as the unexpected added weight caused her to slip a few inches on the root before she caught herself.

Her pack lurched on her back, adding more of a drag to her as something sharp bit into her flesh, digging deep. Warm blood trickled down her leg.

She looked down to see one of the serpent creatures holding

onto her leg. The man's eyes were cruel as his fingers dug deeper.

She was his lifeline, but he still enjoyed torturing her as a grim smile creased his mouth. When she was separated from Brokk, the shadows must have fallen away, and now she was exposed to these things.

Kaylia tried kicking the snake man in the face to get rid of him, but the movement only caused her to slip again. The root abraded her palms and tore away her skin before she succeeded in bringing herself to a stop again.

Jerked to a halt, her shoulder screamed in protest as the creature's weight dragged on her. It felt like she'd fallen far too far, but when she looked above her, she saw she'd only slipped a little over a foot. She was *so* close, yet it seemed like miles away.

She didn't dare look down again as she ignored the pain emanating through her body while resting her forehead against the root. Air surrounded her, and she could feel the looming abyss below as it beckoned to her with its infinite possibilities of death.

CHAPTER TWENTY-NINE

RATTLED from the earth by another round of thunder, dirt and rocks bounced off the side of the wall and tumbled around her. Some of them hit her face as small pieces of debris stuck to her eyelashes.

With a groan, she gathered her strength and pulled herself up the root a little. If she could shrug out of her pack, she would, but she didn't dare let go of the root to adjust enough to wiggle it free.

The monster pulled at her but didn't jerk down again or dig his claws in deeper. He may enjoy tormenting others, but she was his way out of here.

Her arms screamed in protest; she had to take some of the pressure off them, but it was difficult when she had an easily three-hundred-pound asshole attached like a leech to her leg. Wiggling a little, she tried to get her free foot to lodge onto the wall in hopes of bracing herself a little better.

She got it braced against the wall when rocks gave way, and her foot slipped free again. Something cracked in her shoulder.

Inhaling deeply, she tried to breathe through the pain assaulting her. When she felt ready, she tried to get her foot against the wall again, but the strain on her arms was too much, and she fell a few inches again.

"Stupid bitch," the man hissed beneath her.

If Kaylia could use her hands, she would have blasted him in the face with a wall of air or beaten the fucker to death. *He* was the whole reason she couldn't pull herself free from here.

"You're the one relying on a stupid bitch to save you, you lazy piece of shit," she snarled.

When his claws dug a little deeper into her calf, she kicked at him again and managed to catch him in the cheek. He growled but was at least smart enough to refrain from jerking at her again.

Resting her forehead against the cool dirt, Kaylia took a deep breath as the power of the earth seeped into her skin. She inhaled the damp aroma of the soil, relishing its scent as it helped to revitalize her and ease some of the pressure from her hands and shoulders.

"What are you doing?" the man demanded.

Kaylia didn't bother to reply as she absorbed the life teeming against her forehead. It was all so precious and vital, and while she should be trying to drag her ass out of this, she required this flow of life to help rejuvenate her.

She was about to start pulling herself free again when a hand clamped around her wrist. When small tingles erupted across her skin and her breath sucked in, she knew instantly that Brokk held her.

Lifting her head, she couldn't help but smile as she drank him in. He must have released the shadows from himself, and he was the most welcome sight she'd ever seen.

A jagged cut marred his cheek, and blood seeped from it. Something had happened above as more dirt and blood than before covered him. His red eyes burned a fiery shade as they met hers.

Kaylia suppressed a shudder at those eyes. She'd stopped

loathing vampires as much as she once did, but the rage emanating from him made her skin ripple.

Whatever happened up there had *pissed him off.*

A muscle twitched in his cheek as determination etched his features and he pulled her toward the ledge. Dragging her a little upward, Brokk leaned back as he braced his knees further apart and grasped her arm in both of his hands.

He groaned as he hauled her and the shit-for-brains asshole clinging to her toward the edge of the abyss. Kaylia released the tree root to grip his forearm.

His muscles bulged so much that she couldn't get her hand all the way around as she dug her fingers into his skin. She hoped she wasn't hurting him, but he showed no signs of it as the corded muscles in his neck stood starkly out and red crept across his face.

As he worked to pull her free, he edged further away from the pit until he pulled her halfway out. Kaylia fell on her belly as she breathed in the dirt and blood coating the ground. The coppery tang of blood mingled with an ozone aroma so thick it choked the air.

In the hole, the screams of the dying faded away. She didn't know if that was because the blood rushing through her ears had drowned them out, if they'd died, or if they were too far away to hear them anymore.

A fresh round of thunder didn't splinter the earth apart again, but it rattled the ground beneath her and shook the trees until one of them toppled with a crashing bang. Brokk released her with one hand, turned away, and grabbed something she couldn't see.

He thrust a vine into her hand. "Hold this."

Her bloodied and battered fingers encased the vine as he pulled his sword free and ran past her. A few seconds later, the awful grip on her leg shredded deeper into her flesh, and she bit back a scream as the snake's talons raked her.

Then, when she was sure he'd tear half her leg off, the

lumbering idiot relinquished his hold. Kaylia smiled as she imagined him plummeting into the dark before splintering to pieces on some jagged rock.

Now who's the stupid bitch.

Spitting dirt and blood from her mouth, Kaylia clawed her way forward until her feet were out of the hole too. Before she could push herself up, a strong hand encircled her upper arm and lifted her.

Brokk wrapped his arm around her waist and ran as fast as he could with her away from the pit. She did her best not to limp or slow him, but her leg hindered her movements as she ran with him.

Despite the jagged cracks in the earth and the fire coming from their right, more of those snakelike things closed in on them as they sought to get to the immortals behind the wall of fire.

"Are we cloaked in shadows again?" she panted as Brokk weaved them expertly in and out of the trees.

"Yes."

They were moving past the immortals behind the fire and deeper into the trees when shadows slithered forth, and more serpent things emerged from the jungle directly in front of them.

CHAPTER THIRTY

BROKK PULLED Kaylia back against him as more came at them. If they kept going away from the fire and deeper into the jungle, there would be no light for him to keep them cloaked in shadows.

It was as black as the crows who often hung around outside his window in the Gloaming in search of a treat, a pet, and a message to send. Those crows were almost as much a part of the dark fae as the shadows, or at least they were to him.

The shadows didn't move or twist through the darkness, but those serpents did. And there were far too many for him and Kaylia to slip by undetected.

The creatures choked the trees, spilled across the earth, and slithered through the lightning bolts hammering the land around them. Nothing deterred them.

This wasn't a normal storm raging around them, but he had no idea what was causing it and no time to figure it out. He and Kaylia couldn't flee through the trees without encountering some of those things, and once they clashed with one, cloaked in shadows or not, the others would know they were there.

He debated opening a portal, but the serpents would be on

them before they could slip through, and once it opened, the beasts would know they were there. As much as he didn't like it, there was only one option... retreat.

Pulling her back, he led her toward the fire and the shadows dancing across the ground. He had no idea what type of immortals stood behind the flames, but so far, they were holding their own against these reptiles.

While he didn't know if the other immortals could also become the enemy, he *knew* the snake things were.

The enemy of my enemy is my friend.

He hoped that adage held true because they were his only hope of getting out of this... or at least the flames surrounding them were.

Unlike Lexi, he and Kaylia couldn't withstand fire, but a witch and dark fae had some control over the elements. He didn't think that was the same for the immortals behind the wall of flames; otherwise, they would've weaponized the fire further against these creatures.

He and Kaylia could destroy the snakes and have those other immortals turn on them, but Brokk was willing to take that chance.

Pulling Kaylia further back, he held her against his side and bent to whisper in her ear. "Together, we can use the fire against these things. We can't go further into the jungle. There aren't enough shadows there. And we can't open a portal before they're on top of us."

Kaylia's chin jutted out, and she nodded briskly. Brokk would much prefer to be inside the wall of fire while they did this, but beggars couldn't be choosers.

The heat of the inferno caused his clothes to cleave to him as sweat slid down his back and beaded across his forehead as they crept closer. He used the back of his arm to wipe away the water dripping into his eyes and lowered his pack.

He couldn't have the extra weight on his back, and it was one more thing for the flames to possibly catch on. If they did, he'd burn with the pack, and his supplies weren't worth that.

Kaylia set her pack beside his and leaned toward him. Her earthy aroma filled his nostrils as the loose strands of her hair tickled his cheek. She also smelled of sweat and fire, but somehow, she made the combination enticing.

He couldn't believe he was thinking about how alluring her aroma was while the serpents were closing in on them, but it was impossible not to notice her. He dug his fingers into his palm to keep from brushing back a loose strand of hair and tucking it behind her ear.

"I can put a protective spell around us," she whispered.

"Can we move fire through it?"

"No. It would tear down the barrier if we did that."

"Let's use the fire to crisp fry some of these things, and then you can put a protective spell around yourself."

Her eyes narrowed as the cleft in her chin deepened. "I'm not leaving you out here and unprotected while I hide behind a barrier."

Brokk didn't argue with her; he would do whatever was necessary to protect her, but he couldn't force her to do something. He'd have to ensure these things didn't get close enough to harm her.

Brokk edged as close to the flames as he dared before they became too much to bear. Kaylia stopped beside him, and while more thunder rattled the earth and lightning pelted the ground, they found some safety in the shadow of the flames as the storm didn't touch them here.

Closing his eyes, Brokk focused on the power of the flames so close to his right shoulder they nearly blistered his skin. Their heat and energy radiated against him as they devoured the land.

Smoke smoldered from some places where the lightning hit, and more flames leapt to life further in the jungle before sputtering out. So far, the fire remained centered around the group of immortals tucked safely within its circle.

As dozens of the serpents approached, Brokk lifted his hands and opened his eyes. In unison with Kaylia, they moved their hands forward.

Flames followed the movement as they broke away from the fire and crashed into the creatures only ten feet away. The monstrosities released shocked hissing sounds while others screeched as the flames caught on their hair and scales.

A green color filled the air as the fire rose over their tails and sparks shot into the night. Together, they released more flames on the serpents who had turned toward their engulfed brethren, but there was little they could do to put out the inferno as it devoured their friends.

The immortals behind them shouted in disbelief as more snakes burst into flames.

"What the fuck?"

"What's going on?" their confused shouts continued to fill the air.

"Are you doing that?"

"Ryker!" someone else bellowed. "Ryker, you have to get over here to see this!"

Brokk ignored their yelling as he and Kaylia continued to unleash fire on the monsters, who were now edging away from the flames attacking them.

CHAPTER THIRTY-ONE

WHILE THE FLAMES' strength and the earth's power thrumming beneath her feet helped strengthen her, Kaylia could still feel her magical abilities draining. She was injured and tiring fast; she needed to replenish herself before she dropped.

Without thinking, her body instinctively sought the biggest energy source near her... Brokk. Power swelled beneath her fingertips when her hand encircled his forearm.

The power he exuded crackled across her skin as it fueled her abilities and renewed her strength. Releasing him, she gathered more fire and heaved it at the creatures who had started to retreat in confusion.

Lightning pierced through the sky and crashed all around them as it took out more creatures, and a fresh wave of thunder fractured the earth. Some fell into this new pit as commands to retreat filled the air.

The two of them released another wave of fire, sending what remained of the creatures slithering rapidly toward the jungle while more fell beneath the flames. She couldn't see what was happening on the other side of the circle, but the twang of more arrows unleashing filled the air.

Screams came from the other side of the fire, and more cries to retreat sounded. When she swayed, Kaylia grasped Brokk's arm again as she steadied herself. He grabbed her hand and squeezed it as rain started falling.

The fire sizzled and popped when the water hit it. As more of the snakes slithered through the jungle, Brokk released her hand to unleash another ball of fire on them.

Screams erupted from the trees as the fire erupted in the shadows. She let go of Brokk to help him hurl more firebombs at the creatures.

As the fire dwindled behind them, Brokk reached for her, but the immortals from within the flames poured out and raced across the battered field. They pushed her and Brokk further apart as they bellowed while clashing with the remaining snakes.

Kaylia scampered to get out of the way before they trampled her as the fire dwindled to the point where they couldn't use it. She made it a few feet before something hard and heavy crashed into her side and sent her flying.

Brokk lunged for her, but he just missed grabbing her. Her back hit the ground, and she bounced a few feet across the earth before stopping against a tree trunk.

She started to roll away, but the cold tip of a blade against her throat stopped her. Kaylia lay back on the ground as a looming figure towered over her.

The dwindling light from the fire danced in eyes the color of liquid mercury. Dark brown hair fell to the man's shoulders, and thick stubble lined his square jaw. The breadth of his shoulders blocked out the world around him.

His black pants, shirt, and boots blended in with the night, as did his dark hair, but those impossibly silver eyes stood out starkly from the dark. His plain clothes didn't help pinpoint what kind of immortal he was.

Kaylia held up her hands but wasn't sure if shadows still

cloaked her and if he could see her. His next words proved that Brokk remained close enough to keep her cloaked.

"Show yourself," the man commanded.

CHAPTER THIRTY-TWO

KAYLIA GULPED; her throat working against the blade caused it to scrape her skin a little. This man had good instincts or was damn lucky if he'd found her against the tree and managed to point the blade into her neck.

Which meant she wasn't so lucky, and she had no idea how he would react when she didn't reveal herself. She had no control over the shadows and couldn't reveal herself to this mountain of a man.

"Show yourself now!" he barked.

Kaylia lifted her hands to push the air upward, but as she did so, she knew it wouldn't do much, as weakness seeped through her. Her injury and the amount of power she used earlier to control the fire had drained her.

And all she'd succeed in doing was pissing off this guy when she smacked him with a wind current. She lowered her hands and dug her fingers into the ground as she used it to help recharge her, but it wouldn't be enough.

Kaylia didn't feel a difference, but the shadows must have slipped away as the man's eyes went from staring at her chest to clashing with hers. He frowned as his gaze roved over her.

"You're not a dark fae," he stated.

"No, but I am," Brokk growled.

Kaylia had no idea where he was, but the man's eyes widened, and his chin rose a little. The shadows pulled back to reveal Brokk standing behind the man with a knife to his throat. Brokk's eyes were a ferocious shade of red.

"Move your blade, *now!*" Brokk commanded in a nearly unrecognizable voice due to his extended fangs. When the man didn't move, Brokk snapped. "Get your fucking sword away from her!"

The man's jaw clenched. Somehow, his eyes became more silver as his thick muscles bunched and his nostrils flared.

Then, with obvious reluctance, he moved the blade away from her throat. Kaylia breathed a sigh as she wiggled backward to escape the man before rising to her feet.

"Get over here, Kaylia," Brokk commanded.

Normally, she wouldn't have taken well to being ordered about in such a way, but standing here, with many of these unknown immortals surrounding them and the snakelike monsters in the jungle, arguing wasn't the best idea. Besides, she preferred being at Brokk's side rather than away from it.

As she started toward Brokk, the man threw an elbow back, catching him in the side. Air grunted out from Brokk as the man twisted in his arms.

Blood spilled from where Brokk's knife cut across his throat as the man threw his weight into Brokk. The man was a good inch taller than Brokk, had a thicker body, and was probably a good thirty pounds heavier, but Brokk delivered a blow that resonated through the woods.

The strange immortal's arms encircled Brokk's waist and propelled him backward as they tumbled to the ground together. Punches flew, grunts filled the air, and blood spilled as they pummeled each other while bouncing through the thick foliage.

Kaylia's heart leapt into her throat when the jungle swallowed them in its dark depths and she lost view of Brokk. Rushing forward, she sprinted toward where they'd disappeared as more immortals surrounded her.

She could hear the continued sounds of a fight and was almost to them when hands clasped her arms and dragged her back. Kaylia jerked against their hold and kicked at them, but they managed to avoid her blows as they held her away from them.

Exhausted and battered, she wanted to give up but refused to do so as the sounds of a fight continued from the dense foliage. *Brokk.*

The word was a mixture of longing and distress as she pulled forward until her arms and shoulders bent at odd angles. Her shoulder had started to feel better, but now it protested the strain she put on it.

They adjusted their grip on her arms as they grasped under her armpits and pulled her between the two large immortals. Kaylia tried kicking them again, but they were too close for her to do any damage.

"Bastards!" she spat.

They ignored her as they kept their eyes on where Brokk and that man had disappeared.

"What is she?" someone inquired from behind her.

"I'm guessing a witch," another replied. "Don't let her use her hands."

Fingers seized hers and pulled them apart so she couldn't move them. From the depths of the dense jungle, the foliage moved and swayed as the sounds of grunts and fists hitting flesh issued from where Brokk vanished.

Her heart raced, and without thinking, she lurched toward him. She had to see him but couldn't break free of her captors. Frustration filled her to the point where she almost screamed.

She had to see him and know he was okay; every part of her yearned for that reassurance as time slowed to an agonizing pace. When more of the immortals waded into the vegetation after Brokk and that man, Kaylia glanced around and saw the snakelike creatures had all retreated.

It was just her, Brokk, and these other immortals now, and she had no idea what they intended to do with them. She'd used most of her strength to fight off the snakes; if these men and women meant to destroy them too, they were in trouble.

As she stood there, waiting for something to happen, she became aware of the rain pelting her. Her drenched clothes cleaved to her skin, strands of hair adhered to her face, and water trails streamed down her cheeks.

Restrained by the men and unable to wipe it, she tried to blink away the water on her lashes, but the clinging drops blurred her vision. The thunder and lightning had ceased, the crackle of the flames had died, the only noise was the rain pelting the trees and the battle waged within the dark jungle.

Until even that ceased. In the following hush, every frantic beat of her heart thundered in her ears as she pleaded to Hecate for Brokk to emerge. It seemed to take forever, but finally, the foliage parted, and the men emerged.

Held in the grasp of four men, with the man he'd been fighting holding Brokk's sword to his back, they marched Brokk toward her. Bruises marred his cheekbones, blood trickled from his temple and the corner of his mouth, but he didn't look defeated as his eyes blazed a fiery red.

Two welts had formed on the man's temple and cheek. He wiped blood from his nose as he glowered at her and Brokk.

"What do we do with them, Ryker?" one of the men holding her inquired.

"We'll bring them to our camp and find out why they're here," the man replied as he jabbed the tip of his sword into Brokk's back. "Move."

CHAPTER THIRTY-THREE

THE RAIN HAD NEARLY STOPPED when they were led into a small clearing in the jungle. Tucked beneath the thick boughs of the trees, hastily assembled huts and shanties leaned against the branches.

More men and women stood guard around the clearing, but a small group of women sat around a fire in the middle. The scent of spices and herbs drifted from the cauldron one of them stirred.

As they entered the clearing, the women rose from their seated positions. One looked familiar, but Kaylia couldn't place her.

"Kaylia?" the woman inquired as she stepped forward.

Kaylia's confusion deepened as the woman with golden blonde hair and deep brown eyes glided toward her. Then Kaylia remembered the woman was a witch she'd met a few times over the years.

The woman would sometimes come to visit her grandmother in the crone realm. She was much younger than her, but Kaylia had spoken to her a few times.

"Allegra?" she inquired.

The pretty woman broke into a grin. "Yes. *What* are you doing here?"

"What are *you* doing here?" Kaylia retorted.

Allegra's smile faltered when she stopped before Kaylia, and her eyes darted between the guards. Her forehead furrowed as she planted her hands on her hips and scowled at them. "Let her go."

"Fuck no," Ryker retorted. "Not until we learn why they're here."

"You can't keep her a prisoner like this. She's the oldest living witch."

"Well, good for her, but I don't give a fuck."

Allegra's brows drew sharply together over the bridge of her nose as she glowered at him. She had no fear of this man, which Kaylia found a little reassuring since she and Brokk remained prisoners. If someone not of their race of immortals could stand up to them, then they might not chop off their heads.

"She could be extremely useful to you," Allegra stated.

"Or a threat. Until we know what they're doing here and why a *witch* is with a *vampire*, I'm not letting anyone go."

Allegra's eyebrows shot up at this revelation, and her attention shifted to Brokk. His pointed ears standing up through his tussled hair clearly indicated his fae status. The blond hair might throw some off, but it was nowhere near as blond as the light faes'.

Besides, his blond hair now looked brown due to the soaking they'd endured, but he still didn't have the coloring of the dark fae. His gleaming red eyes were those of a vampire, as were the outline of the fangs behind his compressed lips.

Allegra's confusion grew as she studied him before her attention shifted to Kaylia. "*What* is going on?"

Kaylia lifted her chin when Allegra gazed at her with betrayal and disgust.

"I'm more interested in who they are," Ryker stated.

"She's Kaylia Montague, the oldest living witch and the creator of the crone realm. She's extremely powerful." Allegra paused to survey Kaylia and Brokk. "And could be of use to you."

She said this last sentence with obvious reluctance. Kaylia almost rolled her eyes but reminded herself that she'd been a lot like Allegra until recently. She didn't know how this witch didn't know about all the changes in the realms... or maybe she did and didn't care.

There were still some witches and vamps who harbored hatred for each other, and they always would.

Allegra's gaze raked scornfully over Brokk. Whereas she restrained herself from rolling her eyes, Brokk did not.

"I don't know him," Allegra said.

Ryker nudged Brokk with his sword. "Who are you?"

Brokk's lips remained clamped together as he stared straight ahead. Though he couldn't see it, over his shoulder, Ryker's face darkened. Brokk remained expressionless when Ryker pressed the blade a little deeper.

"Stop it!" Kaylia shouted at him.

She jerked against the guards again, but their hold on her only tightened. The tip of one of Brokk's fangs glinted in the fire when his lips curved into a sneer, and an inhuman sound issued from him.

Eyes wide and hand at her throat, Allegra edged away from him. Kaylia felt the tension in the clearing spiraling out of control and toward something disastrous.

"He is Brokk, house of the dark fae!" Kaylia blurted. "Brother to King Colburn of the dark fae and soon-to-be king of all the Shadow Realms."

In the silence accompanying her words, the only sound was the crackle of the flames beneath the cauldron. Even the jungle remained oddly hushed as they absorbed her words.

"Tove is the king of the dark fae," Ryker finally said, "and the Lord rules the Shadow Realms."

Brokk's jaw remained clenched before finally easing enough for him to speak. "My father is dead, and my brother now rules the Gloaming and the dark fae. The Lord is also dead; he has been for months. How long have you all been here?"

"Far too long," Ryker muttered.

"*Why* are you here?" Kaylia asked.

"To save our king," Ryker answered. "Is the Lord really dead?"

"Yes. Many immortals came together to destroy him." Brokk fixed Allegra with a pointed look while he spoke his next words. "Witches and vampires worked side by side to ensure it happened and continue to help each other now."

Allegra's nose wrinkled in disgust as she shook her head.

"It's true," Kaylia stated. "Just look at the two of us. Why else would we be together?"

Allegra's eyes traveled between them, but Kaylia could tell she still wasn't moved by their words.

Ryker rubbed the stubble on his jaw while eyeing Brokk. "Many of King Tove's sons were mixed species."

"I'm dark fae and vampire," Brokk said. "Obviously."

A smile tugged at the corner of Ryker's mouth before he suppressed it. "It seems we have much to catch up on. Bring them to my cabin."

Kaylia didn't protest as the guards led her across the clearing to the largest hut beneath a giant tree.

CHAPTER THIRTY-FOUR

ALLEGRA FOLLOWED them into the hut, along with all their guards. A small table, crafted from wood, sat in the center of the structure, and Ryker moved to sit behind it. One of the guards brushed past them and placed their packs on the table with Kaylia's sword.

Relief filled her at the sight of them. She didn't have many supplies, but she preferred to keep her meager belongings.

Ryker set Brokk's blade in front of him and placed his quiver and bow on the ground before gesturing to the two empty chairs across from him. The chairs had been crafted from logs and sticks twisted together. "Sit."

The guards released their hold on them but remained standing far too close for Kaylia's liking. She brought her hands forward and flexed her fingers to ease the cramped muscles in them.

Beside her, Brokk remained defiant as he planted his feet. Kaylia gulped as she looked from Ryker to Brokk and back again. A battle of wills emanated within the structure barely big enough for all of them.

Brokk was usually far more easygoing than his brothers, but

it was clear he didn't like anyone commanding him. It was also clear that Ryker was used to being obeyed and expected his prisoners to do so too.

With the men against her back and Allegra to her right, the structure felt smaller as their bodies and the walls pressed against her. Sweat beaded her nape as Kaylia remained standing beside Brokk.

Ryker leaned back in his chair, crossed his arms over his chest, and studied them. "Why are you in Doomed Valley?"

"Why are *you* in Doomed Valley?" Brokk retorted.

Kaylia rolled her eyes as she realized they were about to enter a stalemate as each of them tried to prove who had the biggest dick. She wouldn't be surprised if they whipped them out to measure them on the table.

They could stand here all night, spinning in circles and getting nowhere if this continued, and since she was exhausted and sought answers, she wasn't about to let that happen. "We came in search of crudue vine."

She ignored Brokk as she sensed his eyes boring into the side of her head. They could stand here all night and get nowhere or try to figure out what was happening.

These immortals could have answers, and she was curious about what was going on here. *What kind of immortals are they, and why are witches with them?*

"Why?" Ryker inquired.

"To save *the* Queen of the Shadow Realms… the *arach* queen."

Ryker's palms flattened on the table as a murmur ran through those surrounding them.

"The arach are all dead," Allegra said.

"No, they're not. One still lives; she has assumed the throne and control of the dragons. She's also engaged to Brokk's brother."

"Holy shit," someone whispered. "Is that true?"

Kaylia didn't bother to look at the man who spoke as she replied, "It is all true. Thousands of immortals, all working together, managed to destroy the Lord and get her on the throne where she belongs."

"Then why does she have to be saved?" Ryker asked.

"A traitor amongst us nearly killed her with a noxus scorpion. I managed to stop the poison from destroying her, but without the crudue vine, we can't wake her, and the throne is again vulnerable."

"It seems we've missed a lot while here," Ryker muttered as he rubbed at his stubble-lined chin. "Sit."

When neither moved, he leaned back in his chair and crossed his arms over his broad chest. "I know where there's some crudue vine. Now, sit."

Kaylia's heart leapt in excitement, and she took an involuntary step forward. "You do?"

"Yes, but I'll hear *all* of what you have to say first."

Kaylia glanced at Brokk before pulling out a chair and settling onto it. If he knew where there was some crudue vine, she would sit and learn its location.

Ryker ignored Brokk as his attention shifted to her. "Tell me everything. Starting with how it's possible an arach still lives."

Kaylia held up her hand. "I'll tell you all that, but first, what kind of immortals are you?"

She wasn't about to reveal any more, not even for crudue vine, if there was a possibility these immortals could turn on them and invade Dragonia while Lexi was at her weakest. There were thousands of different immortals throughout the realms; some were far more power-hungry than others. If she knew what they were, she would better understand their character.

She might have already revealed too much by letting them know the crudue vine was for Lexi, but they'd be in for a rude awakening if they tried to take over Dragonia and encountered the Shadow Reaver.

Cole and the dragons would tear them to shreds before they made it anywhere near the castle. But she had no intention of telling them any of that. She'd give Ryker enough to get what she wanted in return but never reveal all their secrets.

Ryker smiled at her. "We are known as the amsirah."

CHAPTER THIRTY-FIVE

KAYLIA'S EYEBROWS rose at this revelation, but she should have guessed it from the unnaturalness of that storm. She'd been a little too busy at the time to put all the pieces together, and the amsirah rarely left their realm.

She hadn't seen or heard about them in centuries. Although, she'd spent a good portion of that time shutting herself away from the happenings of the realms.

"What are you doing here?" she inquired.

Ryker tilted his head to the side while studying her. "I'm the one asking the questions."

"You want answers, then you'll also have to give them," Brokk stated from behind her.

Ryker smiled while stretching his legs before him. "You're not exactly in the position to make demands. I know where to locate what *you* want."

"So you say, but we have no proof."

Ryker looked at Allegra. "Do you still have some of the vine?"

"Yes."

"Please show it to our guests."

Allegra spun and pushed past the curtain covering the entrance to leave the hut. The curtain rustled as it settled back into place.

Kaylia eyed Ryker with interest as she recalled what she knew about the amsirah. "Does Leonidas still rule Tempest?"

A muscle twitched in Ryker's clenched jaw at the mention of his king and realm. "He does."

"I met him once, many, *many* years ago. He was a good man then."

"He still is."

"Good. The years have a way of corrupting immortals… especially those with power."

"They do, but Leo remains just in his rule and stalwart in his convictions to protect his realm and people."

Kaylia didn't miss the fact this man had called his king by a nickname, one most likely reserved for only those closest to him. That meant this man held a lot of power in Tempest and probably in himself.

An amsirah. She marveled over this revelation. It was so rare to see them outside their realm; they mostly kept to themselves and were a powerful race that could rain down hell on those who crossed them… literally.

They could control the weather, but not all of it. Each of them possessed certain weather-controlling abilities. Some held power over the rain, others fog, some held sway over the wind, or lightning and thunder, and others could control snow, ice, and hail.

And some could control more than one weather element at a time. King Leonidas could control four different weather types, but none of them had ever possessed the ability to control all five.

"How much of the weather can *you* control?" she asked Ryker.

A corner of his mouth twitched toward a smile. "How much do you think?"

The power emanating from the man crackled against her skin. "I'm guessing two or three different elements." *At least.* "And someone here is a lightning bearer."

His lips twitched again. "Maybe more than one someone."

It was possible, but she doubted it. "I know that's the rarest ability for any of you to possess. Your king isn't a lightning bearer."

Some of his amusement faded. "You know a lot about us."

"I'm one of the oldest living immortals; I've learned a *lot* about many things over the years and at least a little about even more."

"I see."

"*You're* the lightning bearer."

"I am many things."

But as he said this, his eyes started clouding like a storm passing across the sky. The color seeped into their whites as they turned so dark they were nearly black when lightning bolts shot down the center of them.

No other lightning filled the room, but it became so electrified her hair stood on end. When she glanced at the others, she saw the same thing happening to them. Brokk remained stone-faced, but his eyes narrowed on Ryker.

Except, it didn't happen to Ryker. He remained the same except for another set of lightning bolts zigzagging through his eyes.

It was a wonderous, frightening spectacle that enchanted and unnerved her. With one flick of his hand, he could unleash a torrent of power and death. They were far better off with this man as an ally than an enemy.

As the storm left Ryker's eyes, the electricity in the air dissipated until it returned to normal. When he sat back in the chair again, his eyes held hers, but there was nothing smug in his gaze.

"Impressive," she murmured. "How many elements can you control?"

"Four."

"And they are…?"

A smile curved his lips. "Do you really expect me to answer that?"

Before she could reply, Allegra returned to the hut. The curtain swished as it settled into place behind her. The young witch strode over to the table and set something down between Kaylia and Ryker.

Kaylia finally tore her attention away from the powerful man sitting across from her. When she did, her eyes settled on the small piece of crudue vine between them. She gasped and lurched toward the vine, but Ryker pulled it away before she could grasp it.

"This is ours," he stated. "It's necessary to counteract the ophidians' venom."

Kaylia was too busy staring at the vine to process his words. *There it is! Right there! The key to saving Lexi!*

Her fingers flexed as she resisted the urge to tear it away from him, but as she contemplated doing so, she knew it wouldn't be enough. They required more than that small piece of vine to save Lexi.

This man held the key to getting it for them. She was certain of it.

"What are ophidians?" Brokk inquired.

Kaylia finally tore her attention away from the vine as she focused again on the conversation around her. She had to fight to keep herself from looking at the vine again.

"The ophidians are those snakelike immortals you just encountered," Ryker answered. "They're hunting us, and their venom is toxic and kills in less than an hour. The crudue vine is the only thing that counteracts it."

"Why are they hunting you?"

"Because their emperor has imprisoned our king, and I'm *going* to get him back."

CHAPTER THIRTY-SIX

BROKK WAS BECOMING MORE intrigued by Ryker's revelations and less irate with every passing minute, but he still wanted to pummel the man sitting across from Kaylia. He'd like to finish what they'd started in the jungle, but that wouldn't happen.

He glanced at the guards surrounding them; if they hadn't intervened in their fight, he would have gotten him and Kaylia away from these immortals. *But maybe that was for the best,* he thought as he eyed the vine in Ryker's hand.

If this man knew where there was crudue vine, Brokk would do everything it took to get the knowledge from him. At least it didn't seem like these immortals would kill them, but Ryker was after something; Brokk was sure of it.

"Now," Ryker said, "tell me about the new queen of Dragonia. The *arach* queen."

Brokk crossed his arms over his chest as he studied the man. Whatever Ryker wanted from them, it had something to do with Lexi and his brother; Kaylia hadn't revealed much, but it was enough to intrigue this man.

Kaylia clasped her hands in her lap as she stared at the vine before looking at Ryker again. "I can do that if you promise to tell us where there is more crudue vine."

"No," Brokk interjected. "He'll give us *that* vine. I don't care if they need it or not."

Ryker twisted the vine in his hand as he contemplated this.

"It doesn't matter," Kaylia said. "That piece may be enough for the ophidians' venom but not for the noxus scorpion. We need more... unless you have it somewhere?"

"That's the last of it," Allegra said. "We were planning to gather more again soon."

Kaylia's shoulders fell.

"Not only will I tell you where there's more." Ryker set the vine on the table, clasped his hands on it, and leaned toward Kaylia, "but if I like what you say, I'll take you to it."

"Why would you do that?" Brokk inquired.

"For your help. Your brother is the king of the dark fae, and you"—Ryker pinned Kaylia with his steely gaze—"if you were near enough to this new arach queen to save her from the sting of a noxus scorpion, then that means you're close to her." His silver eyes shifted to Brokk. "And if your brother is engaged to her, then you're practically family."

Kaylia lifted her chin. "Lexi is a queen, not a pawn."

"Lexi, is it? Not Queen Lexi, her Majesty, or any other term indicating you're nothing more than just one of her subjects. I doubt I could get away with calling her Lexi."

"You are now," Kaylia bit out through her teeth.

"But I wouldn't do it to her face. I suspect *you* would."

The creatures of the jungle called, squawked, and screamed as they hunted and killed in the night. Brokk eyed the man across from them as he tried to decide if he was someone worth trusting or an obstacle to destroy.

Guards surrounded them, but he would find a way to get him and Kaylia out of here if necessary. The shadows beckoned to him as they danced in the glow of the lantern sitting on a table beside the cot.

"Like you, I call my king by a nickname. When we aren't in a formal setting, I call him Leo because he's my friend *and* my ruler, and we have fought many battles together. I won't leave here until he's free."

Kaylia remained rigid, but Brokk saw what Ryker was angling toward. If he helped them get the crudue vine, he expected help in saving his king.

It was a fair enough trade and mutually beneficial. "You've met their king, Kaylia. Is he worth saving?"

She turned in the chair to look at him as she pondered this. "I knew him as a fair man. That could have changed—"

"It hasn't," Ryker interjected.

"That is true," Allegra murmured. "King Leonidas is a great man and ruler."

A murmur of agreement went through the guards. Kaylia's pewter eyes held his while she spoke and thrust her thumb over her shoulder at Ryker. "That doesn't mean we can trust *him*."

"General Ryker is a good man," one of the guards grumbled, and a murmur of agreement and irritation ran through the others.

"We don't need them," another growled.

When Ryker held up his hand, silence descended over those in the hut. Brokk wasn't entirely sure about this man, but his followers were as they came to attention.

Brokk studied the stony faces of the men and women surrounding them. He still wasn't sure about Ryker or the rest of them, but Ryker and his followers hadn't tried to kill them, and they could have.

If it helped save Lexi, then he would give this man a little to get what they sought. He glanced at the thorny crudue vine before striding forward, pulling out the other chair, and settling next to Kaylia.

He didn't care what it took; he'd save his future sister-in-law.

Besides, Ryker couldn't use anything he planned to reveal against her or Cole.

"Lexi is the last living arach, and we helped her reclaim the throne that was rightfully hers," Brokk said.

He filled Ryker in on as many details as the man required. When he finished speaking, the hut remained silent as everyone absorbed his revelations.

CHAPTER THIRTY-SEVEN

"There's no more Lord," Allegra breathed. "The realms are… *free.*"

"Yes, but if we don't get the crudue vine to Lexi, then someone else could try to take that throne, and it will all start over again." Brokk held Ryker's eyes as he said this.

Ryker glanced at the vine before shifting his attention back to Brokk. "We'll take you to the vine and get you as much as you need to save the queen, but, in exchange, I want your help… no, I want *her* help freeing Leo afterward. Dragons would go a long way against the ophidians and accomplish much more than we have."

"Lexi will help you," Kaylia vowed.

"Are you able to speak for her?"

"*No one* can speak for her, but we're looking to build allies to solidify peace in the realms," Brokk said. "We're all tired of the fighting. If you think King Leonidas would agree to pledge his allegiance to her, I'm sure she would help."

"I don't see why he wouldn't," Ryker said. "As long as she doesn't turn on everyone like the Lord and start slaughtering anyone who stands in his way."

"And even those who don't," a guard muttered.

"Lexi would never do that," Kaylia said. "That throne is hers by birth; it won't corrupt her as it has the previous rulers who didn't belong on it."

Ryker pinned her with his gaze. "As you said, power corrupts."

"I'll never say that couldn't happen; we can't know the future, but she's strong, caring, and has a lot of immortals who love her to keep her grounded. She *is* the rightful ruler of the realms, and not just because of her birth."

"I'll take your word for that. How did you end up in the middle of our fight with the ophidians?"

"We were in a mirror realm and emerged from a tree into the middle of your battle."

"That's unfortunate luck for you."

Kaylia looked pointedly at the crudue vine. "Or good luck, depending on how you look at it."

"Very true. There are many mirror realms here; I've lost more than a few men to them. I'm not sure if they ever emerged again or not."

"We encountered gremlins there but were able to avoid them. I suspect there are more monsters there too."

"Most likely."

Ryker ran his hand tiredly over the thick stubble lining his face. Brokk studied the man as he tried to ascertain his thoughts. He'd never encountered an amsirah before, as they mostly kept to themselves, and he'd never had a reason to travel to their realm.

"What are *you* doing here?" Brokk inquired. "I understand these creatures have your king, but how did that happen? The amsirah rarely leave Tempest."

Ryker lowered his hand. "About two years ago, an army of ghouls invaded Tempest. During our last battle with them almost a year ago, we finally succeeded in driving the monsters from

Tempest, but that victory came at a steep price. The ghouls captured our king and handed him over to the emperor of Doomed Valley; they knew how difficult it would be to free him from here. King Leonidas has been a prisoner ever since, and I *will* get him back."

"You've been here for almost a year," Kaylia said.

"Yes. We've returned for supplies and more fighters when necessary, but I haven't left Doomed Valley since they brought Leo here, and it's been almost six months since we returned for anything."

"No wonder you don't know about the Lord."

"Why are the witches here?" Kaylia asked as she glanced at Allegra.

The witch wasn't quite as hostile as she was before Brokk told them their tale, but she still shot him a look before clasping her hands before her. She stared at the wall while she spoke.

"We've been paid well for our assistance. We're here to make the potion that counteracts the ophidians' poison, and we set protective spells around the areas where camps are established."

"They've been a big help," Ryker stated, "and were also a part of the war against the ghouls in Tempest."

"Do you know that the Lord destroyed Verdan?" Kaylia asked Allegra.

The woman's lips parted. "*What?*"

"He unleashed his dragons on it. Some parts still stand, but much of the realm was destroyed."

Tears brimmed in Allegra's eyes. "I didn't know. How many died?"

"Too many."

"If you need to return…." Ryker said.

Allegra wiped away the tears rolling down her cheeks. "No. I will see this through. Some may wish to return to find their loved ones, but I'll remain."

Brokk was a little surprised by this response but didn't say anything. It wasn't his place to judge her choices.

"If you'll excuse me, I must inform the others," Allegra whispered.

"Of course," Ryker said.

After the witch left the hut, Brokk focused on Ryker again. "I never knew a war was going on between the amsirah and ghouls."

"Our war was small compared to the one the Lord waged against the human realm and anyone who stood in his way. The realms are vast, mysterious places, but now that we know each other's plights, we can work together to save our rulers."

Brokk smiled at the man's confidence. "If you get us to that crudue vine, you'll have all the help you need."

Ryker grinned. "Good."

"Will we open a portal to get there?" Kaylia asked.

"No," Ryker answered. "You may not have been here long enough to realize this, but Doomed Valley is constantly changing. What was in one place today may not be there tomorrow, or it will have changed somehow. Portals are useless for traveling in this realm."

"Then how will you get us the vine?"

"It doesn't change so much that we can't travel there on foot. It may not be in the exact same spot as when we were last there, but it will be close. And the vine is guaranteed to have changed. It's been different every time we've seen it."

"How often have you found it?" Brokk asked.

"Four times, and I have no doubt I can find it again; it's just going to have to be the hard way."

"Why don't you camp closer to it?"

"We have to move around here constantly. We've been trying to advance on the ophidians' pyramid, but we keep getting pushed back, or the ophidians find and ambush us... as they did tonight while we were hunting. I wish we could bring more men here to help us rescue Leo, but we must leave most of our soldiers behind to protect Tempest in case the ghouls decide to attack again."

"Then we'll do it the hard way."

"Good. Now, I think it's time for a drink. It's been a long day, and we'll start our journey tomorrow. Would you care to join me in a glass of wine?"

Brokk wasn't going to say no to that.

CHAPTER THIRTY-EIGHT

THE DRAPE SETTLED into place with a swish as the guard vanished from the small hut she'd escorted Brokk and Kaylia to. On the way to the hut, Kaylia had seen Allegra and the witches huddled together and crying while consoling each other.

None of them had left... at least, not yet. She'd much prefer their help for the journey to the crudue vine, but that was a problem for tomorrow.

With a sigh, she studied the hut. The space was barely big enough for the two of them to lie down, but it was the most shelter she'd experienced in days, or maybe a week or more, as she had no idea what day it was.

She cast a silencing spell over the structure with deft fingers as Brokk set the lantern Ryker had given them down near the back of the hut. The flames cast shadows over the dirt floor.

Kaylia finished her spell and lowered her hands. "Do you trust him?"

"Is it safe to talk?"

"Yes."

"No, but I don't distrust him either, if that makes sense."

"It does, but only because that's how I feel too. I don't think they intend to hurt us."

"I don't either, but they'll do whatever's necessary to get their king back, and that makes them untrustworthy."

"We'll do whatever it takes to save Lexi."

"And that's what makes us untrustworthy to them."

Kaylia set the pack Ryker had returned to her on the ground. Rolled-up blankets were placed against the wall inside the curtain. Whoever's place this was before them was probably not happy to have been routed from their home.

Too bad for them. It was small, but she was grateful for a safe, sheltered place to sleep for the night.

Ryker had said it would take at least a couple of days to arrive at the place where the vine grew, but Kaylia's fingers itched to have it in hand.

They were so close to getting what they required to save Lexi; they just had to make it there. And once they did, they could return to Dragonia, and she could create the potion to counteract the noxus' sting.

Kaylia was so focused on everything she would have to do to create the potion to save Lexi that she didn't realize Brokk had taken off his green fae tunic until it landed on the ground with a barely audible swish.

When she realized he stood in this small space with *her* without a shirt on, Kaylia kept her eyes on the piece of dirty clothing as she willed herself not to look at him. It was nearly impossible as the magnetic pull of him felt stronger inside these small confines.

"I'm going to the stream," he stated. "I have to get some of this grime off me. Do you want to come?"

Kaylia couldn't speak as he lifted his sword and swung it onto his back. They might not be able to trust Ryker and his men completely, but he'd given them back all their possessions and weapons.

Unable to resist looking at him anymore, Kaylia's eyes darted from the shirt to him. She kept her attention on his face and its intriguing angles as he strode toward her.

I will not look at his chest. I will not touch him.

Her fingers dug into her palms as she restrained herself. Ryker had shown them the stream running along the outskirts of their camp and told them it was safe to wash there as it was within the confines of the witches' protective barrier.

He could go alone; she didn't have to go with him, but she didn't like the idea of him being alone. Plus, she would give anything to scrub herself clean. She'd never been this dirty; a bath and clean clothes sounded better than heaven.

Despite that, she couldn't get her feet to move after him. He was going to the stream to bathe, which meant he'd be naked and wet and oh-so-tempting.

Her fingers dug further into her palms as she tried not to lick her lips at the tantalizing images racing through her mind. She tried to breathe through her body's traitorous desire, but it was impossible when her lungs refused to cooperate.

"Kaylia?" he inquired.

She looked like an idiot, standing there without saying anything. Managing to swallow, she choked back the lump in her throat before speaking. "Yeah?"

"Are you going to come with me or stay here?"

Her brain had no idea, but apparently her mouth already knew the answer as she said, "Let me gather some of my things."

This was such a very bad idea.

Then why are you so excited?

She knew the answer to that, even if she'd never voice it.

∽

BROKK STUDIED their surroundings while waiting outside the hut for Kaylia. Creatures moved about, branches and limbs broke beneath their weight, and trees shook as the things in the night bounced off them.

Some of the things screamed while others made soft cooing noises that almost sounded rather pleasant. He'd spent enough time in the human realm to know he enjoyed the songs of the crickets and peepers.

Some of these creatures reminded him of those as they made their music. But the song only broke through the endless noise of death and suffering on occasion as the night animals hunted and fed.

What he didn't hear were the whispers that haunted them during their first days in Doomed Valley. He hadn't heard them since entering the mirror realm, and he was fine with that.

Amsirah guards stood in the shadows of the huts. The flickering fire from the torches illuminated the spaces between the shanties but didn't illuminate much beyond them or the guards.

The power of the spell the witches cast to keep the camp safe prickled against his skin and vibrated the air. While the shield over the camp wouldn't deter everything, it would keep most of the monsters at bay.

A rustle from behind alerted him that Kaylia had emerged before she stepped beside him. He kept his eyes on the night, but every part of him was aware of the warmth and life she exuded, as well as her enticing, underlying scent.

And despite her vitality, power, and sexual appeal, she'd locked herself away after the loss of her fiancé and only recently reemerged into the world of the living. He couldn't imagine her heartbreak after losing her love, but, to him, the real travesty was that she'd hidden herself from the world like she had.

Finally, he turned his attention from the night to take her in. His breath caught a little as the radiance of the moon and torches emphasized her stunning beauty.

Even still covered in dirt and blood, and with her hair matted around her features, she was exquisite. Unable to stop himself,

Brokk brushed a strand of hair back from her face and tucked it behind her ear.

Her eyes widened when his fingers lingered on her silken chin before falling away. His hand still tingled from where he'd touched her skin.

He was battered, exhausted, and had taken a beating tonight, but hunger crept through him as he rubbed his fingers together. "How's your leg?"

She glanced down at her wounded leg with confusion, but then her brow cleared as if she'd just recalled the injury. "It's healing. It will be fine once I clean and put some ointment on it."

"Good. Are you ready to go?"

"Yes."

Maybe it wasn't the best idea to bathe in the stream right now, but there was no way he would sleep tonight, covered in filth, when he could finally be clean again.

CHAPTER THIRTY-NINE

THEY WALKED side by side down to the stream. The witches had retreated from their huddle in the center of the clearing; the fire beneath their cauldron had gone out, but they remained standing outside a couple of huts, their arms around each other.

"Do you think they'll leave?" he asked Kaylia.

"No. I think they would have already if they planned to do that."

"Do you think it's odd they've chosen to stay?"

She bit her bottom lip as she pondered this. "A little, but they've been a part of this for a couple of years and have a lot invested in whatever happens. They're probably also being paid well."

"I'm sure they are."

He turned his attention away from the witches as they approached a guard. The woman nodded to them as they passed, and Brokk did the same in return.

He still wasn't overly fond of these weather-controlling douchebags, but if Ryker could get them to the crudue vine, then he would ensure they helped rescue the amsirah king.

"What do you know about the amsirah?" he asked as the jungle closed around them again.

"Not much. I know they can control the weather, and Tempest is a beautiful place, but it's been many centuries since I've been there or met Leonidas. However, anyone who fosters the kind of loyalty that Ryker and these men exhibit toward him must mean he's still a good man."

"I have to agree."

"The amsirah mostly kept to themselves throughout the years. I assume that didn't change much when I retreated to the crone realm."

"No, it didn't."

"Do you know much about them?"

"A little more now."

She smiled as she pushed aside a low-hanging leaf the size of her. "There's so many different creatures in the Shadow Realms; it's impossible to know them all."

"So many mysteries out there."

"It's wonderful, aweing, and frightening when you think about it."

"It is," Brokk agreed. "All this talk about kings, emperors, and rulers reminded me of something I've pondered off and on through the years."

"What's that?"

"Why did the witches never have another queen after that vampire killed the last one?"

"There was talk of appointing another one. Like the dark fae, family heritage never dictated who would rule over us; a voting council appointed our queen."

"And that council never voted on a new one?"

"They did."

"So… what happened?"

A small, wistful smile played at the corners of her lush, inviting mouth—a mouth he'd give anything to taste.

"I didn't want to be a queen."

"So, *you* turned it down."

"I did, and this was centuries before what happened with Fabian, so it wasn't because of that. I believed we were doing fine on our own and didn't require a central figure who could become corrupted by power."

"Was the last queen corrupted by her power?"

"No, but things were working well after her death and have continued to do so for years. A council of witches still represents all the different covens, so everyone has a voice and democracy rules."

"Were you good friends with the last witch queen?"

"Not *good* friends, but we got along well."

"Not many would have turned the position of queen down."

"I'm not many."

"No, you're not," he murmured.

Kaylia cast him a sideways glance from under her lashes as his gaze ran appraisingly and hungrily over her. She was so amazing.

The sound of running water drifted to him a few seconds before the stream came into view. Beneath the moon's glow, the water glistened as it meandered through the jungle, over rocks, and around tree roots.

It wasn't a large stream, but big enough for them to wade into, sit down, and scrub themselves clean. Brokk's skin prickled with excitement as he kicked off his boots.

Next to him, Kaylia edged away a little and crept further down the bank. There wasn't much here to shield himself, but nudity wasn't something he'd ever cared about.

Recalling her dead fiancé and how sheltered she'd been for these past centuries, he hesitated with his hand on the button of his pants. "Is this okay?"

"Oh… ah… yeah… yes, of course it is. I'm going to go a little further downstream."

Brokk stepped after her before stopping himself. She needed privacy, and she was as safe as him along the river's shore, but he didn't like the idea of her being out of view.

She would probably leave if he followed her, though, and she wanted this bath as much as him. No matter how badly his protective instincts screamed at him to stay close to her, he couldn't take that from her.

"Don't go far. The witch's spell is strong, but we don't know what is out there," he told her.

"Don't worry about me. I can take care of myself."

While this was true, he couldn't help but worry as she moved further away from him and into the shadows.

CHAPTER FORTY

KAYLIA REFUSED to look back at him until she was certain she was far enough away not to see much. Finally, when she was sure not to glimpse Brokk and all his naked glory—and she knew it was glorious—she stopped and looked over her shoulder.

Through the thick canopy of trees, she glimpsed him wading into the water, but she was far enough away and it was dark enough that she couldn't make out many details. She told herself she was extremely glad about this, even as disappointment crashed through her.

Shaking her head, she berated herself for this strange, newfound weakness when it came to him. Not only was her desire for him a betrayal to Fabian, but Brokk was part vampire.

Yes, she'd worked side by side with vampires to overthrow the Lord, but a vampire killed Fabian, after all. For some reason, the wrath this knowledge used to arouse didn't come screaming to the forefront like it once did.

Not all vampires were bad, and she didn't have that kind of hate inside her anymore; she couldn't. It was exhausting to hate that much all the time.

With a sigh, she admitted defeat when it came to being a

pissed-off, hostile witch. Just like her time in the crone realm had ended, so had that part of her, but life was ever-changing and evolving. The flowers bloomed, died, and bloomed again... and so did she.

She would still be hostile when necessary, but that woman who had seethed in the crone realm for centuries wasn't there anymore. Someone new, who had forged bonds with immortals as strong as the ones she once shared with her family, replaced her.

Those immortals, like Lexi and Cole, needed her to be strong and not angry. They required her help, not her fury. It had taken her a while to learn that, but it made her a lot happier when she did.

And while that was true, guilt still tugged at her. Fabian's life was ripped away from him; he could never enjoy it again, and while she had no choice but to keep living, and she had a right to do so, it still made her feel like she was betraying him.

She couldn't change that and refused to hide, but she didn't have to ogle other men; she could stop herself from doing it.

Stripping out of her clothes, Kaylia tore her gaze away from Brokk and splashed into the water. She'd hoped for it to be freezing so it would douse some of her unwanted lust, but it was warm and inviting as it sloshed around her calves.

Kaylia removed her soap from her pack and walked up to her thighs in the water. That was as deep as the water went, and it felt wonderful as it swirled around her.

She used the soap to scrub away the grime caked onto her. The bar she'd made was great for her skin and hair, and she spent a long time washing herself and carefully cleaning the healing cuts on her leg.

She twisted her calf to examine it more carefully, but the jagged slices had stopped bleeding and were knitting together. It would completely heal by the time they left tomorrow.

When she finished cleaning the wounds, she sat on the soft

riverbed and slid down to dunk her head underwater. She held her breath as she stared up at the trees and skies from under the clear water that caused the landscape to blur around her.

She should finish bathing and get out of the water, but it was all so soothing and beautiful. The water flowing around her and sliding across her skin was marvelous as well as… arousing.

Kaylia burst free of the surface and inhaled a shaky breath as she tried to ignore the tingles racing over her skin as her nipples pricked. Now was not exactly the time, and she had to get clean and get out of there before some horrible monster broke free of the jungle and tried to eat her.

Yes, she'd have a warning before that happened, and the creature would have difficulty breaking through the protective spell, but she had to move. With trembling hands, she lifted her arms and washed her hair.

She was grateful for shorter hair as she cleaned it before letting it fall around her shoulders. When she finished, she pulled herself from the water and trudged toward the riverbank as she tried to ignore the sensation of the water streaming down her, trickling between her breasts and legs.

With no towel, she shook off her hands and hopped from foot to foot as she tried to drip-dry faster, but it wasn't helping. Unwilling to put her only clean clothes on while still wet, she removed her blanket from her pack and laid it on the ground.

She glanced back at where she last saw Brokk, but he was still in the river, mostly hidden by the trees bowing low over the water. It looked like he would still be a bit, so she had time to relax while she dried.

Lying on her blanket, the warm air caressed her drying skin as she spread her arms over her head and relished the beat of the earth beneath her. At the river's edge, the trees weren't as thick, and silvery rays of moonlight filtered through their thick leaves.

It had been far too long since she'd run naked through the woods, absorbing the power of the earth, moon, and stars. She'd spent many nights dancing in clearings and releasing all her tension, but those nights happened centuries ago.

She'd forgotten how freeing it felt... until now. Kaylia gave herself over to the power, the life, and the freedom coursing through her veins as every part of the world imbued her with strength.

They were trapped in Doomed Valley, with who knew what lurking in the darkness, but she felt more alive than she had in centuries. *Everything* was fresh and exciting. The rest of the world fell away as power crackled over her skin, her heart raced, and a bubble of laughter caught in her throat.

She was free, alive, and very aware of the newly awakened desire she'd experienced for Brokk as her nipples hardened and an ache spread between her legs. Small beads of water continued to trickle between her thighs.

Closing her eyes, she couldn't stop herself from imagining that water was his hands as he stroked between her thighs while kissing her. Unable to resist, she feasted on the energy around her while her hand caressed her nipple.

She gasped as the familiar sensation of pleasure speared her. Only, it had been very unfamiliar to her over these past centuries.

The last one to touch her like this was Fabian. She'd been so deadened since his death that she hadn't given any consideration to sex or the ecstasy it brought. It had been one more thing she completely closed off from her life, but now, in this strange world and in the last place anyone should be waking, she was.

Like most witches, she'd always enjoyed sex before Fabian and, of course, with him. She was free with her sexuality and embraced the power that came with it, even if she was choosy about her partners. The men she'd chosen, she enjoyed.

But Brokk wasn't like any of them. He was far more wild, powerful, and the things he'd do to her....

She moaned, and her back arched off the ground as her hand slid down her belly. Alive. So alive. And aching so badly for release, for life, for the ecstasy that would unravel through her, the cries of joy, and the abandon that came with giving herself over to the pleasure.

As her skin crackled with energy, the moon invigorated her, and the earth pulsed around her, Fabian's handsome face rose to replace Brokk's. Her eyes flew open as the new awakening of her body crashed around her.

Like a band pulled too tight, the energy pulsing through her snapped and was ripped away. It all vanished as swiftly as a shadow from light.

CHAPTER FORTY-ONE

STARING up at the towering trees above and the stars poking through, an icy chill seeped into Kaylia's body. That chill wasn't from the warm air encompassing her but the self-hatred churning inside her.

Sitting up, Kaylia hugged her knees against her chest while staring at the stream. She should get up, dress, and move, but she didn't have the energy. Seconds ago, she'd teemed with vitality; it was gone.

She was in Doomed Valley, exposed to anything that could be watching her from the woods, yet she didn't care. For the first time in months, she felt as deflated as when she retreated to the crone realm.

And Kaylia also felt robbed. Robbed the joy she'd just experienced, the abandon she'd forgotten she could possess, and the release she so desperately needed.

Tears brimmed in her eyes and slid down her cheeks as conflicting emotions battered her. She would *never* move on from Fabian or forget him, but that breathtaking moment of coming alive again reminded her of the woman she once was… and could never be again.

It was almost as painful as his death.

"Kaylia."

She closed her eyes against the shiver Brokk's voice sent down her spine. It was so... *sexy.*

His gravelly tone and the way he said her name caused butterflies to erupt in her belly. She could listen to him say her name a few dozen times a day and still never get enough of it.

However, she was naked in a jungle, and despite the allure of his voice, it also held a note of concern. And he was coming closer.

She wiped away her tears as she spoke. "I'll be right there."

Shoving aside her self-hatred and guilt, Kaylia pushed herself to her feet. She couldn't sit here and wallow; she'd done that for centuries and refused to do it anymore.

She'd most likely never know the touch of a man again, and she could live with that. Even as she told herself this, her body mourned her decision, and the air caressing her skin brought back the memory of her hands doing so.

She bit her bottom lip as she pulled out a pair of brown fae pants and tugged them on. Next, she removed a black bra and green tunic she hastily donned. She missed the comfort and freedom of her dresses and skirts, but they weren't the most convenient clothing for running for her life through a jungle.

Lifting her pack, she shrugged it onto her back and strode to where Brokk stood, half hidden in the trees. She was still so focused on her misery, she didn't remind herself not to look at him.

It was a mistake.

The second her gaze fell on him, she came to an abrupt stop while she drank in the tantalizing sight of the man leaning against a tree with his arms folded over his chest. His disheveled dark blond hair stood out around his handsome face and nearly touched his shoulders. He'd shaved while in the water, and without the stubble, the striking handsomeness of his face was completely exposed.

The tips of his pointed ears poked through his hair. She fisted her hands against the overwhelming impulse to touch those ears and trace their contours while drawing him closer.

He hadn't bothered to put a shirt back on, and chiseled muscle etched *every* inch of his lithe build. She didn't think he had an ounce of fat on him, something his eight-pack abs stood testimony toward.

His pants hung low on his hips, showing off a perfect V, pointing straight toward what lay below his pants. She'd bet his cock was as enticing as the rest of him.

In the dark, his dark fae ciphers nearly blended into the night, but she could make out some of the sharp edges and gentle waves of the markings running across his shoulders and down to his wrists. Those marks indicated his power; the more a dark fae possessed, the stronger they were.

She suspected, as did most immortals, that the dark fae kept at least some of their markings hidden to mask how much power they possessed. That rumor had never been substantiated. Judging by the number of ciphers and the energy he exuded, she'd be willing to bet that rumor was very true.

Despite the shadows concealing him, Brokk's aqua eyes stood out starkly against the night. And as those eyes roamed down her, her skin prickled everywhere they touched.

He emanated an impossible-to-ignore sexuality as the awakening she experienced earlier returned. If he touched her, she might tear his pants off and pounce before having any thought of doing so.

"Are you okay?" he asked.

Her eyes fell to his full lips before darting away. "Fine."

He hesitated before speaking again. "We should head back."

Not trusting herself to speak, Kaylia could only nod in

response. When he turned away from her, she spotted the ciphers running down his back to his waist. She couldn't help admiring how they flexed and bunched as he strode toward their hut.

CHAPTER FORTY-TWO

BROKK TRIED to shut out the picture of Kaylia sitting on the ground with her arms wrapped around her legs and her chin resting on her knees. He'd hated the anguish radiating from her but knew it wasn't his place to get closer to comfort her.

However, he couldn't leave her there, not in this place. The first couple of times he'd called her name, she hadn't heard him, but he'd gotten through the third time.

Interfering in her suffering had been the right thing. If something somehow managed to slip past the witches' defenses, she was so lost in her thoughts she might not have heard it coming.

He didn't understand why she'd gone from hedonistic abandon to such misery so fast. When he first came upon her, lying on the ground with her arms and legs spread wide, she'd been reveling in pleasure.

The vision of her, so beautiful and ripe for fucking, had stopped him in his tracks. His dick instantly hardened as his fangs elongated. The overwhelming compulsion to sink his shaft and fangs into her had nearly propelled him toward her, but he'd been too enraptured with her to move.

As a dark fae, he'd seen and experienced many erotic things

in his life, but none had turned him on as much as Kaylia reveling in nature and herself. He shouldn't have been there, but his feet remained planted as she arched off the ground, and her head fell to the side.

She was so exquisite and held him captive, and he swore he was about to come in his pants from watching her. Then, she'd suddenly stopped, sat upright, and drew her knees against her chest.

He didn't understand the abrupt change, but the sadness exuding from her doused his lust, and his fangs retracted as his erection softened. Inexplicably, it felt more wrong watching this, and he had to stop it, even if he couldn't comfort her.

Retreating noiselessly through the trees, he took some time to compose himself before calling to her again. This time, when he approached, he made sure to make more noise, but it had still taken her a while to realize he was there.

But though the image of her sorrow haunted him, so did the memory of her body. It had been at least a week or two since he last fed on sex; he could go longer without any consequences and had planned to do so, but *every* part of him thrummed with awareness for this woman.

He pushed past the drape covering the doorway of their hut and entered. Before, the small space had seemed like a good place to shelter; it was safe and protected from the elements. Now, as Kaylia entered behind him, it felt far too cramped.

The scent of the stream and nature clinging to her permeated the small space and made it impossible for him to ignore her presence. *This is going to be a long night.*

He should go sleep outside. He could remain close to ensure she stayed safe while also giving himself the space he required, but no matter how much the walls closed in on him, he couldn't part from her.

He set his pack and sword on the ground as he tried to ignore the hunger coursing through his veins. Both the dark fae and vampire halves of him craved her... badly.

Bracing himself to face her again, he turned and edged around her toward the blankets bundled near the curtain. He was almost past her when her hand fluttered up. He stopped as her palm seared into his flesh.

"What happened here?" she asked.

Brokk froze as she stroked his chest, and his shaft stirred again. He was so focused on her touch and nearness that he didn't respond to her question.

Her sweeping lashes fluttered up to reveal her translucent, pewter eyes. Her lips parted a little as their gazes held, and the air between them crackled.

When her fingers twitched on his chest, they drew his attention to where they rested over his heart. The scar beneath them had faded to a white starburst.

His jaw clenched at the memory of how he received it. "A dark fae ran me through with a sword."

A glimmer of apprehension shone in her eyes. "Good thing it wasn't made from dark fae metal."

"It was."

Her jaw dropped as her gaze shifted from his face to the scar and back again. Not only had he somehow miraculously survived that, but a dark fae using a dark fae sword against another was something that never happened.

"How... how are you still alive?" she gasped. "It's *directly* through your heart."

Brokk's lips twitched toward a smile. "Being a half vampire has its advantages."

Reminding her that he was part vampire would probably drive her away, but he needed space from her. He couldn't think when she was this close and her scent was everywhere.

Instead of pulling away at the reminder of his half-vampire

nature, she stared at the scar while caressing it. He almost gripped her hand and moved it—there was only so much a man could take—but though her touch made him crazy, he didn't want it to stop.

"Amazing," she murmured.

When she licked her lips, he became fully erect. She was fascinating, beautiful, and he wanted her so badly that lust pulsed through him with every beat of his heart—a heart that pounded faster as she continued to caress. He wasn't sure she was aware of what she was doing, but her touch made him wild.

Unable to resist her lure, he cupped the back of her head. Uncertainty filled her eyes, but she didn't pull away.

Her fingers stilled on his skin as her breathing ceased, and she swayed toward him. They gazed at each other for a second, but Brokk could no more resist her than the sun could resist shining.

Bending his head, he waited for her to tell him to stop, push him away, and look at him with disgust and loathing, but she remained unmoving as his lips brushed hers. A bolt of electricity coursed between them as he deepened the kiss while still giving her time to push him away.

When his tongue stroked her lips, she opened to him. She tasted as refreshing and freeing as she smelled. She was nature and passion rolled into one, and the heady combination was one he couldn't resist.

When his other hand fell to her waist, he pulled her flush against him. She gasped a little when his erection prodded her belly but didn't recoil from him.

She was kissing a vampire and didn't care as their tongues entwined, and she rose onto her toes to thread her fingers through his hair. A low growl emanated from him when she rubbed the tips of his sensitive ears.

She had no idea the fire she played with or the savagery with which he wanted her. His hand slid down her back and inside the waistband of her pants to cup her firm ass.

Her skin was like silk against his palm, and the scent of arousal became her most prominent as it permeated the air. He hadn't realized how *much* he wanted her until he held her.

It had been there for a while, building over time, but she'd awakened something primitive inside him, and it wouldn't be denied. He'd never experienced this unraveling, this borderline loss of control, but it built toward a crescendo only she could unleash and sate.

Releasing her ass, he slipped his hand free to find the button on her pants; he undid it. He pushed them down her hips, and they slid down to pool at her feet.

He was reluctant to break the kiss, but he had to taste her, fuck her, and hear her cry his name as he finished what she started with herself by the stream. Worried she might come to her senses, he went to his knees before she could stop him.

Grasping her slender thighs, he nudged them further apart and lifted his mouth to her core. She tasted of Heaven and sin, a delicious mix that shattered his remaining restraint.

CHAPTER FORTY-THREE

KAYLIA'S HEAD spun as Brokk's mouth settled against her, and his tongue did the most deliciously wicked things she'd ever experienced. The man weaved magic with his mouth, and she rocked against him until her legs quaked.

A dim, distant part of her tried to speak up and remind her why she shouldn't be doing this, but as she gripped his ears and pulled him more firmly against her, she didn't care what it tried to say. All she craved was *him* and the ecstasy he created.

Even if she could recall why this should stop, she wouldn't end it. It felt far too good.

Her head tipped back, and she moaned as she rode his tongue. A long-forgotten tightness clenched her belly, her toes curled, and the world filled with rapture as she came apart with a cry.

Feeling as if the bones were pulled from her body, she would have fallen to the ground if he hadn't caught her and scooped her into his arms. Kaylia smiled as her head fell against his shoulder, and tremors continued to roll through her.

The thick wall of his muscles bunched around her as he

moved. Cradled against his chest, she'd never felt so secure and protected as when he held her.

He shifted her in his arms, and she didn't know what he was doing until he settled her on the ground. Except, he'd somehow managed to get a blanket down.

Still trapped in her haze of rapture, she stretched languidly as he pulled off her boots and pants before removing his own. Freed from its confines, his shaft stood proudly out from his body, and her mouth watered at the sight of it. It was as rigid and thick as she'd imagined, and she couldn't stop herself from squirming at the idea of having it inside her.

Her euphoria faded as desire surged back to an all-consuming intensity that she couldn't deny. Needing to feel all of him against her, she tugged off her shirt and undid her bra.

His eyes held hers as he settled himself between her thighs and removed her bra. Once he had her completely naked, his gaze raked her body before hungrily latching onto her breasts.

"You're gorgeous," he murmured, "and I'm going to own *every* part of you."

Goose bumps broke out on her arms, and her breath hitched at his words. It was a promise she knew he would keep.

His head bent to her chest, and he claimed one of her nipples. Ready for more, Kaylia lifted her hips to him. The motion brought the head of his cock into contact with her; he pressed a little deeper, teasing her entrance but not entering.

Growing irritated by his refusal to give her what she wanted, Kaylia lifted herself further, but he still held back. Then he raised his head from her breast and reclaimed her mouth.

Brokk kissed her like it would be the last one he'd ever experience; he kissed her like she was the most desirable woman he'd ever encountered and the only one who mattered.

He kissed her as if he'd claimed her as his and she so badly wanted to be claimed by him, and feel him moving within her as he made her scream. Growing impatient, she tugged on his ears and lifted her hips to him again.

This time, he gave her what she sought and thrust forward. Him filling her created such an overwhelming sensation of rightness that she screamed against his mouth.

The awakening she started to feel on the riverbank erupted in a wave of power that shook the stacked wood around them. She barely noticed as she latched her legs around his waist and reveled in the feel of his body moving against hers.

She gave herself completely over to him as he possessed her in a way no other ever had. The memory of why she should stop this tried to surface again, but Brokk's scent, the way he moved around her, and the enticing feel of his body sliding against hers shut out everything except for him.

Sweat slicked their bodies as she moved faster against him. She demanded all of him too as she gripped his ass and her mouth found his again.

When she felt his fangs against her lips, she didn't recoil. Instead, curiosity made her brush them with the tip of her tongue.

She'd *never* been with a vampire before, and she marveled at the way they extended with her ministrations. When she pushed her tongue more firmly against them, his breath sucked in when his fangs pricked her and a bead of blood formed on her tongue.

As soon as it formed, it vanished when he consumed it. Such a thing should repulse her, but she yearned for more.

Breaking the kiss, her head fell back, and she turned it to expose her vein. His mouth found her neck, and his fangs grazed her skin, but he didn't bite.

Growing impatient, she clasped the back of his head and held it closer to make it clear what she wanted from him. "Do it."

He stiffened, but the call of her blood must have overwhelmed him as, a second later, his fangs pierced her neck. Another burst of power erupted from her as the vampire part of him consumed her blood while the dark fae feasted on the energy their sex created.

And he wasn't the only one strengthened by their joining. This unrestrained, gorgeous man emanated so much strength that it was impossible for her not to drink it in.

Grasping his ears, she held him against her as she whispered, "Fuck me harder."

He bit deeper as he grasped her hips, lifted her ass off the ground, and thrust into her. His fangs retracted from her vein as any pretense of restraint between them melted away. They grasped and pulled at each other while demanding more until they both came apart with a savage cry that Brokk muffled with a kiss.

CHAPTER FORTY-FOUR

WHEN REALITY SETTLED back over her, it was a cold, monstrous beast that left her shaken while Brokk's arms remained locked around her. The warmth he created against her back should have been uncomfortable, given the cloying humidity of the jungle, but she welcomed it... until she didn't.

In his arms, she'd forgotten the one man who had mattered most to her. The one man she'd vowed *never* to forget.

But she hadn't thought of Fabian while allowing Brokk to sweep her up in a haze of ecstasy. She stuck her knuckles in her mouth and bit down as horror and self-hatred swamped her.

How could I have forgotten him?

But worse than that... *how did I give myself more freely to Brokk, a man I haven't known for long, than to the man I planned to bind my life to?*

Sex with Fabian was always pleasurable. She'd enjoyed it, she really had, but not like she did with Brokk, and that only made her feel worse.

Yes, Brokk was part dark fae, a race known for their prowess in the bedroom, but that still didn't explain how she'd given herself so completely to him.

I forgot Fabian!

Her hand stifled her sob as her heart twisted in her chest and guilt threatened to choke her. She'd completely forgotten him when he'd been an ever-present companion for over three hundred years.

The man she'd loved and lost was always on her mind, even if she wasn't consciously aware of it. Fabian was a part of her that never left... until tonight.

And she'd forgotten him for hours as Brokk took her over and over until they'd both been too tired to continue. He'd fallen asleep, but reality had returned to grasp her within its icy tentacles.

She'd also allowed him, a *vampire*, to feed on her. While her hatred toward vamps had greatly lessened, one of them *did* murder Fabian, yet she'd allowed another to feast on her in every way possible.

At least somewhere between their second and fourth time together, she'd managed to rouse herself to awareness enough to ask him about birth control. It had been centuries since she'd worried about such a thing, but ever prepared, as most dark fae were, Brokk had assured her that he took a monthly potion for it.

Careful not to disturb Brokk, she drew her knees up to her chest as anguish twisted in her gut. The worst part was she could move out of his arms but didn't. He felt warm, strong, and secure as he held her close while his soft, sleeping breaths stirred her hair.

She hadn't experienced this kind of contact with another in centuries and didn't want it to end. But she didn't kid herself into thinking it would be like this with any other man; something about this man captivated and enthralled her.

Her inability to pull away only made her hate herself more. The only good thing was that since he was half dark fae, he'd be more than happy to move on to someone else tomorrow.

Once he diverted his attention from her, she could return to her life. It may be a bit lonely, but it was the one she'd accepted.

As she told herself this, sorrow rose to battle with the guilt. She hated the idea of him moving on, but it would be best for them.

However, she couldn't help questioning if it was the best thing for her. The guilt rose again as turbulent emotions battered her.

She had to get her shit together, or she would die in this place.

As she lay there, listening to the sounds of the jungle, whispers drifted to her. Kaylia gripped Brokk's arm as she tried to understand what they said, but it sounded like a bunch of murmured gibberish until her name and Brokk's pierced through.

The night had been silent in the mirror realm, but back in the jungle, the whispers found them.

CHAPTER FORTY-FIVE

BROKK WOKE to discover Kaylia missing from their small hut. Panic shot through him as he bolted upright and rose.

Her pack was gone. With jerky movements, he tugged on the pants he'd tossed aside and buttoned them.

He didn't bother with a shirt or his pack before ducking through the curtain and stepping into the bright, sunny day. He immediately spotted Kaylia on the other side of the small clearing, talking with the witches.

The sun shining off her silvery blonde hair caused it to shimmer. Its rays danced all around her, shining a spotlight down on her.

He didn't move as he drank her in. She was strikingly beautiful, and last night, she'd been *his*. He'd had countless women over the years, so many they'd all blended into each other, but she would never be like one of them.

Last night was different in some way. He didn't know how to explain it, but something inside him had changed. Usually, he was glad to say goodbye to all those other women the next day, and many times, he hadn't done that, but he'd hoped to find her still beside him.

He buried his disappointment over discovering her ready to go, and he suspected it was because reality had returned, and she'd recalled her dead fiancé.

He didn't know if guilt had driven her from his arms or if she only meant for it to be a one-night thing. Either way, he wouldn't let it stand. There would be other times and nights; he'd make sure of it.

When Allegra pointed at something in the jungle and Kaylia turned her head to look, Brokk was disappointed to see that the bite marks he'd left on her had already healed. The next chance he got, he would leave them again.

Excitement and power crackled through him. The energy she'd exuded during sex, and the strength of her blood, continued to course through his veins.

No one had ever invigorated him the way she had. Yes, she was an extremely powerful immortal, but he'd been with plenty of those before. This was different; *she* was different. He didn't know how or why, but he would figure it out.

Sensing his gaze, Kaylia turned toward him. When their eyes met, she held his briefly before shifting her attention to the ground.

Something about how she'd reacted to seeing him didn't sit right, but he didn't have time to address it as he spotted Ryker striding toward him from the corner of his eye. Brokk turned to face him.

"Are you ready to go?" Ryker inquired.

"I have to get my pack."

Ryker's attention shifted to the trees. "The sooner we get started, the better we'll be. It's much hotter but safer to travel during the day."

Brokk had a feeling it didn't matter much in this realm, but Ryker had been here a lot longer than him. Few survived a week in this place; he gave Ryker and his men credit for lasting almost a year.

Turning, he pushed back past the curtain, used the mouth-wash for his teeth, finished dressing, packed the extra blankets, and shrugged on his pack. He returned to the clearing to discover Ryker only a few feet away.

Brokk walked over to stand beside him. "What about the shelters?"

Ryker glanced around the clearing. "They stay. Sometimes, if we find them again, we return to some of our old camps for a night or two, but not often. It's best to stay on the move here."

"So, you establish camps when you intend to stay in an area for a little while?"

"If we plan to be there for more than a few days, yes. It gives us a little sense of normalcy in a place where there is none."

"I can understand that. What about the table and chairs in your hut?"

"Sometimes we build more, sometimes we don't. It depends on the situation. We've built some camps near the crudue vine, but we won't stop at those."

Brokk frowned at him. "Why not?"

"They might not be where we left them, and I've learned not to waste time searching. It's a good way to die."

"Fair enough."

"This jungle is alive around us. Never forget that."

The leaves of the trees, rustling in a slight breeze, empha-sized Ryker's words.

CHAPTER FORTY-SIX

BY THE TIME the sun was high in the sky, Brokk was fighting his growing irritation with Kaylia as she went out of her way to avoid him. They had yet to speak, and she remained clustered with the witches.

Normally, he wouldn't mind that she wanted to be with them, but she wasn't with them to catch up. She was there to avoid *him*.

Anytime their eyes met, she didn't acknowledge him before glancing away. It was something he planned to remedy when he got the chance, but first, they had to get out of this area of Doomed Valley.

His teeth ground together as he used his sword to chop through the dense foliage surrounding him. The leaves here were bigger than him, and they all sought to drown him in their cloying depths.

He had no idea where Kaylia was in this mess. He'd lost sight of her a few minutes ago and was trying to work his way back into view of her, but the more he carved away, the more the jungle clung to him.

Screams didn't pierce the air, which meant nothing was

attacking them and no one was stuck in white muck, but he hated not being able to see her and assure himself that she was safe. His muscles tensed to spring at the first indication she was in trouble; he just wished he knew which way to go.

Finally, the density of the jungle eased a little, and he could see Kaylia again. She stood a few feet to his right, pulling bits of leaves and branches from her hair.

Tired of being ignored by the witch, he strode over to stand beside her. She swayed a little toward him before stiffening and bowing her head.

A muscle in his jaw ticked at her reaction. No *fucking* way was he putting up with being ignored because she'd come... *many* times.

She may feel guilty because of her dead fiancé, but he refused to let her shut out the world again. She deserved far better than that.

"Are you okay?" he asked.

She plucked another piece of leaf from the short braid she'd pulled her hair into. Without looking at him, she flicked the leaf aside. "I'm fine."

He looked around, but the witches she'd surrounded herself with earlier were half hidden in foliage ten feet away. A few of Ryker's men stood a few feet away and were engrossed in conversation as Ryker examined his compass.

"We're in this together," he told her. "We're the only ones we can completely trust."

"I know."

She may say she knew it, but she'd been going out of her way to avoid him and didn't seem willing to change it any time soon. Frustration mounting, he stared at the top of her head as he willed her to look at him.

He didn't know what to say or do to change this, but that was because, even though she was avoiding him, it wasn't about *him*. This was because of her emotions about her dead fiancé.

Brokk shifted his gaze away from her as he took in the dense jungle while all around them animals screamed in pain and skirted through the foliage. Something was probably hunting them, but they wouldn't know until it was on them.

One of the snake symbols was etched into a trunk the size of a giant's calf. After their time in the mirror realm, he'd forgotten about them, but here was another.

Now that he was finally close enough to smell her earthy aroma again, he didn't want to move away, but he sought answers and she required time—not too much time because he suspected she'd use it to run. He wouldn't get anywhere pushing her, especially not when surrounded by others.

Striding over to the tree, he rested his fingers against the mark of a snake eating its tail. "What is this?" he asked. "And why is it carved into different things throughout the jungle?"

Ryker came to stand beside him. "It's the mark of the ophidians. They use it to delineate their territory."

"But we've seen it ever since we arrived here."

"As far as I can tell, they consider *all* of Doomed Valley their territory."

"Of course they do."

Brokk resisted looking at Kaylia. Instead, he shifted his pack, wiped the sweat from his brow, and followed Ryker into the dense jungle.

Brokk swatted away a few bugs buzzing in his ears as his lip curved into a sneer. "Do you plan to return home at some point?" he asked to distract himself from the annoying insects while carving through the jungle.

"I swore to protect my king, and while I failed in my oath, I *will* remain here until he is free."

Brokk suspected that meant Ryker had no family he cared about at home. Even a man who'd sworn an oath of loyalty to his king would return to see his wife, children, parents, or siblings.

Or at least most of them would… if they had strong bonds with him.

Hell, he'd return to see Orin, and he was still pissed at the self-centered asshole. While he knew the Lord's command killed his father, he also placed some of that blame on Orin's shoulders. Orin loved his family, Brokk was certain of it, but he was reckless, selfish, and never thought about anyone other than himself.

Still, Brokk loved his older brother, even if he'd prefer to shove a sock in his mouth and beat him senseless most of the time. Thinking about it made him smile.

The day crept onward as he hacked through branches, vines, and other obstacles. He was sure things sprang up between him and Ryker that hadn't been there before or shifted to block his way. The jungle had a way of changing around them.

He often lost sight of Kaylia as they moved through, but not for long as she stayed to his right and at the same pace. Though he sensed creatures creeping through the trees, nothing attacked them.

Maybe the larger numbers of Ryker's men kept them at bay, or they would wait until nightfall to pounce. Either way, Brokk was ready for them.

The sun was setting when they emerged from the woods to stand at the edge of a clearing full of stone ruins.

CHAPTER FORTY-SEVEN

SOME STONES REMAINED positioned across two or three others to offer shelter and protection, but most of the massive rocks were scattered across the ground or tilted haphazardly against each other and trees.

All the stones were long and flat and had to weigh at least a thousand pounds. It had taken a lot of work to get the rocks positioned on one another, and he suspected many of the fallen ones were also once built up in such a way.

A hundred-foot circle of cleared land surrounded all the stones, and while it didn't look like anyone had been here in years, as none of the ground was disturbed, the jungle hadn't crept in to reclaim the stolen land. He wasn't as connected to the earth as a witch, but power thrummed beneath his feet.

"What is this?" he asked.

"I have no idea," Ryker answered. "We've never seen it before."

"Are we going in the right direction still?"

"Yes, but there are many paths to take to the crudue vine, and don't forget, the jungle has a way of changing."

"That it does," Brokk murmured.

"We'll still find the vine; we always have."

Brokk believed Ryker's conviction, but he couldn't help contemplating if the jungle might prevent them from doing so.

"It looks like an ancient temple or place of worship," Kaylia said. "It's been destroyed, but a *lot* of power remains in this land."

The other witches were hushed as they stood around her, their heads bowed as if in reverence, and their hands clasped before them. If he could feel the power here, he could only imagine what *they* sensed from this land.

Kaylia gazed around the clearing before dropping her gaze to her hands. She lifted them before her and turned them over as awe flitted across her features.

Something deep inside him shifted while watching her. She was so amazing, and for the first time in his life, he found himself wanting a woman as *his*.

Brokk had never given much consideration to marriage and families. He suspected one day he'd have children because he liked them and wanted to be a father, but he'd always believed it would be with a woman who would prefer to move on afterward, like his mother.

Whenever he considered a family for himself, he imagined it would be much like his—a single father raising his offspring with love and guidance—and he'd been more than happy with it.

But now, he wondered what it would be like to have a woman who stayed with him, helped him raise his children, and loved him. And he couldn't help picturing that woman as Kaylia.

Shit. He ran a hand through his hair and tugged at the ends of it. *Slow it down, and stop being such an asshole. One good fuck does not equate to a lifetime.*

It had been more than one fuck, but it was still the truth. He had no idea what was wrong with him or why she affected him so deeply, and he was starting not to like it.

But he wasn't going to let her go, not yet, at least.

Kaylia closed her eyes and inhaled deeply. "So much power."

"Even I can feel it," Ryker murmured.

"So can I," Brokk said.

Brokk was about to turn away when Kaylia's eyes opened and met his. The passion blazing from their pewter depth froze him as an answering rush of lust flooded him, and something sizzled in the air between them.

Despite their surroundings, his dick stirred, and he almost went to her but stopped himself. He couldn't take her in the middle of the clearing with everyone watching. However, if he touched her now, that's what would happen.

"We'll stay here for the night." Ryker's words shifted Brokk's attention away from Kaylia.

"Yes," Kaylia murmured. "We can form a strong protection spell over this area."

"Good."

Brokk didn't look at Kaylia again as he helped the others set up a makeshift camp for the night. There would be no huts in this clearing, but many of Ryker's followers claimed shelter beneath the stones.

Unwilling to sleep with them, Brokk removed a piece of canvas from his pack and draped it over a low-hanging branch. Once settled into place, it created a small shelter where he placed his bag inside.

When he finished, he turned to discover Kaylia and the witches working to weave a protective barrier around them. Her movements and words entranced him as power crackled on the air and more power vibrated up through his boots.

After they established the barrier, the witches turned to creating their own shelters. Brokk buried his disappointment when Kaylia went with them instead of coming to place her things inside his space.

He'd suspected she wouldn't return to him tonight, but he

hadn't realized he'd still retained hope she would. She was determined to establish a wall between them, and he was as determined to demolish it.

In the end, he would win.

CHAPTER FORTY-EIGHT

KAYLIA SAT at the edge of the clearing, her legs crossed and her hands on her knees as the earth around her hummed. That energy left a crisp, almost ozone taste on her tongue while vibrating so loudly it created a song in her head.

Despite the vast power pulsing beneath her, the earth didn't emit a happy song. It was one of sadness and loss.

Tears pricked her eyes as the melancholy notes tugged at her heart. Whatever happened in this clearing, whatever destroyed the monuments that once stood here, it was swift and brutal. Time hadn't knocked the stones down. Monsters did.

She had no idea what happened to destroy what once stood here, but blood soaked the earth beneath her. That blood wasn't visible, but it was there, deep within the ground and creating much of the sorrow surrounding her.

Beneath the song, screams also resonated in her ears. The earth didn't reveal what occurred, but because of the blood, she could imagine the horror that unfolded and the devastation wrought upon those who once resided here.

Her eyes closed, and her shoulders hunched forward as

waves of sadness wracked her. This wasn't her sadness from her loss of Fabian; it was the grief of the earth weeping around her.

She should get up and walk away to save herself from more suffering, but someone had to offer comfort to a land that had been crying for far too long... or at least she did the best she could to try to do so. She hadn't eased the earth's weeping yet, but it understood she was here for it.

So, she sat alone in the shadows of the giant trees surrounding the clearing and allowed the earth to share its mourning. The power of the magic once thriving here kept the jungle from encroaching, but it hadn't stopped a murderous rampage from unfolding.

Whatever entered this clearing and destroyed these monuments was brazen, vicious, and powerful. She suspected it was the ophidians but couldn't be sure.

If the ophidians came now, the protective spell they'd cast over the clearing would help keep them at bay, but *not* out. They'd gotten here and destroyed this place once; they would get in again.

The barrier would alert them to the presence of invaders, and that was what mattered most. She suspected that whoever once lived here hadn't expected an attack; they wouldn't make the same mistake.

A nearby footstep caused her eyes to fly open. She didn't have to see Brokk to know he'd arrived; she smelled him, and the energy he emitted caused her hair to stand on end.

He'd stayed away for most of the day, but she'd often felt his eyes on her. Despite being a dark fae who often bounced from one bed to another, he didn't understand why she'd shut him out.

Even if he didn't want to keep her as a lover, and was most likely already looking to move on, they'd become friends. Yet, she'd distanced herself from him.

It was wrong of her to pull away from that friendship, especially since they really could only trust each other in this realm, but being near him was a battle between self-hatred and lust. And that war was battering her down so much she could barely breathe through it.

Still, though it was best if they kept their distance, she would miss his lopsided, endearing smile and unwavering loyalty to all those he cared about.

"Why are you crying?" he inquired. "Is it because of what happened last night?"

She shook her head, though she had cried over that. She wouldn't do so again.

What they did made her feel like she'd betrayed Fabian, but she wouldn't beat herself up about it anymore. Life was a journey with many detours, dead ends, roadblocks, and lots of joy.

Despite her distress following her choice last night, there were times of pure bliss before then. She couldn't and wouldn't change it.

Last night, Brokk gave her the gift of being free from sorrow, if only for a brief moment in the vast expanse of time with which she'd lived. It was one of the best gifts she'd ever been given.

"No," she whispered. "It's not because of last night."

He tilted his head and studied her like he didn't believe her, but still he approached. He wore a loose-fitting brown tunic and pants that hugged the corded muscles of his thighs and his taut ass.

Kaylia couldn't see his ciphers, but she vividly recalled every dip and sway in the markings running across his shoulders and back. She'd spent a lot of time tracing and kissing them last night.

He stopped a couple of feet away and gestured at the ground near her. "May I?"

She should have said no and distanced herself from him immediately, but now that she was in his presence again, she didn't want him to go. Plus, absorbing the sorrow of this land had made her feel unbelievably lonely.

And she was tired of being alone. She'd isolated herself for centuries and couldn't do it anymore.

"Yes." The word was barely more than a breath, but he heard her.

Coming closer, he settled on the ground across from her. He was so close she could smell him, but not so close they touched; she appreciated that. She didn't like being alone, but she wasn't looking for anything more than company right now.

He rested his hands on his knees as he imitated her position. "Do you want to talk about it?"

"Something terrible happened here."

She didn't realize she was crying until a tear dripped off her chin and landed on her hand. She didn't bother to wipe away the ones still trickling down her cheek. Those lost here should be mourned by someone other than the earth.

"Their blood stains the earth," she continued.

CHAPTER FORTY-NINE

BROKK'S FOREHEAD furrowed as he looked around the clearing.

"You can't see it anymore, but it's there, ingrained into the soul of the earth."

When his gaze came back to hers, understanding and sympathy shone within it. "Do the other witches know this?"

"They might, but I haven't asked them about it. We each feel and experience things differently."

"Of course."

"I feel those who lived here should be acknowledged and mourned; the other witches might not feel the same."

As if it were the most natural thing in the world, he rested his hand on top of hers, and some of her burden eased. She'd never experienced anything like it, as his touch was like an instant balm to her soul.

She stared at his hand, so big and strong with its marks from the many battles he'd waged and the work with his sword today. His hands had killed many immortals throughout his lifetime, but they offered her comfort and had touched her with such gentle reverence last night.

"The suffering of others shouldn't be your burden," he said.

"Many carry burdens they shouldn't, but they face the world every day and continue with their lives because they must. It makes some stronger while breaking others."

"And what will this burden do for you?"

"It will teach me not to let down my guard and remind me that I must have sympathy for the plight of others.... far too many don't possess that anymore. Their ability for empathy has been stripped away by wars and fear. The Lord and so many others like him have unleashed their terror on the realms for far too long. This place is a reminder to be ever vigilant against becoming indifferent to suffering."

"I think that's a reminder we all need from time to time."

Her fingers turned over and clasped his even as she told herself to let him go. Talking with him again felt so right; it was so easy, and he was her friend.

But it was more than that, and she knew it. Guilt lingered over last night, but it had changed her. It was an experience she would never forget, and while she tried to deny she wanted it again, she couldn't hide from the truth.

She did want him again... *badly*.

As a dark fae, what happened between them last night probably hadn't registered much on Brokk's radar, but it was life-changing for her. It had awakened her, but though she felt more alive than she had in centuries, she couldn't repeat last night... with anyone.

She squeezed his hand before removing hers from Brokk's. With a sense of serenity she didn't feel, she clasped her hands together and placed them in her lap.

"You believe last night was a mistake," he stated.

"I didn't say that."

"But you think it."

Her eyes darted away from him. "No, I don't, but I once pledged myself to marry a man who I love deeply."

"And he died."

She couldn't stop herself from flinching at his words. "He was murdered."

"Yes, but you still live."

"I know that. I've done so for centuries now."

"No, you haven't, but you already know that. You locked yourself away and only emerged from the crone realm because of Lexi and the hope she promised for all the realms. You'd still be there otherwise."

She almost protested his words, but she wasn't a liar. If Brokk and Sahira hadn't come to the crone realm in search of the harrow stone, she wouldn't be here. She'd still be in the crone realm, locked away, and simply existing in a sheltered world instead of living in the realms.

"I will always love Fabian," she stated.

"And you should, but he died, *not* you."

Kaylia looked to the guards standing in the shadows, staring resolutely ahead. For years, she'd been dead but still living, yet...

"A part of me died with him."

"I can't know how that feels; I understand loss, I've had plenty of it over the years, but not like what you endured. You'll never forget him, but you shouldn't beat yourself up over living again."

She couldn't tell Brokk that she *had* forgotten Fabian last night. Somehow, he made her forget the one man who had been on her mind for centuries. It was too close to her heart and too painful.

"You're a powerful, beautiful woman who exudes life and relishes it, Kaylia. It would be a travesty if you buried yourself in guilt and regret; it's not fair to you."

Her eyes shot back to him. "It's not fair that a vampire took him from me."

Brokk sighed as he rested his hands on his knees. "It's not, but you're not the first to lose a loved one, and you won't be the last. My father moved on after losing his wife."

"Having sex with and fathering sons with other women isn't moving on. If he had truly moved on, then he would have fallen in love with one of those other women, like he did with Cole's mother. Sex isn't moving on."

A flicker of something... maybe sadness... passed across his eyes, but it was there and gone too fast for her to tell. He pondered her words before bowing his head a little.

"You're right, it's not, but my father didn't allow guilt to fester and destroy him because he continued to embrace whatever small moments of happiness he could still find in life from his children, his realm, and other women."

"Your father was a dark fae; he had to feed to survive. What if he didn't have to feed? Do you think he still would have been with other women?"

She was genuinely curious about this. She'd met Tove a few times but always in passing and never spoken more than a few sentences with the man.

Brokk rubbed his chin while contemplating this. Then he lowered his hand and lifted both to hold them before him.

"My father used to hold my hand while on walks. We'd stroll the grounds, examining the gardens, the guards' houses, and the fields of the Gloaming. We'd talk about the dark fae who lived there and worked the land; he said they made the Gloaming what it was, not him, not us, but *them*.

"It was our private time together, but he did something similar with all my brothers. We were always gifted time alone with him. We also had family time, with all of us, and far more of it than our individual time with him, but those times were so very special."

Kaylia couldn't stop herself from settling her hand on his leg as love shone from his eyes. She'd known Tove as ruthless and relentless, or at least that was his reputation, but Brokk painted an entirely different picture of the man.

"He loved all of us deeply. And I think, in the end, that yes, he would have had sex with other women because I think once my father had Cole and realized how much he loved his child, he wanted more, even if it wasn't with the woman he cherished. He chose life after Cole's mother... my brother's lives, *my* life, and never regretted it."

Kaylia's lips parted. She hadn't known where his story was going and hadn't expected it to come to this conclusion, but once it did, she saw he was right.

Brokk gave her a sad smile as he rested his hand over hers. "As I've said, you're a beautiful, vibrant woman who can choose to embrace that and move on with love for Fabian still in your heart, or you can allow guilt to reign."

He was right. *She* was the one who would decide what course her life would take and how she'd let it affect her. Ever since Fabian's death, she'd felt as if she didn't have any control over her life, but she did, even in this forsaken land of monsters and death.

And while she wasn't sure how to handle the guilt or if she'd ever get used to it, she didn't want to give up what she'd rediscovered last night. The only problem was, she couldn't imagine being with anyone other than Brokk.

He was the one who'd awakened her, and *he* was the one she wanted. However, that wasn't the way of the dark fae, unless they sought something more from the relationship... and that was something she could never give.

CHAPTER FIFTY

BROKK WAITED for Kaylia to say something, but when she didn't speak, he knew she'd had enough. Her shoulders remained hunched and her skin paler, but this time, he knew it had nothing to do with what passed between them last night and everything to do with this land and the sorrow she'd decided to take into herself.

He understood this was something she had to do, but she'd acknowledged the destruction here for long enough. It wouldn't do her any good to continue draining herself.

Patting his hands off his knees, he rose and extended his hand to her. "It's probably time for you to rest. Tomorrow will be another exhausting day, and we might make it to the crudue vine."

When her gaze fell to his hand, he waited to see what she would do while preparing himself for rejection. Seconds passed in which he once again became aware of the creatures moving through the jungle as night set in, but none of them screamed, hissed, or made their strange calls.

It was quieter than normal out there, as if the creatures in this area were as awed by the power here as him. And so far, there were no whispers.

Finally, Kaylia stretched out her hand, and their fingers entwined. A spark shot through him, and his fangs pricked as his gaze fell to her neck.

He easily recalled the ambrosia of her blood filling his mouth and the way she moved against him with such abandon. He wanted more of both but wouldn't push her. She'd avoided him all day because of what happened last night, and no matter what happened between them after this, he still wanted her friendship.

"Where are you sleeping tonight?" he asked.

She released his hand to point to a cluster of fallen rocks not far from where he'd established his tent. "I set up my shelter over there."

"You'll be safe there." However, he'd far prefer to have her at his side again. He kept that to himself as he strolled across the clearing with her. "The jungle is quiet tonight."

"I don't know if that's a good or bad thing."

"Neither do I."

He stopped outside the canvas she'd draped between the rocks and stepped back while she ducked into the shelter. After she vanished from view, he remained outside, his feet planted into the ground as everything in him screamed against leaving her alone.

She should be with *him,* and they should be enjoying each other again. But he didn't know if that would ever happen again.

He hadn't known it was possible to hate a ghost, but he loathed the one between them. What would have happened if he'd met her before Fabian?

That's a strange, pointless thought. It certainly wasn't anything he'd contemplated about the other women who'd come and gone in his life.

Besides, it wouldn't have made a difference if he met her before Fabian. Back then, the witches *loathed* vampires simply for their existence; Kaylia wouldn't have looked at him twice, and he wouldn't have bothered with her either.

It was only now, after things had changed so much, that there could have been something between them... but he wasn't sure that was what he wanted anyway. He didn't embrace his dark fae nature over his vampiric one, but he enjoyed playing the field and experiencing all the realms had to offer.

He could also admit a part of him was envious of what Cole and Lexi shared. How could he not be?

They loved each other deeply and would share their lives. They would get married and have children, and those children would be raised in a home full of love, like he was.

Finally, he mumbled good night to her and walked away. He'd almost crossed the ten feet separating their shelters when the whispers started.

The guard directly across from him stiffened but showed no other reaction to the insidious sounds. Brokk was determined to shut them out as he ducked into his shelter, but their mutterings taunted him as he settled onto his blanket and clasped his hands behind his head.

He detected his name, Kaylia's, Ryker's, and some of the others in the whispers, but most of the words remained unintelligible as he stared at the thick branch above him. Closing his eyes, he tried to listen more carefully to the words, but they remained elusive.

He wasn't sure if they were speaking another language, muttering nonsense, or talking over each other so much it became drivel. It would be his turn to stand guard in a few hours, and he required rest, but between the whispers and Kaylia, he wouldn't get any sleep tonight.

CHAPTER FIFTY-ONE

RYKER CAME to wake him for his guard shift, but he was already awake and still trying to decipher the whispers. When Ryker hit the side of his canvas, Brokk crawled from his makeshift shelter and rose.

He stretched his back as he surveyed the clearing with its handful of torches set around the perimeter. The moon had risen, but it was waning, so its dim radiance didn't bathe the clearing in much light.

From the jungle, the whispers rose in volume before lowering back to barely heard mutterings. If he thought he could find the source and not get killed in the process, he'd hunt them down to have some silence.

"Where do the whispers come from?" Brokk inquired.

"I don't know. I've never seen whatever causes them, but they never go away. So far, whatever causes them hasn't attacked us, so they could be harmless assholes."

"Nothing in this realm is harmless."

"Very true."

They fell into step beside each other as they walked across

the cleared land. "Kaylia said a lot of blood stains the ground here."

Ryker looked down at the earth. "A lot of blood stains everything in this realm."

"There's more of it here."

"And it was most likely the ophidians who spilled it. They terrorize everything in Doomed Valley."

"You said they have a pyramid; how close have you gotten to it?"

"We've been really close a few times, but those fuckers always push us back before we can get inside. They're vicious, and their poison will knock you down fast."

"Aren't all immortals vicious?"

"Not the light fae."

"The light fae fought against the Lord. They didn't wield weapons, well... one did, but they stood against him."

Ryker's eyebrows rose at this revelation. "Interesting."

Brokk couldn't stop his gaze from traveling to Kaylia's makeshift structure when they passed it; he hoped she was getting some rest tonight. Tomorrow was going to be a long day, but it wouldn't be the first he'd face without sleep, and it wouldn't be the last.

As they approached one of the guards at the edge of the jungle, Brokk removed his sword from its sheath and assumed the position Ryker's follower vacated. The leader of the amsirah army relieved a guard fifteen feet to Brokk's left.

Brokk stepped back and faded into the shadows created by the moon. There weren't enough shadows to conceal him completely, but it would be difficult for anyone to see him.

From behind the witches' protection spell, the whispers continued. As much as he loathed them, they were a welcome distraction from Kaylia and everything that could never be between them.

Though the whispers mostly spoke nonsense, other than

names, their insidious tone and incessant noise raised the hair on his nape. Whatever created those whispers couldn't pierce the witches' protective bubble without them knowing, but they were out there, watching them, and he felt their eyes boring into his neck.

Brokk ignored them as they moved closer before creeping further away again. Their mutterings grew louder with their movements, and he sensed them circling the barrier.

He'd never heard them so close before. Certain that one of the whisperers stood directly behind him, Brokk turned to search the woods.

All that greeted him was the dark, endless spaces between the trees and the jungle. Nothing stood outside the barrier, staring at him as it waited to pounce, but he could feel it beyond the veil, salivating as it watched him.

Brokk smiled. He started to turn away when he spotted red eyes to his left, watching him.

He held those ravenous eyes until they blinked, and blackness briefly encompassed where they once stood. Then the red flared back to brilliant life as it continued to watch him from the trees.

He didn't know if these seemingly free-floating eyes were part of the whisperers or belonged to some other creature, but they continued to stare at each other until it blinked again and vanished into the night.

Brokk tried to follow its movements but soon lost it in the dense foliage. He felt it out there, watching and waiting for its opportunity to strike.

And when it did, he was going to slaughter it. He'd had enough of this valley, whispers, emotions, ghosts, and all the other shit plaguing him since arriving here.

Brokk grinned as he tightened his hold on his sword and turned to face the clearing once more.

CHAPTER FIFTY-TWO

KAYLIA DIDN'T GO OUT of her way to avoid him as much the next day. She was still a little hesitant to meet his gaze, and her smile was shyer, but at least she'd stopped acting like he was the enemy.

As soon as the sun rose, they packed up their small camp and resumed their journey to the crudue vine. Brokk couldn't get the image of those red eyes out of his head as they traversed through the cloying jungle.

As they traveled, he saw no signs of the creature from last night, but that didn't mean it wasn't out there. It was entirely possible it stood only a foot away from him, hungrily watching, and he didn't know because the jungle hid it.

Brokk glanced back at Kaylia, who had fallen into line behind him. He'd been keeping a close eye on her to assure himself she was still there.

She smiled, but her brow creased as she studied him. "Everything okay?"

"Yes," he assured her.

She'd pulled her hair into a ponytail that bobbed against her nape, but loose strands cleaved to her flushed face. Loose-fitting clothes adhered to her curves.

Sometimes, the jungle was so dense he lost sight of her and the amsirah in front of him, but more often, he kept them in view. The sun reached its zenith in the sky when a grunt, followed by a shout, came from ahead of him.

Brokk stopped and held up his hand to let Kaylia know to stop too. From ahead of them came a sharp cry followed by a startled yelp.

His attention shifted to the thick green leaves, vines, and trees surrounding him as more sounds of an attack came from ahead. Grasping Kaylia's arm, he pulled her against his chest and locked her back against him as he swiftly drew the shadows around them.

"Shadows," he whispered so she would know she was cloaked.

Holding her in his arms again caused a sense of rightness to envelop him. How was it that even now, while something stalked them from the jungle and others died, she could affect him like no other woman?

His fangs throbbed as the rush of her blood pulsing through her veins filled his ears. He'd never considered the vampire and dark fae sides of himself as opposing each other. They'd always been cohesive as he made his way through life, but something about Kaylia caused the vampire half of him to surge to the fore-front as it sought to protect her.

She'd probably *hate* to learn that.

Kaylia might not despise vampires as much as she once did, but he doubted she would like hearing that she aroused the vampire half of him in such a way. But he couldn't deny his relentless impulse to feast on her again as his heart matched the rhythm of hers.

From his right, the loud crack of bone was accompanied by

the screech of an injured immortal. No, not a crack; something had chomped on that bone and continued to do so as more screams and crunches filled the air.

The leaves before them rattled and parted as a sleek, black creature emerged from between the trees. Twice the size of the jaguars in the human realm, the catlike creature's muscles rippled as it prowled toward them.

Its five-inch-long claws didn't make a sound against the rich earth as it lifted its boulder-sized head to sniff the air. Two front teeth, at least a foot in length, hung over its lower jaw, and when it lowered its head, its golden eyes shone in the sun.

It wasn't the creature he'd seen last night, but it would gladly eat anyone in its way. Its nostrils flared, and its head swiveled back and forth as it sniffed the air. The creature sensed them nearby, but the shadows kept them concealed.

Brokk brought his other hand forward, the one with the sword, and clasped it in front of Kaylia's belly when its head swiveled toward where they stood. Though it couldn't see them, its eyes locked on their location, and it sniffed again.

When another beast emerged from the thick foliage, the first animal snarled at the new arrival. They growled at each other, but the second remained crouched in the vegetation as a shriek came from somewhere behind them.

A lightning bolt broke free of the clear blue sky and slammed into the ground ahead of them. The crackle of electricity caused the hair on his arms to rise as an animal screeched before going silent.

The two near him and Kaylia swiveled their heads toward the sound but didn't retreat to help their brethren. It was already too late for help as Brokk was certain Ryker hadn't left the beast alive.

When the first animal lowered its head and crept closer to them, Brokk carefully shifted his hold on Kaylia to push her behind him. She stiffened against him and probably would have protested his repositioning, but she couldn't do so without giving them away.

Brokk lifted his sword and prepared for an attack when the creature lowered its front feet and its ass rose in the air. Brokk's attention shifted to the second one as it crept further from the jungle.

He'd have to remove his sword from the first one fast if he was going to take down the second predator. Thunder rolled across the sky, shaking the trees and ground as the first one sprang into the air, seeking to pounce.

It was only six inches from him when it started to twist, changing its trajectory and trying to get under his defenses. Brokk hadn't expected the move, but his reflexes had him pivoting in time to plunge his sword straight through its massive skull and out the back.

He bashed the creature into the ground with enough force to spray debris out around him. Planting his foot on the beast's jaw, he pulled his sword free as the second one sprang at him.

Jaws wide and with claws extended, the cat flew toward him with a grace that belied its colossal size. Brokk brought his sword up, but before he could swing at the creature, power swelled behind him as Kaylia lifted her hand and pushed a wall of air at the beast.

The cat yelped as it soared into the jungle before crashing into a tree. The crack of its back breaking filled the air as the tree rattled and the creature fell to the ground.

From behind him, someone screamed. Kaylia lurched toward the sound, but Brokk grasped her hand and pulled her against his side.

"Stay with me, or the shadows won't cloak you anymore," he said.

Not that they did much good against these creatures, as they could scent them out, but it was still some protection from them.

"We have to help them," Kaylia whispered.

"We will, but stay with me."

He took her hand as he led her toward the screams. He'd much prefer to get her somewhere safe first, but that was impossible in Doomed Valley.

CHAPTER FIFTY-THREE

KAYLIA'S HEART raced as she stayed close to Brokk while walking through the jungle they'd already traversed and toward the screams of the dying. Despite the foliage having already been chopped away by numerous swords, it was still difficult to navigate their way back to the others as trees and leaves had fallen in to block the path again.

They only made it a few feet before coming across one of those giant cats feasting on a witch. Kaylia's hand fluttered to her mouth as her stomach churned and everything inside her revolted.

Brokk struck the beast down with his sword, and they side-stepped the remains as they hurried back through the jungle in the hopes of helping those who remained. Brokk lifted a leaf out of the way, and Kaylia ducked beneath it as something to her right caused a rustling in the trees.

Brokk rested his hand on her back. If the beasts were in the jungle, watching them, then the movement of the leaf would have given away their location, but they couldn't exactly hack their way through here. That would be far more noticeable.

When nothing sprang at her, Kaylia inched her way under the

leaf, and Brokk followed her through. The leaf settled back into place with a tiny swish that set her teeth on edge.

Creeping further down the path, she rounded a corner and spotted an amsirah woman and witch standing back to back as two beasts circled them. With a flick of her hand, the witch used her powers to throw out a blast of air that flung one of the cats backward.

It bounced across the ground but rebounded swiftly as it leapt to its feet. The witch clasped her spear in both hands and planted her feet apart as she braced for the creature's attack.

The other cat leapt at the amsirah guard, but the woman ducked its flight and drove her sword up to catch the beast in its belly. She flung the cat over her head as another one emerged from the underbrush and pounced on the guard before she could recover in time to defend herself.

As the cat dragged the woman to the ground, Kaylia and Brokk raced forward. Brokk brought his sword down across the beast's nape. Kaylia whispered a protective spell while moving her fingers in an intricate pattern that created a wall of air between the other creature and the witch, who didn't have enough time to cast one herself.

The cat crashed into that wall and hit the ground. Rising, it staggered back as a mewl of confusion issued from it.

With her sword in hand, Kaylia rushed over to join the witch. When Brokk growled, she looked back to see him a few feet away, his eyes narrowed on her.

"Stay close."

He was only trying to keep her safe, but she had to help. Her barrier would keep the creature at bay for a little bit; she didn't know how much time they had before it pierced through.

Kaylia stepped beside the witch whose name she couldn't remember. The woman's frightened blue eyes searched for her while the cat stalked toward them.

"Where are you?" the witch whispered.

"Beside you."

The woman twitched a little as Kaylia's nearness startled her, but she kept her attention on the cat. On the other side of Kaylia's protective wall, it spit while clawing at the barrier. They didn't have much time before it succeeded in breaking through, and as much as she hated the idea of killing such a magnificent animal, she would destroy it when it did.

Behind them, Brokk tossed the other cat aside. The guard let out a startled gasp when he seized her arm.

"It's okay," Brokk assured her. "It's us."

Kaylia realized he'd released the shadows around them when the witch touched her arm and spoke. "Thank you."

Kaylia smiled at her, but the cat drew her attention again when it emitted a roar, backed up, and crashed into the barrier again. Brokk helped pull the guard to her feet as the cat swiped at the bubble again.

This time, its claws pierced the protective shield, tore it apart, and surged forward. In less than a second, Brokk was at her side as he teleported the few feet separating them.

As soon as the cat sprang, Brokk plunged his sword into the beast's throat. The witch staggered back as Brokk spun and flung the creature away.

The large cat hit the ground and started to rise before collapsing again. Kaylia stood and stared at the creature as Brokk lowered his sword.

A hush descended over the jungle; she'd never heard it so quiet before, and somehow, the absence of sound was more deafening than all the screams and awful noises; even the thunder had stopped rolling. Holding her breath, she waited for more cries of death, but none came.

Either the creatures had all retreated or been destroyed, and now it was time to discover how much devastation they rained down first.

CHAPTER FIFTY-FOUR

AFTER THE ATTACK, Ryker called a halt to their journey to deal with the devastation of the cats' aggression. After all the bodies were recovered, they learned they'd lost three amsirah and two witches. Ryker didn't suggest turning back as Brokk believed he might.

"We don't have a choice. We need more crudue vine too," Ryker told him as they worked together to set up a new camp near a slow-moving river. "We don't have much left to save us from the ophidians' venom."

"Have you ever been attacked by those cat things before?" Brokk asked.

"No, but there's no end to the monsters in this realm."

Brokk hadn't been here for anywhere near as long as Ryker, but he knew the man was right. "Have you camped here before?"

"No, we usually make it further than this or to the crudue vine before calling it for the night, but I think everyone could use a break after what happened earlier."

"So do I." Brokk stopped gathering wood to study the river. "Anything in there that's going to eat us?"

A smile tugged at the corner of Ryker's lips, but there was no humor in it. "We've crossed it to get to the crudue vine, and nothing has tried, but that doesn't mean there isn't something in there now."

There was a time when coming to Doomed Valley and learning its secrets was his biggest dream. Now, he'd give anything to get away from the choking jungle, unrelenting humidity, the fucking bugs, and countless enemies stalking them.

He glanced over at where Kaylia had formed a circle with the remaining witches. They all held hands as they bowed their heads and whispered words he couldn't hear; tears streaked their faces.

"Will the witches leave now?" he asked.

"They haven't left yet. We're paying them well, but I think it's become a mission for them to rescue Leo and defeat the ophidians too. More than a few witches have already died here; if they were to leave now, those lives would have been lost in vain. I think they would see it as a disgrace to the memory of those who have perished if they left now. Plus, Allegra had a thing with Leo."

"They were sleeping together?"

"Yes, but I think it meant more to her than him. She and the other witches were there for the ghoul war. They've been through a lot, seen a lot, and shed a lot of blood; I think they intend to see this through to the end."

"And Allegra is in love with your king?"

"Maybe, and if she's not, she's at least something."

Brokk's gaze shifted back to the mourning witches. Witches had always hired out their services to other immortals; most of them made a living by working for others, selling their potions, and casting spells, but it surprised him that they continued to put themselves in jeopardy for money.

But love could make someone do the craziest, bravest, worst, and best shit ever.

Love was why he and Kaylia remained here. Him, for his

oldest brother, best friend, the man he admired and loved deeply as he did the future sister-in-law he'd come to care for a lot. Kaylia was here because she'd grown to love Lexi and because she couldn't stand the suffering others would endure if they lost the queen of Dragonia.

And everyone in *all* the realms would suffer because Cole would unleash destruction on anything in his way. Without Lexi, the Shadow Reaver could never be stopped.

Brokk finished gathering wood and carried it over to the ever-increasing pile they'd stacked in the center of their newly established camp. He set his sticks on top of the others, stepped back, and rubbed his hands together to get rid of the bark and debris adhering to them.

Makeshift tents and shelters had already been set up beneath the trees; many were created from their limbs. Guards already stood around the perimeter, keeping watch of the safe space the witches established before they gathered to mourn.

When he looked back at Kaylia, his heart clenched. She was beautiful; he desired and admired her, but the swell of emotion he experienced around her was a new sensation.

He didn't understand what it meant or why she caused the vampire part of him to rise to the surface so strongly that his fangs tingled. He gritted his teeth against the unexpected hunger she'd awakened and returned to the river.

He stopped at the edge again and surveyed the brown water flowing past them. Tree roots and rocks poked above the surface, and branches dipped into the water. Leaves swirled as they floated leisurely past.

"At least it looks clean," he muttered.

Ryker chuckled. "The bottom is muddy, but the water's clean. I've bathed in it before, and it's a far better option than being covered in sweat and smelling like shit."

Brokk wasn't so sure, but since he couldn't stand the smell of himself anymore, he planned to find out.

CHAPTER FIFTY-FIVE

KAYLIA FINISHED WASHING herself the best she could in the river and sat back to study the sluggish current. In some sections, ripples radiated outward as the water moved around tree roots and rocks.

She saw no signs of life within the water's murky depths, but because she imagined it was full of gators, snakes, and leeches ready to devour them, she'd stayed on land and dipped her hands into the river to wash herself. Entering the water was not something she was willing to brave after the earlier events of this day.

Kaylia glanced back at where the witches had assembled their sleeping quarters for the night. They'd draped tarps over the trees and gathered close to the trunks to find solace in the life flowing through the jungle.

Verdan was in ruins, but they'd returned the bodies of the fallen to the witches' realm and buried them in the sacred land of the dead. While there, they hadn't encountered any other witches, and a palpable hush hung over the weeping land.

Verdan would be rebuilt, and the witches would see to it, but that rebuilding hadn't made it to the land of the dead yet. They hadn't encountered anyone else while there and returned through the portal they'd left open and heavily guarded on both ends.

When they finished, Ryker and his men carried their fallen into Tempest. They didn't stay to bury them but returned to Doomed Valley before seeing the bodies claimed by their families.

It seemed a little cold, but Ryker was in a hurry to close the portal again. No one liked the idea of leaving one open with so many monstrous things in this land, and the amsirah were used to returning their dead in such a way.

Too many have died in this land.

Unwillingly, her gaze traveled to where Brokk had assembled his small shelter near the river. He was a little further away from the others but well within the barrier of the protection spell they'd cast earlier.

Still, she didn't like him being by himself, even if he wasn't far from the other immortals. Her fingers dug into her palms as the crackling fire created shadows within the trees swallowed by the night.

On one side, they had the river, and on the other three sides, the jungle pressed against them. She felt the weight of it bearing down on her chest, and though it was unusually hushed, she felt the hunger of those beyond the protective veil while they watched and waited.

Kaylia tugged at the collar of her shirt. She had no idea what was out there, but there was something, she was sure of it. They had their bubble to keep them safe, but instead, she felt suffocated and trapped.

Behind her, Ryker's men spoke in hushed whispers while roasting one of the beasts that attacked them over the fire. The smell of cooking meat turned her stomach.

Normally, even if she didn't eat meat, she didn't mind its scent, but *everything* felt wrong tonight. Probably because the events of this day, the casting of spells, and her work on the barrier had left her drained.

The witches didn't have to stand guard at night; they spent that time resting and rejuvenating after expelling so much energy, creating the veil at night, and casting spells. She was glad for this as she required time to recuperate, but she was used to being worn down after expending too much energy.

That wasn't why something felt off. She didn't feel right in her own skin anymore because she craved something she shouldn't have.

Despite the awful events, all she wanted was to get up and disappear into Brokk's tent so she could forget all about this day and this *hideous* place. However, that couldn't be, and not because everyone would see her, but because she had no idea *what* this was or *why* she wanted him so badly.

There could never be anything serious between them. She could never give her heart away again, and Brokk was part dark fae, so serious wasn't something he did, but she thought about him too much for this to feel like a casual, already-ended fling.

She'd had plenty of casual in her life before Fabian. As a young witch, free from the bonds of a relationship, she'd thoroughly enjoyed exploring her sexuality and had bedded a dark fae or two.

There was *no* way she wasn't going to explore the most sexual beings in all the realms. But while she'd enjoyed her time with them and many other men, none of them had caused her body to react the way Brokk's did.

Witches didn't have fated mates; if they did, hers would have been Fabian, but she couldn't deny the explosive chemistry between her and Brokk, even as she denied herself the pleasure of it.

He was the sun, and she was Icarus flying too close as the wonder of him called to her. And like Icarus, she could end up burnt and ruined, and she would be the one to do it to herself.

As if he knew she was thinking of him, he emerged from beneath the canvas he'd draped over the low-hanging limb of a tree. Her stomach did a little flip as the fire danced across the handsome planes of his face, turned his hair a paler shade of blond, and emphasized the striking beauty of his aqua eyes.

CHAPTER FIFTY-SIX

A TINGLE RAN through her as the earth pulsed with more energy beneath her knees. It could be the water and the power of this valley calling to her so strongly, or at least that's what she tried to tell herself, but she knew it was *him*.

For some reason, Brokk affected her in this strange, beautiful, yet overwhelming way. She relished it as much as she hated it.

When guilt rose to replace her desire, she lowered her gaze to her hands. Hecate, she *hated* this new constant companion, but she didn't know how to come to terms with her feelings for Brokk and her love of Fabian.

Rising, she glanced at the trees as she contemplated walking into the jungle so she could be alone for a bit, but in this place, not having allies equated to certain death. No matter how badly she craved solitude, she preferred having a life to not having one.

Kaylia bent to retrieve her tunic from the ground. She'd found a secluded spot under a tree to wash herself, but while she hadn't gotten completely naked, she had removed her tunic. She pulled it over her head and tugged it into place as she walked back toward the camp.

When she emerged from the trees, Brokk's eyes latched onto her, and red flashed through them as they ran ravenously over her. Kaylia sucked in a breath as his gaze caused her skin to prickle everywhere it touched.

If she could move her feet, she'd run to him, throw her arms around his neck, and quite possibly fuck him in front of everyone, but the heat of his gaze kept her legs locked in place as excitement thrummed through her.

Their eyes briefly met again before he shifted his attention away. With the connection broken, Kaylia's shoulders sagged as she gasped in a few panting breaths. No one had ever made her body come alive with just one look before, and she didn't know how to react to the *yearning* his gaze created within her.

～

KAYLIA TOSSED and turned back and forth on top of the small blanket she'd used to cover the earth. Despite every intention to keep them buried, memories from her night with Brokk refused to remain deep in the hole she'd dug for them.

They intruded on her thoughts, caused her heart to hammer, and made it impossible to sleep. Flopping onto her back, she stared at the tree limb overhead as her heart thudded against her ribs.

Magic vibrated through every part of her. It seeped up from the ground and coiled its way inside her as she tried to ignore the lust pulsing through her.

Nothing she did would ease it, not even her own hand. The second she came, a gulf of discontent opened inside her. She swore that moment of release only made things worse as her body craved the touch of another.

No, it craved *Brokk*.

With a sigh, she flipped onto her stomach and peered out the front of her small shelter to the clearing beyond. The fire had been doused, but a couple of torches remained burning beneath some trees.

Their firelight barely illuminated the guards watching over them. Brokk was out there now; she'd seen him relieve one of the other guards, but his shift would end soon... and then what?

And then nothing. Nothing more can happen between you. Once is forgivable. Twice is intentional.

But as she told herself this, her body rebelled against her brain, and her skin prickled with the need for his touch. She couldn't stand this aching that made her skin feel too tight.

What has he done to me?

She definitely hadn't been shadow kissed by him and never would be. She knew how to resist having a dark fae turn her into one of their mindless sex slaves, but if she didn't know better, she'd almost think Brokk was half warlock instead of dark fae and vampire.

Unable to stand it anymore, she slipped out the back of her structure and walked to the edge of the protective barrier. She stood there with her hands fisted and shoulders heaving as she tried to calm the acute sexual frustration hammering her.

It didn't work.

What is wrong with me?

She had no answer for that, but she couldn't rid herself of the sensation that her growing feelings for Brokk would tear her in two. Maybe she'd spent too much time locked away from the world.

She'd been out of the crone realm for a while but hadn't really gotten the chance to think about her life, men, or anything else. She'd been a little too preoccupied with the Lord, war, preparing for Lexi's wedding, and now the possibility of Lexi's demise.

Doomed Valley and the mirror realm had changed the rapid pace of her life. Here, while death lurked around every corner and kept rearing its ugly head, there were also moments of peace when she woke to find herself in the arms of a man who made her feel alive again.

When she first woke to find herself in Brokk's embrace that morning in the mirror realm, something shifted inside her. Since then, she'd gotten to know more about him.

He was so different than his remaining brothers. Orin was a complete asshole, and Cole was harsher, more distant, and intense. Varo was reserved and wounded, but Brokk... Brokk had a smile meant to disarm, and he was charming and open in a way few others ever were.

Yet, a steel rod of strength, determination, and viciousness ran through him. He was loyal and loving but also willing to kill when necessary, and he refused to take anyone's shit.

And she liked it. Not all the men she'd been with were like that. Some were too weak for her, and she quickly moved on from them.

Even Fabian, when she first met him, had come across as too proper. He didn't like to get his hands dirty with blood or earth. They were so different in that way; she was a creature of nature and loved sinking her fingers into the soil to feel the worms, trees, plants, and all the other insects teeming with a life that nourished her.

She didn't like killing but had done so a couple of times before to save herself. During the war against the Lord, she killed many, but she would do whatever was necessary to survive. Fabian would do the same but often had others do the killing for him if he could.

As she got to know Fabian more, while he never displayed an ability to let his guard down and enjoy life like she did, she'd grown to like and eventually love the differences between them. Instead of their opposites working against each other, they somehow combined into a perfect team.

Brokk was nothing like Fabian. Maybe he didn't plunge his hands into the earth and relish it as Kaylia did, but he embraced the wilderness and beauty of it. She'd seen that when she caught him trying to touch the stars in the mirror realm. The awe on his face had enchanted her.

Maybe that's why she was so attracted to him. He was nothing like Fabian, and therefore, when she was in his arms, she could forget the anguish of losing her love because she was with a man who was his exact opposite.

With her mind focused on Fabian, the tide of passion she'd been unable to control earlier, faded away. She should be happy to finally have a reprieve from it, but as she stared into the darkness, all she felt was a sense of loss.

While that inescapable need for Brokk had been too extreme, it also made her feel alive. Now, emptiness rushed in to fill veins once teeming with life, and her heart slowed to a dull rhythm.

.

CHAPTER FIFTY-SEVEN

SHE TURNED AWAY from the edge of the protective barrier and started back toward the camp. She was almost there when the whispers began.

Kaylia froze as that first indiscernible whisper pierced the silence. It was then she realized how abnormally hushed the jungle was tonight. Nothing screamed as it hunted or died, and the insects didn't sing their endless songs.

At first, the words remained as unintelligible as always, but then she caught her name. As more whispers joined the first, she made out a few more names, and someone hissed, "Hungry."

The hair on Kaylia's nape rose as that hunger beat against her skin. She didn't want to look but refused to let these things think they frightened her.

Turning, she searched the jungle behind her. She didn't see anything, but they were there... watching her.

A shiver raced up her spine, but while whatever was out there unnerved her, they couldn't be much of a threat if they hadn't attacked already. Could they?

Sure, they had a barrier in place, but she'd heard them since the very beginning, before she'd ever put a bubble around their campground. At first, they'd been foolish enough to think they could handle whatever came at them at night.

Then the dwarf was stolen, and they'd known Doomed Valley had far more hazards than they could have imagined. After that, though it weakened her, she'd placed a barrier over them every night, but whatever was behind these whispers could have gotten to them in the beginning, and they hadn't.

Kaylia eyed the barrier. It was invisible to anyone who wasn't a witch, but she saw the colors dancing through the magic the witches had weaved.

She walked back to the edge and rested her fingers against it. A thrill shot up her arm from the power thrumming through the bubble. There was so much of it here, and it was all still intact. Nothing was draining or weakening it.

She leaned closer as the whispers grew louder and mingled into one chaotic mess that didn't mention their names anymore. Turning her head, she leaned forward to rest her ear against the bubble to see if she could understand them better.

When she was only inches from the barrier, something lashed out of the night and crashed into the barricade.

CHAPTER FIFTY-EIGHT

KAYLIA STAGGERED a few feet away from the protective barrier as a small, cylindrical, slimy *thing* crept across the surface. From the shadows, bright red eyes blazed out from the night.

Unable to breathe, Kaylia watched the monstrous creature making its way over the surface before retracting. The whispers became an excited, almost frenzied babble of nonsense as they grew louder.

The hair on Kaylia's nape rose; there was a reason for their increased excitement, and it couldn't be a good one.

When she caught another flash of red eyes to her right, she realized these monstrosities were surrounding the bubble. Kaylia backed away from the barrier as the colors swirled with more intensity.

The spell would hold against them for a while, but she sensed they were plotting something as they sought a weakness in the shield. Ten feet away, another one hit the barrier with a thud. It left a slimy trail behind as it felt its way over the surface.

Kaylia didn't take her eyes away from the protective barrier as she edged closer to the camp. On her left, another cylindrical thing smacked into the wall. From this angle, she could tell it was an appendage as a three-inch wide, red, circular attachment ran from the slimy tentacle and deeper into the jungle toward a set of unblinking, red eyes.

Is it a tongue? How is that possible?

She couldn't answer those questions, but she shouldn't be here. None of them should. They'd entered the domain of something extremely lethal, and it was looking to feast.

Kaylia had almost retreated to the camp when another presence stopped her. She didn't know how, as she couldn't smell or see him yet, but she was certain Brokk stood nearby.

Tearing her attention away from the jungle, she turned to find him about ten feet away from her. His forehead furrowed as he studied her. "Is everything okay?"

"No. There's something out there."

His gaze flicked past her, but when she looked at the jungle again, she didn't see any of those *things*.

"They're out there," she told him, "and they're hunting us."

"They can't get in here."

"I think they're plotting something."

"Like what?"

"I don't know."

Brokk removed his sword from its sheath as he strode toward her and held out his hand. She didn't hesitate to take it, and the second her fingers entwined with his, a sense of security crept through her, and some of her terror eased.

Together, they would figure this out and get through it.

Brokk pulled her closer and locked her against his side. As soon as she was nestled securely against him, red eyes flashed through the night.

"It's them," he murmured.

"Them who?"

"I don't know, but I saw them watching us last night too."

"They're doing more than watching us now."

"Like what?"

As soon as the question left his mouth, one of those sucker-like things hit the barrier. The tentacle it was attached to pulsated like it was trying to drain energy from the shield.

Is that possible?

Before coming here, she would have said absolutely not, but she had no idea what kind of monsters resided in this place. They could be capable of doing anything.

No, it can't be possible. If it were, they would have broken through the protective barrier long ago.

The witches had told her they'd also heard the whispers ever since arriving, and they'd been here for almost a year. After all that time, if whatever was creating the whispers could have gotten through the barrier, it would have by now.

But what if something changed?

The second sucker broke away from the bubble and vanished as another one hit it to the right. Outside the barrier, the whispers grew more frantic as the excitement of the creatures increased.

"What if no one has encountered them before? What if they can get in?" she asked.

"We've heard the whispers since the first night we arrived, and the others have all heard them for months. They have been around us since we arrived here."

"Maybe not. We've heard their whispers, but until last night, no one had seen them. Maybe we've only been able to hear them but have never been close to them. Maybe we've wandered into their territory."

"We have to talk to Ryker."

Brokk said this, but neither of them moved as another tonguelike appendage hit the barrier. Almost immediately, ten more thudded against it from all different directions.

They wiggled up and down as the suction cups moved along the surface. She didn't want to move away in case these things somehow managed to get through, but they had to alert the others to their presence.

Stepping back, she tugged on Brokk's hand a little. "We have to go talk to Ryker."

Brokk glanced at her before focusing on the barrier again. "You go and get them; I'll stay here."

The idea of leaving him here created a flutter in her belly. What if those things broke through with only him here to stop them?

She had no idea what was on the other end of those disgusting appendages, but she sensed it was something awful. "No, come with me."

"Go on, Kaylia. I'll be fine, but someone has to stay and keep watch."

She couldn't bring herself to release his hand. However, the longer she stayed here, the better chance the creatures had of breaking through while he was here alone.

"Be safe. I'll be right back," she vowed.

With that, she released his hand and fled into the jungle. Every part of her yearned to look back, but she kept her attention forward as she ran faster than she ever had before for help. She wouldn't leave him alone for long.

CHAPTER FIFTY-NINE

"HAVE you ever seen anything like this?" Brokk asked as Ryker and Kaylia came to stand at his side.

It took Ryker a good minute or so to respond as he observed the strange appendages making their way across the barrier. "No."

The whispers increased. They weren't making progress on getting through the barrier, but something had excited them.

"You've always heard the whispers, though," Kaylia said.

"Yes, but that doesn't mean the creatures who issue them were ever near us, as I think we're finding out. You've been here for enough time to know nothing is what it seems."

More of those sucking, tonguelike appendages hit the barrier with a wet thwack. From the dark, six red eyes burned bright, but not all the creatures were revealing so much of themselves.

When Kaylia started forward, Brokk grasped her arm. "What are you doing?" he demanded.

"I have to feel the barrier."

He didn't release her but moved with her until they made it to the edge of the protective bubble. Ryker stayed close to her other side.

Kaylia steadied the tremble in her hand when she stretched out her fingers and rested them against the invisible surface. As soon as she touched it, one of those suckers slapped into the barrier on the other side of her palm.

He doubted anyone else saw it, but she twitched beneath his palm. She didn't yank her hand away from the barrier as she refused to back down from these things. It took all Brokk had not to rip her hand away and move her back to safety.

Finally, she lowered her fingers and looked at him. "It's still strong."

"I'll send some guards around and have them check to see if there are more out there or if they're focused here," Ryker said.

Brokk remained where he was as Ryker went to talk with his men. He watched as the tentacle-like things moved across the barrier in search of a weakness.

He had no idea what Ryker's men would find, but, like Kaylia, he suspected these things were plotting something.

CHAPTER SIXTY

OVER THE NEXT FEW HOURS, no one got any sleep as a steady stream of guards patrolled the area while Brokk remained where he was with Kaylia and some guards. They never found more of these creatures outside the perimeter, but he suspected they were there, hiding and waiting.

He had no idea how long these things had been following them, but after discussing it with the others, he learned he was the only one who'd ever seen any sign of them. And all he'd seen before this was that brief glimpse last night.

Brokk suspected they hadn't meant for him to see them then. They'd meant to reveal their presence now, and there was a reason they'd concentrated their efforts on this section of the barrier.

He had no idea what that was as they weren't progressing on taking it down.

His gaze shifted to the night sky; dawn was coming soon. He didn't know if the day's arrival would illuminate the monsters. He had a feeling that, like him, these beings thrived in the shadows and would retreat at dawn, but that didn't mean it would be safe for them to move on.

These things could have set traps out there or planned to attack as soon as the witches lowered the barrier. And since they had no idea what these creatures were, they could be in for countless surprises.

A footstep from behind alerted him to Ryker's return. The amsirah general kept going with the others to check the barrier and ensure it remained safe.

"What if you bring a lightning bolt down out there?" Brokk asked. "We might be able to see them better for a second or two. Maybe get a better idea of what we're dealing with."

"I have to gather the energy inside the barrier to bring the lightning down; would that disturb the protection spell?" Ryker asked Kaylia.

"I'm not sure."

"It's not worth taking the risk," Allegra said tersely.

Brokk gritted his teeth; the witch was right, but he wished he could get a better look at these beasts. They couldn't stay here and had to know what they were dealing with. The whispers went away at dawn, but that didn't mean these things would.

Brokk rubbed the stubble lining his chin as he contemplated his options. "I can cloak myself in shadows and go out there. At least then I can get a better idea of what we're facing."

"No," Kaylia stated. "You're not going out there alone."

"I won't be gone long and have to stay close to the barrier to maintain enough light to keep the shadows around me."

"If something goes wrong and you're pushed further out, you'll be exposed to them."

Brokk frowned as her voice became higher pitched. "I won't be in danger."

"Of course you will. We have no idea what they can do, what they're plotting out there, or what exactly the appendages are. I'm assuming it's a tongue, but we have no idea how far they can launch it or what kind of senses they possess.

"It might not matter if they can *see* you; they might be able to *smell* or *hear* you. Or maybe they have senses we don't know about; maybe that tongue can find you anywhere. Those cats sensed us even while cloaked in shadows. They'll go away when the sun rises; we can wait it out."

"We *think* they'll go away at dawn. This is the first time they've ever exposed themselves to anyone; we have no idea what will happen when the sun rises. More of them could come then, or they could grow more powerful."

"We should wait and see."

"I could go out there, discover what we're dealing with, and possibly eradicate the enemy."

"We have no idea how long they're going to stay out there, and we can't stay here," Ryker said. "They're not the only danger we have to worry about in this jungle. The ophidians will come too if we stay here."

Kaylia shot him a look that caused Ryker's eyebrows to rise. His lips twitched toward a smile before he suppressed it.

Brokk was too smart to share in Ryker's amusement as an irate Kaylia glared at them. He also enjoyed that she was concerned about him going out there.

Maybe I'm not the only one who feels something here. Her fiancé's ghost would always haunt them, but perhaps they could have something more… if they survived this place.

"I might be able to take them out with relative ease instead of risking the lives of everyone here," Brokk said.

Kaylia glowered at him. "It's a bad idea."

"It's one of the few we have," Ryker said. "Can I go with you?"

Brokk studied the shadows beyond the barrier. There weren't a lot of them, but there was enough to keep them concealed.

"Yes, but if something goes wrong, we could lose the shadows and be exposed."

"I'll unleash some lightning if that happens."

"I'm coming with you," Kaylia stated.

"That's too many of us out there." There was no way he was going to risk her getting hurt. "We could create too much noise, or I could have a tough time keeping the shadows around us."

"If you're going out there, then I'm going too. Besides, you could have a difficult time keeping the shadows around you anyway. At least, if I'm out there, I can cast a protective spell to keep us all safe until we return here. You have no reason to argue, especially since I'm right."

Normally, he liked it when she was bossy and determined, but he wasn't a fan when it worked against him. "And if I say no?"

Her chin jutted out. "That's not an option."

"But it is."

Behind him, Ryker chuckled as he muttered, "Brave bastard."

When Kaylia's eyes narrowed, Brokk pondered if she was contemplating turning him into a toad.

"I won't let you out of the barrier," she stated.

"Allegra will."

They all looked at the witch, whose mouth parted as she looked between him and Kaylia. She held her hands up as she backed away a couple of steps. "Don't put me in the middle of this."

"Someone has to let you out," Kaylia said.

Brokk could ask Ryker to command the other witches to do it, and they would. Kaylia was the oldest, but Ryker paid them. He couldn't bring himself to do that to her.

He hated the idea of her out there, but she'd survived many years and knew how to take care of herself. He grated his teeth together as he bit out his next words.

"You're to stay by my side. If you don't, I'll drag you back in here kicking and screaming if I have to."

"You can try."

"And I'll succeed."

They glowered at each other before she broke into a beautiful smile that melted his heart while irritating him.

"We should go," she said.

Brokk didn't like the idea of this at all, but with the three of them working together, they should be able to destroy whatever was out there or return safely. And he'd make sure that no matter what happened, Kaylia survived this.

CHAPTER SIXTY-ONE

KAYLIA STAYED CLOSE to Brokk as they slipped away from the suckers moving over the barrier and back toward their camp. They ducked into one of the shelters, and once there, Brokk wrapped the shadows around her and Ryker.

When he nodded to let her know they were all set, they emerged from the shelter and crept toward the barrier. Kaylia rested her hand against it as the rest of the camp continued behind them as if nothing had changed.

They had to maintain the appearance of normalcy while the monsters watched from the shadows. Whatever those things were out there, they couldn't see her pulling back the barrier for them to step through together.

Kaylia turned as the colorful bubble settled behind them before they moved deeper into the jungle and away from the river. They'd exited the barrier on a side where they hadn't seen any creatures.

As they emerged, she still didn't see anything lurking in the night, but that didn't mean they weren't there. Kaylia kept her hand on the small of Brokk's back as they moved through the jungle.

Outside the protective barrier, she felt exposed, even if those things couldn't see them. However, she'd been the one to point out they had no idea what these creatures could do, and there was a chance they *could* see them.

She debated casting a spell to shield them but decided against it. The trees, dense foliage, and other obstacles around them would either destroy or hinder her magic, and the last thing they needed was anything slowing them.

After so many nights of endless noise and screams from the many animals residing in Doomed Valley, the jungle was oddly quiet except for the whispers. And the unintelligible words wove beneath her skin where they festered like a splinter that wouldn't come free.

They hadn't irritated her as much before, but they'd never been this close to whatever created them.

The three of them stayed near the barrier and the light created by torches within. Sometimes they had to move away to navigate obstacles, but they never got so far that they risked losing the shadows.

Ryker stayed close to Brokk's shoulder, but sometimes he fell back to walk beside her when a tree or branch forced him to do so. They only made it fifty feet before Brokk stopped and raised his hand.

In front of them, about thirty feet away, one of those tentacle-like things limbs was latched to the protective barrier. It swayed up and down a little seemed to try to suck out whatever power kept the protective shell in place.

So far, they hadn't been successful, but they were determined to keep trying. With an uneasy feeling in the pit of her stomach, Kaylia rested her fingers against the barrier. It had remained strong when she pulled it back to let them out, but something could have changed.

Thankfully, a strong wave of power continued to vibrate against her fingers. The barrier didn't feel any weaker than before, but why did these abominations keep trying to penetrate it like this when it wasn't working? Were they too dumb to realize they weren't succeeding, or did they know something she didn't?

Her hand fell limply back to her side. From where they stood, she still couldn't see what the appendage was attached to, and since that's why they were here, it was a bit of a problem.

She'd prefer not to go anywhere near that thing, but they had to get closer. When Brokk started forward again, she was extra careful about where to put her feet. Making a noise now could prove deadly.

Her fingers twisted into Brokk's shirt as he moved to the left and deeper into the darkness. Kaylia glanced anxiously back at the torches and their much-needed light as they faded further away.

After about fifteen feet, Brokk stopped. Kaylia pressed against Brokk's right side while Ryker remained close to his left.

They couldn't move any further away from the light; she was certain of it, but that didn't matter as the creature had finally been revealed. Kaylia gulped as she stared at the monstrosity that she could somehow tell was a woman.

The creature stood between two trees. Its greenish-gray skin looked like it had hung in the blazing sun for years. Sucked tight against the woman's body, that leathery, cracked skin revealed the sharp bones sticking out from her hips, rib cage, and shoulders.

No fat filled out the creature; it was all skin and bones. Flattened and deflated, the woman's breasts were the only signs of excess tissue, and it was very little.

Her red eyes burned like lava from the dark, and when her elongated jaw opened, one of the suckers erupted from within the cavernous depths of her mouth. Tufts of straggly hair stuck up from the woman's head.

Some hairs were a foot long and waved around her hollowed-

260 BRENDA K DAVIES

out cheekbones. The woman's coloring and skin reminded Kaylia of dead things that would fall apart beneath her fingers.

Brokk glanced over at her, and she shook her head at his questioning look. She had no idea what this being was or what it could do. When they both looked at Ryker, he shrugged and looked as confused as Kaylia felt.

Brokk waved his fingers around them before pointing to her and placing his index finger against his lips. Kaylia knew he was asking for a silencing spell, and she quickly worked to create one.

She glanced nervously at the woman as she reminded herself they didn't know what abilities these creatures possessed, but they had to test the spell. "All set," she whispered.

Some of the tension in her shoulders eased when the woman showed no reaction to her words.

"Neither of you know what that is," Brokk stated.

"No, and I could have gone my whole life without ever seeing it," Ryker replied.

"Do we kill it?"

Kaylia studied the strange, repulsive creature as she debated the answer to this. "They only make their presence known at night, but what if they still hunt us during the day?"

"There's a good possibility they'll follow us," Ryker said.

"Plus, I don't feel any difference in the shield."

"They could be searching for a weakness," Brokk suggested.

It was a good possibility, but the problem was... "What if they find one?"

"They haven't yet."

"*Yet*," Ryker said. "And if they follow us, they'll have more time to learn and attack. We can't let them find a weakness we don't see. Besides, I don't like keeping anything alive that wants to kill me."

"I agree," Brokk stated.

"But once we attack one of them, the others will know we're out here," Kaylia said.

"You should return to the camp."

She crossed her arms over her chest. "We're not having this discussion again."

"We can move faster if only two of us are here."

"Then Ryker can go back."

"I'm not going anywhere until these monsters are dead," Ryker replied.

Brokk scowled at her. "I'm trying to keep you safe."

"I'm not weak or helpless, and we protect *each other* here; we have from the start," she retorted. "We don't have time to argue over this."

Brokk closed his eyes and bowed his head in acquiescence. "Fine, once we take out the first one, we have to be prepared for the others to converge on us."

"I'm prepared to kill them all," Ryker declared.

Kaylia was too, even if she didn't like killing, but it was pretty clear these things weren't here for tea and friendship. She would do what was necessary to survive. "Should we get the others?"

Ryker glanced back at the barrier and the guards there. Some were still patrolling, but a handful stood, looking at the jungle.

"If we get in trouble, they'll see it and come, but let's find out if we can do this without putting anyone else at risk," he finally said.

"Let's get it over with then," Brokk said.

Kaylia pulled her sword from her scabbard and followed them deeper into the jungle and away from the light. She knew the second the shadows slipped away as the creature's red eyes shifted toward them.

Instead of looking alarmed, it smiled.

CHAPTER SIXTY-TWO

BROKK IGNORED the fiend's smile as he rushed forward. With a speed he hadn't expected, the creature's tongue whipped back toward its head. Before it retracted completely, it swung to the side and lashed out at him.

When Brokk ducked the appendage, it thunked off the tree behind him. Before the monster could retract it again, Brokk brought his sword down against the tentacle and sliced off the hideous member.

A scream that could rival a banshee's pierced the air as what remained of the creature's tongue sucked back into its head. The woman's mouth didn't shut as she continued her awful shrieking noise.

It took all he had not to slap his hands over his ears as it was almost too much to bear, and his eardrums vibrated until he was sure they would rupture. Kaylia cringed, her shoulders hunched, and pain etched her delicate features.

Her fingers worked, and her mouth moved, but he couldn't hear what she said until a beautiful, deafening silence descended over him. Kaylia relaxed as relief washed over Ryker's face.

The quiet was welcome but also dangerous, as they couldn't

hear if the others were approaching them. They had to end that spell soon.

Rushing forward, Brokk charged the creature. She snapped her jaws closed and lifted her clawed fingers as she lunged at him. He had no idea if her screaming had stopped and didn't care as he sliced off the hands stretching for him.

The woman's jaw opened again, but he wasn't sure if she screamed as what remained of her tongue lashed out. With a wet thud, it hit him in the forehead at the same time he brought his sword down, cleaving it straight through the top of the woman's head.

With her head split in two, the woman's arms flailed as blood sprayed from her. A hot wave of it hit him when he yanked his blade free and swung at her neck, slicing her head from her shoulders.

When her head landed with a thud, he kicked it into the shadows as more of the monstrosities emerged from the jungle. They'd kept themselves mostly concealed and had only revealed a small fraction of their presence in the trees.

His heart sank as he spotted dozens, if not more, of them. The ground vibrated, and a swell of power radiated through his feet a second before lightning split the sky and hit the ground with a sizzling pop.

Kaylia must have released the silencing spell as that pop resonated in his ears while power emanated outward. His hair stood on end while three creatures fell beneath the onslaught of the lightning splitting open the sky and pummeling the earth.

Some of Ryker's men and the witches poured out from within the bubble to help as more hideous beings emerged from the woods. Shouts of war, death, and thunder filled the air as the sides clashed.

Another one of the beasts screamed. By the time this ended, none of them would have any hearing left, but if Kaylia kept silencing the world around them, they'd all get killed. The best they could do was take out the screaming ones as soon as possible.

He looked back to discover Kaylia standing behind him with her sword at the ready and determination etching her features. Unease tugged at his heart as he resisted dragging her back to the safety of the barrier. He'd only succeed in pissing her off, and he couldn't make her do it.

He had to be content knowing she was strong, powerful, and a good fighter, even if she'd prefer to live in peace. She'd survived the war against the Lord; she would survive this too, but he couldn't shake his concern for her.

You better shake it, or you'll end up dead.

Those truthful words spurred him into motion. Lifting his sword, he charged at one of the creatures as it emerged from the jungle.

Ducking low, he took out its legs. The second it hit the ground, and before the screaming could start, he severed its head from its shoulders.

A guttural shout pierced the air before being silenced. Brokk looked up at one of Ryker's men. The man's back bowed, and his hands spread out at his sides; his toes pointed down as he hovered a few inches over the ground.

Attached to the man's neck, one of the tongues wiggled in the air as it sucked something from the guard. Brokk wasn't sure if it was the man's blood or something else as the man's fingers and toes curled up, his face thinned, and his clothes grew baggy on his shriveling frame.

His veins and muscles stood starkly out against his pale skin. His mouth parted as if he were trying to scream, and his whole body spasmed so hard it looked like his bones would break.

It all happened so fast that Brokk barely had time to jump to his feet before the man's skin wrinkled. His eyes rolled up into his head to reveal the yellowed decay underneath.

When the appendage unlocked from the guard's neck, his

body crumpled to the ground. Brokk didn't have to get any closer to know the man had died a fast, agonizing death.

Brokk expected to discover the woman who slaughtered him filled with life, but she remained a revolting, shriveled beast... one who was still ravenous as her tongue shot at him.

"Fuck," he muttered as he threw himself to the side.

The appendage glanced over his back as he rolled away from it. Kaylia rushed forward and drove her sword down, pinning it to the ground. The thing jerked, and blood spilled from it as it tried to pull itself free of her blade.

Leaping to his feet, Brokk lifted his sword and severed it. The beast's scream blended with the rolling clap of thunder as more lightning pummeled the creatures.

The noise and flashing lights made things more chaotic as each flare illuminated the deeper recesses of the jungle and more creatures. Thankfully, the scream ended when Allegra decapitated the beast.

A startled cry drew his attention to Kaylia as she ducked an appendage, but another one lashed out of the night. Before it could hit her, Brokk dove forward and caught it. His momentum carried him to the ground as he rolled with the slimy tongue.

It was a thick and solid muscle as it throbbed beneath his palms. Brokk released it with one hand and used his sword to slice across it. He was about to cut all the way through when something smashed into the side of his neck.

The impact knocked him to the side, but before he could hit the ground, something latched onto him with a brief sucking, crunching sound. Brokk had barely processed the noise when he was jerked to an abrupt halt.

Whatever had attached itself to him pulled him back a couple of steps. Brokk reached for whatever it was, but before his fingers could connect, a fierce pull, as if something were sucking the very essence from him, froze his movements.

The next pull rattled his bones as he gritted his teeth against the bellow echoing inside his skull while the thing seemed to draw the very marrow from his bones. Whatever it was doing, it crept into his cells and twisted them into something new, something broken. Something that battered against his veins, sliced into them, and tore him apart.

This thing delved into the core of who he was while pulling his soul from him.

.

CHAPTER SIXTY-THREE

"No!" Kaylia screamed as one of the horrific tongues latched onto Brokk's neck.

She saw what that thing had done to Ryker's man and knew she didn't have much time before nothing remained of Brokk too. Her heart smashed against her ribs at the idea of losing him, and she could barely breathe as her chest constricted.

Lifting her sword, Kaylia raced toward Brokk, who already looked thinner. She had no idea what would happen if she severed the creature's tongue and its connection to Brokk, but she knew what *would* happen if she didn't.

Gripping her sword in both hands, she lifted it over her head and brought it down on the appendage. It jerked and swayed as black blood spewed forth; that wasn't Brokk's blood, she was sure of it.

She didn't succeed in cutting all the way through on her first swing but did on her second. Another scream rose to join the others as the appendage spewed more blood while recoiling deep into the trees.

Kaylia dodged another tongue as she raced after the creature.

She'd make that *bitch* pay for what she'd done to Brokk as he staggered and went down to one knee.

Sprinting forward, she dodged the creature's eviscerating claws as it launched its broken tongue at her again. Kaylia twisted to the side to avoid the bloody, slimy stump before plunging her sword into the woman's hollow belly.

The bitch's hands grasped the blade, trying to pull it away from her as Kaylia yanked it from the monster's belly. She succeeded in slicing off some of the woman's fingers. They hit the ground as Kaylia lifted her sword, and screaming, she took off the woman's head too.

The head hit the ground with a thump, and when it rolled toward her, she kicked it into the jungle, where it bounced off a tree before skittering out of view. Terror and rage continued to fuel her as she raced back to where Brokk remained, kneeling on the ground.

His head bowed as he rested a fist on the earth. He tried to rise but staggered to the side and went down again.

CHAPTER SIXTY-FOUR

ARRIVING AT BROKK'S SIDE, Kaylia knelt beside him and draped her arms around his shoulders. She tried not to give in to the anxiety threatening to take over. She had to get him out of there before another abomination attacked, and she couldn't do that if she was too panicked to think clearly.

"Easy," she soothed. "Are you okay?"

"Wh... wha... what did that bitch d-do to me?" he stammered.

Kaylia didn't know, but she gripped the sucker still stuck to his neck, yanked it off, and threw it aside. A gruesome, circular red welt remained, as did smaller, circular holes in his flesh.

"You're going to be okay."

Kaylia didn't know if she was saying this to reassure him or herself, but she hadn't been this scared since she opened the door to discover Fabian's brother on the other side. The look on his face immediately told her something terrible had happened.

Brokk isn't Fabian!

No, he wasn't, and whereas she hadn't been there to save her fiancé, she was here to help Brokk, and she would.

Gripping his arm, she draped it around her shoulders as more lightning bolts pummeled the ground. Thunder shook the earth until a jagged crack ran across its surface.

More monsters screamed as they tumbled into the pit the amsirah created. She had to get Brokk out of here before one of the lightning bolts or the splintering earth came for them.

She slid her arm around his waist. "Can you stand?"

A muscle twitched in his jaw as his lips compressed into a thin line. As he pushed himself up, he tried to stay strong and not show any weakness, but a tremor ran through him and into her.

His hip bone prodded her hand as he swayed briefly before righting himself. She didn't know how it was possible, but he'd lost at least ten pounds in the few seconds that *bitch* had a grip on him. He planted his feet apart as he lifted his sword.

"Let's get you back under the protective barrier," she said.

"No, I'm not retreating from this fight. Besides, I already feel better."

She didn't believe him, but before she could argue, the first rays of the sun peeked over the horizon. The whispers intensified, and judging by the tone of their insidious voices, they were arguing over something.

Some creatures tried to slip back into the trees, but more lightning pierced the night. It struck them dead while Ryker and the others worked to cut off more of the creatures' escape.

The whispers grew louder, more frenzied, as the emaciated monsters became frantic to flee. Their nonsensical words were hysterical screeches nearly as painful as the screams.

As the sun rose higher in the sky, the women ran to and fro as they sought a way out. Kaylia edged Brokk toward the barrier and glanced back at the few remaining witches who stood on the other side, ensuring that anyone who retreated to the bubble could return inside it.

They waved to her, but when she tried to move Brokk, his feet remained planted. "Brokk—"

"Not until they're all dead," he vowed.

His stubbornness would get him killed, but though weakened, he was still too strong for her to budge. But it might not matter as the rays started dancing through the trees, the screeching whispers grew louder, and something started changing.

The sun had the monsters in a flutter of frenzied movements as they ran from Ryker's men, the lightning, and the sun. Some appendages still shot out, but not as many because the women were... changing.

At first, she couldn't quite believe it, but as the sun rose higher, she was more certain her eyes weren't playing tricks on her. The creatures actually *were* changing.

They didn't burst into flames and die like vampires in the sun's rays. No, instead of becoming smaller and turning to ash, they were filling out and changing into something less monstrous.

They were also much easier to slaughter as what remained of them was taken out by the witches and Ryker's men. When one of them ran toward her and Brokk, he pulled away before she could stop him and lunged at the creature.

His hands encircled the woman's throat, cutting off her air as they tumbled to the ground and he brought her down beneath him. He pinned the woman to the earth with one hand on her throat while he brought the other one forward to place his sword against her neck.

When the blade pierced her skin, blood rose to bead on her pale flesh. The woman didn't try to fight him off as he leaned over her; instead, she smiled a charming smile that would probably beguile many men.

Brokk's lips curved into a sneer as he scowled down at the stunning woman beneath him. Despite how hideous the woman had been only minutes ago, Kaylia couldn't find a single flaw in her delicate features or lush body.

What lay before them now was the exact opposite of the

monster who existed only minutes before. Tears rolled down the woman's cheeks from eyes so green they outshone an emerald.

Gone were the wild tufts of hair once framing her sunken face. In its place was a thick, black mane that shone in the sun.

As the last sounds of battle faded away, Kaylia looked around to discover another woman also remained. She was as beautiful as the first, with a shock of red hair that was more orange in the sun; it spilled down her back in a cascade of spiraling tendrils.

Ryker gripped the orange-haired woman by the neck as he held her above the ground and carried her over to them. The rest of his men and witches gathered closer as the protective barrier came down.

The bodies of the other creatures remained scattered through the woods. Most were caught in their decrepit state, but a few were trapped in a state between desiccated and lush. Only these two had transformed completely.

Gone were the lethal beasts, and in their place were two beauties seeking some way out of this. They didn't have the same lethalness as their monstrous counterparts; if they did, Kaylia was certain those tongues would be lashing out at them, and their claws were gone.

Ryker shoved the orange-haired woman to the ground beside Brokk. Before the woman could rise, Ryker pointed the tip of his blade at her throat. She lifted her chin while tears streamed down her face.

"Please spare us," the orange-haired woman pleaded. "We cannot help ourselves. We have no control over what we become."

As she spoke, tears dripped off her chin. Somehow, the woman was still lovely while weeping so profusely.

Despite her tears and words, her hands roamed over her naked body, clasped her breasts, and moved in an enticing way that made it seem as if she were on the finest bed, instead of the ground with a sword pointing at her throat. Kaylia had no idea what the woman was doing or why… until she looked around.

While the woman moved seductively, Kaylia noticed those surrounding her became slack-jawed and their eyes glazed over. She felt the tug of something close to desire but couldn't quite put her finger on it, and she didn't feel anywhere near as enraptured as the rest of her group looked.

What the fuck?

Kaylia glanced toward the witches who had remained behind the barrier as they crept closer; one of them licked her lips. From her position, she couldn't see Brokk's face, but the woman behind him smiled as tears slid down her face and her hand slid between her legs.

Someone behind her issued a guttural groan that prickled her skin. Kaylia couldn't look back; she was too scared of what she would see if she did.

But looking down at the woman, she had no idea what to do as her brain battled with her body for control.

CHAPTER SIXTY-FIVE

BROKK'S COCK stirred as the woman moved erotically while issuing a low, throaty moan that conjured images of sex. It brought to mind some of the orgies he'd attended where he couldn't separate one body from another.

That sound brought his dark fae hunger surging to the forefront as the scent of sex rose to ensnare him. Her lids half lowered over her eyes as she licked her lips. There was no sign of the repulsive appendage now, only a glistening tongue that could suck his shaft dry.

She's so beautiful....

Her fingers brushed his side as her hips rose beneath him. A shudder went through him, except this wasn't one of pleasure.

Instead, revulsion rose from the depths of the lust trying to consume him. Her touch wasn't right... it wasn't the one he wanted....

Closing his eyes, he shook his head to clear it of the fog trying to creep in and muddle his brain. When he opened his eyes again, he found himself staring into the woman's clear green eyes as she smiled seductively at him and caressed her nipple.

"I can make you feel better than anyone else ever has. You can do whatever you want to me, wherever and whenever you want. I'm yours to please, and I'll make you feel so good."

When she touched his side again, Brokk sneered at her, and a flicker of unease flashed through her eyes while she continued to move in that seductive way. Those weren't the eyes he wanted to see beneath him.

I want… I need…

He couldn't quite put his finger on what he sought, but he knew it was out there somewhere. And it was close.

Keeping the blade against the woman's throat, he turned to discover Kaylia standing behind him, her face etched with confusion as she rubbed her temples. She took a step back before freezing.

Her. He longed for her far more than the naked, entirely willing woman beneath him.

Kaylia's apprehension sent a jolt of adrenaline through him as she started to lift her sword before lowering it again. Whatever these things did to him, it had left him weakened, but he'd die to keep her safe.

His attention shifted to the others as the witches also crept closer to the orange-haired beauty beside him. With their faces slack and their attention riveted on the women, they were entranced by their movements.

Ryker still had his blade to the orange-haired woman's throat. When she spread her legs and slid her fingers between them, he licked his lips, and his sword dipped a little.

Brokk had no idea what these monstrosities were, but he had to stop them before they destroyed everyone here. Enclosing his hand on the black-haired beauty's throat, he kept her pinned to the ground as he lifted his sword and, with one violent motion, brought it down across the orange-haired woman's neck.

A short scream broke from her before Brokk succeeded in decapitating her. Blood seeped free to stain the ground, and when her head rolled toward him, Brokk flicked it away with his sword.

For a second, no one moved as they all gawked at what remained of the woman. Then, fury clouded their features, and Brokk prepared himself to leap up, grab Kaylia, and envelop them in shadows.

He was weak but would use the last of his energy to get her away in case they all decided to turn on them. These women were dangerous; they clouded minds and turned rational immortals into mindless drones.

Brokk kept his eye on them as he brought his blade back to the other woman's throat and tensed to flee. He'd kill her first. He had no idea what she'd done to Ryker and the others, but he wouldn't leave them to her mercy, and he wouldn't have her pursuing them if she managed to escape or kill everyone here.

Blinking, the confusion cleared from Kaylia's face, and their gazes met. They stared at each other until Brokk shifted his attention to the confused others.

Kaylia whispered some words as her fingers wove their magic. While he couldn't see it, he felt the swell of her power as it rose to surround them. She'd prepared to protect them from Ryker and his followers.

CHAPTER SIXTY-SIX

RYKER'S EYES SQUINTED CLOSED. He opened and closed them again before resting his hand against his temple. Confusion flitted across his features before it cleared away.

"What the fuck?" he muttered.

Behind him, the others were also emerging from the depths of whatever spell these creatures had woven. Brokk shifted his attention to Kaylia. "Keep an eye on them."

When she rested her hand on his shoulder, Brokk pushed his blade deeper into the woman's throat, drawing a trickle of blood from her pale flesh. She sucked in a breath as her body arched a little beneath his and licked her lips again, but he felt no stirring of desire.

He didn't check on the others; if they were falling victim to her again, it wouldn't last, as she'd soon be dead, and Kaylia's spell would keep them protected for a bit. The woman's beautiful eyes flicked between him and Kaylia before a look of resignation settled over her face.

Then she twisted her head a little to look at her friend. As she did, a trail of blood appeared across her neck, but she didn't notice as she gazed at the headless body beside her.

She emitted a small sob as she rested her hand against her friend's arm. Tears slid down her face, but no sympathy stirred within Brokk.

"What are you?" he demanded.

The woman didn't speak as she went still beneath him, closed her eyes, and tears slid down her face. After a couple of minutes, she finally started talking. "A monster."

No shit. But Brokk kept those words to himself.

"What did you do to me when that *thing* stuck to my neck?"

"I didn't do anything to you."

She gasped when Brokk pushed the blade a little deeper into her neck. "Don't fuck with me."

She gulped. "My sister sucked out part of your essence. It's what we feed on."

"Will he be okay?" Kaylia demanded.

"I don't know. No one has ever escaped us before."

"I'm going to be fine," he assured Kaylia.

She nibbled on her bottom lip while gazing at him. Finally, she responded. "Yes, you will."

"*What* are you?" Ryker demanded.

"We... I...," she breathed the word. "*I* am a mandaru."

"A what?" someone else inquired.

"A mandaru," the woman said again. "We are a race of ancient creatures who have resided in this valley for as long as we can remember. This is *our* home... or it was."

"And you feed on any unsuspecting victims who enter it," Brokk stated.

"We cannot help who we are," she retorted.

Brokk understood that, but while he fed on sexual energy and blood, he didn't suck the essence from others and leave them a hollowed-out, shrunken mess.

"So, by day, you're beautiful women who seduce unsuspecting victims into your bed, and by night, you're hideous monsters who suck the life from them," he said.

Her eyes narrowed on him. "We do what we must to survive, but it wasn't always this way."

"How else was it?"

"We have always borne the curse of what we are with dignity and grace, but when the sun goes down, we cannot change what we become. However, we found a way to contain ourselves at night. Because while it feels *so* good to feed, we never liked killing. Our darker nighttime natures relish it, but during the day, we regret what we do. So, over time, as we grew stronger, we pulled our magic together and created a sacred space to contain ourselves at night."

"The stones," Kaylia said. "That's why there's so much power in that clearing."

"The stones," the woman confirmed. "And for centuries, the stones worked. We survived on animals—"

"You had sex with animals?" someone blurted.

The woman recoiled in disgust. "No, of course not. We don't require sex to feed; it's just a way to lure our victims in to protect ourselves." She looked pointedly at Brokk. "Few can ever resist us, and we can often either run from them if necessary or lure them in and kill them.

"Every day, just before nightfall, we'd return to the stones and the magic there to keep us from hunting. We brought any animals we caught during the day there so we could feed. Then, one day, those *monsters* arrived in the valley, and everything changed."

Brokk didn't get a chance to ask why some could resist them before Ryker asked, "Do you mean the ophidians?"

"Yes. They attacked us, destroyed the stones, and eradicated half of our number. We fled into the jungle and have lived a nomadic lifestyle ever since. We've had no other choice. A few times, we tried to settle into a new area and claim it as ours, but they always found us and destroyed it. We lost all hope of ever knowing peace again after the last time."

A bit of sympathy tugged at him for this woman and her brethren. They had tried to contain themselves, but predators made it impossible. That sympathy wasn't going to stop him from killing her though.

"Why did we hear your whispers throughout the valley?" he asked. "Were you stalking us the whole time?"

"No. As I said, we've been here for as long as we can remember. We are *one* with the valley, a part of it. We speak with the trees; they listen to us and spread our message."

"Did you ever think of telling those trees to inform people to stay away from this area instead of making nonsense noise?"

He knew the truth when the woman's gaze moved away from him. They didn't like what they did at night and tried to contain themselves, but once freed from the stones, they also embraced their darker nature.

They were torn between the thrill of the kill and their conscience. After so many centuries, he was surprised their bloodlust hadn't buried their conscience, but somehow, they'd maintained one... or pretended to.

"You figured if anyone made it this far, they were fair game," he stated.

Her chin lifted defiantly. "Just kill me. Without my family, I have nothing; I *am* nothing. We both know you're never going to let me live, and I don't want to be alone in this world. I can't imagine being the last of my kind and having no one to share this burden with."

Brokk wasn't going to argue with her. She was right; he wasn't going to let her live. Holding the woman's gaze, he pushed down on the sword. She didn't try to fight him as she stared up at the sky until he severed her head.

CHAPTER SIXTY-SEVEN

KAYLIA HID her fear for Brokk as she sat beside him in the small shelter he'd created. He'd managed to walk back to the protective barrier on his own, with his head high and a steely look of determination on his face, but once inside the shelter, his shoulders slumped as his head bowed forward.

Kaylia rested a hand on his shoulder. "Are you okay?"

"I'm fine. I just need some rest. I can't remember the last time we had a good night's sleep."

"Neither can I. I have an ointment that will help heal the injury on your neck."

He lifted his fingers and felt across the wound; his brow furrowed as if he'd forgotten it existed. "Okay."

"I'll be right back."

She ducked out from under the shelter and hurried to her small space. Before she got there, Ryker intercepted her.

"How is he?" Ryker asked.

Kaylia had no idea, and the uncertainty of it was chewing at her like a rat on wires. She kept hearing what that woman said about no one ever escaping them before and having no idea if he would recover from this.

She resisted wringing her hands. "He's tired, but he'll be fine after some rest." She really hoped this was true. It *had* to be true. "I'm getting an ointment for the wound on his neck."

"Good. We'll spend the day and night here. We have to return our dead to Tempest, and we could all use some rest too, especially after last night, but we have to move on tomorrow. We can't stay here; it will only spell more death for us if we do."

Kaylia gulped as she glanced back at Brokk's shelter. She had no idea if he would be ready to move on tomorrow but didn't voice her doubts. There was no reason to when a night of rest might make all the difference.

She told herself this, but she wasn't so sure. However, she'd do everything she could to help him heal and get through this.

"I'm sorry for your losses," she murmured.

Ryker looked away from her, but not in time to hide the sadness in his eyes. "Thank you."

Not knowing what else to say, Kaylia rested her hand on his arm as she started to pass him.

"Kaylia." She lifted her head to meet his turbulent, mercury-colored eyes. "How could he resist them, and we couldn't?"

Kaylia didn't tell him that she hadn't felt the effects of those things as strongly as them either. And it hadn't been only the amsirah who felt the impact of the mandarus; she'd seen the glazed look in the witches' eyes too.

Those monsters had entranced everyone... except her and Brokk, and she had no idea why.

"How could he fight them off and kill them?" Ryker asked.

"I have no idea."

"Maybe it's because he's a mixed breed."

"Maybe."

Though Kaylia knew that wasn't the answer, *she* wasn't a mixed breed after all. And she suspected Ryker didn't buy the explanation either, but neither of them had a better one.

"I'll see you soon."

With those words, he turned and walked away. Kaylia entered her shelter, gathered her things, hastily packed them into her bag, and tossed it on her shoulder.

When she left the shelter, her gaze went to the witches who were erecting a new barrier as Ryker's men carried their dead into an open portal. Sadness hung heavily in the air as more dead were transported back to their families.

They had to be here, but she hated this place.

Kaylia kept her head high as she hurried back to Brokk's side and set her pack on the ground next to him. She removed the ointment and leaned forward to dab it onto the raw, red, circular wound.

Dozens of smaller circles peppered the larger one. Those circles reminded her of an octopus's tentacles with all its little suction cups.

They literally sucked the life from him.

Kaylia shuddered at the reminder and recapped her ointment before returning it to her pack. Brokk's far-paler-than-normal skin was clammy to the touch as she smoothed the cream over the wound.

When she finished, she kissed just behind the injury and her ointment. She had no idea why she did it other than she had to connect with him.

He stiffened against her then relaxed. She inhaled deeply, savoring his scent, before moving away and placing her hand on the ground beside him.

His fingers found hers and intertwined with them. The strength and warmth of them were a little reassuring but not enough to ease the worry churning inside her.

When the memory of Fabian rose into her mind, she pushed it down. Ignoring the reminder of him did nothing to ease her guilt, but this wasn't the place for it. Brokk needed support in his weakened state, and she would give it to him.

CHAPTER SIXTY-EIGHT

"Ryker was asking about you," she told Brokk.

He removed his hand from hers and settled it in his lap. "Tell him I'm fine."

"I did. He said we're going to stay here tonight. They're returning their dead to Tempest now."

"How many did they lose?"

"Five, I think. I didn't ask, but that's how many bodies I saw while we were returning after the attack."

"That's too bad. How about the witches?"

"I don't think they lost any."

"Good."

Kaylia fiddled with the edge of his blanket as she recalled her conversation with Ryker. There was something she had to ask Brokk, but she wasn't sure she wanted the answer.

But it wasn't a question that could go unanswered. "He asked how you withstood the seduction of the mandarus when they couldn't."

Kaylia couldn't bring herself to say *when we couldn't*. She hadn't felt the pull of those creatures as badly as the others either and could have withstood it. She couldn't say the same for the others as they were all far more enthralled than her by those women.

Brokk's eyes remained fixed beyond her shoulder on the canvas wall of his shelter. While she waited for him to speak, her heart hammered in anticipation of *something*... but what that something was, she didn't know.

She could feel the explanation there, the knowledge of what she needed from him, from her... from the entire world and all the realms at the tips of her fingers and the edge of his tongue. What she sought was *right there*, seeking to break free, but she couldn't quite figure it out.

Maybe he knows.

She bit her bottom lip while waiting for him to say or do something; finally, his gaze met hers again. Tension built inside her as the connection between them became so palpable, she was half convinced she could touch it.

A lump formed in her throat, and her fingers twitched within his. He was so close, yet an unfathomable distance separated them.

She could breach it, but she had no idea what the result would be if she did or if that's what she wanted. For so many years, she was so certain of everything in her life. A solitary existence was her saving comfort, and *all* vampires deserved to burn in a fiery oblivion.

Then Sahira and Brokk arrived in the crone realm and forced her from isolation. And more unbelievable, the two half vamps actually made her *like* them. Now, Brokk had made her do more than like him—she could no longer deny she had feelings for this man—and now, she wasn't certain about anything in her life.

When she didn't move or speak, Brokk's eyes settled on something behind her again. "I'm not sure why they didn't affect me as much."

Kaylia's breath hissed out. She'd been expecting something more from him, but if she didn't know the answer for why they didn't affect her as much either, then why would he? And it wasn't like the beasts were still around to question them about it.

But though he'd given this answer, she suspected it wasn't the full truth. There was an answer for her to grasp, and he may already have an idea of what it was.

It just wasn't something he was willing to reveal. That only made her more curious and determined to piece it all together.

Her eyes narrowed as she carefully studied every nuance of his profile to see his reaction to her words. "There are always mysteries in life."

"Yes, there are."

She continued to stare at him while he ignored her for the wall. Finally, his head turned toward her.

The exhaustion and pain radiating from his eyes caused her anxiety to melt. She leaned toward him, seeking to help in whatever way she could, but his words froze her.

"Do you know about Allegra and King Leonidas?"

Kaylia was so thrown off by the strange question and the abrupt change in topic that she leaned away. "Know *what* about them?"

"After that last attack, when some of the witches were killed, I asked Ryker why they remained. Why didn't they go home where they would be safer? He told me they paid the witches well, and they sought to revenge their dead, but there might also be something more to it."

"Like what?"

"Allegra and Leonidas were having an affair. Ryker thinks the relationship means more to her than his king, but he suspects it is part of the reason the witches remain when they could easily return home."

"He thinks she's in love with Leonidas?"

"That's what I gathered from it."

Kaylia pondered this. "That makes sense. I mean, of course, the witches want money, and selling our services is one of the main ways we earn an income, but I'm sure they considered leaving after the first time one of them died in this valley.

"They might have stayed to get revenge on those who killed their friends and for the money, but a witch being in love with the man they're trying to rescue would keep them here. Witches would never leave a loved one to an unknown fate, and the others would stay to prevent Allegra from suffering."

She waited for him to say something more, to explain why he felt it necessary to divulge this information. Instead of expanding further, he laid down on his makeshift bed and draped his arm over his eyes.

He should rest, but Kaylia had to know...

"Why did you ask me about them?"

"After what happened with the mandarus earlier, I was wondering about Allegra," he murmured.

"What about her?"

"Did they affect her too?"

His voice became groggy and a little slurred while speaking. She didn't think he would have muttered the question if he'd been fully awake, but Brokk was asleep as soon as he finished talking.

His mouth slackened as his head tipped to the side, and his breathing softened. He'd relaxed, but his question made it impossible for her to do the same as his words hung heavily in the air.

CHAPTER SIXTY-NINE

KAYLIA'S MIND spun as his question ran on repeat in her head. Why would he question such a thing? What difference would it make if the mandarus didn't affect Allegra too?

Kaylia lifted Brokk's blanket and settled it over him; she tucked it around him to ensure he stayed warm for the night since his skin was so cool and clammy. Again, she couldn't stop herself from kissing him as she rested her lips against his forehead and inhaled his comforting scent.

"Rest. You'll feel better after some sleep."

It took more time than it should have to move away from him as she finally sat back on her heels. She shifted to look outside while also keeping an eye on Brokk.

For hours, she watched the steady rise and fall of his chest as she nibbled her nails. When she had nothing but nubs left for fingernails and had drawn blood, she scowled at the destruction she'd wrought.

In all her many centuries of living, she couldn't recall a time when she'd bitten her nails, never mind chewed them to the quick. Shoving her hands under her ass, she sat on them to ensure she didn't touch them again.

Outside, the others lit torches to combat the growing darkness. Ryker's men and women moved around the clearing as the familiar sounds of night set in, but the whispers didn't come.

Kaylia kept waiting to hear those awful murmurs again as Brokk's strange words looped through her mind, but all she heard was the call of insects and the screams of those hunting and dying. Not hearing the whispers was a welcome reprieve after everything they'd endured, but it was also a reminder of what happened today.

Why did Brokk ask me about Allegra and Leonidas?

No matter how much time she spent pondering it or how many angles she looked at the question from, she couldn't figure out the answer. But two things were for sure... he asked the question after she inquired about his ability to resist those women, and he didn't know they hadn't affected her as badly either. None of them did.

She tried to deny it and tried to think of any other reason, but she kept coming back to one conclusion: he was curious about whether Allegra had withstood the mandarus too because Allegra might be in love with King Leonidas.

But Brokk wasn't in love. He couldn't be.

And she most certainly wasn't. It was impossible.

Her heart bashed against her ribs as a tickling sensation made its way down her throat, and the hair on her arms stood on end. A strange creeping, like that of an insect making its way up her nape, sent tingles down her spine.

She couldn't tear her eyes away from his pale countenance as her thoughts fragmented into hundreds of pieces and scattered around her brain. She swore she felt them battering the inside of her skull.

Her fingers twitched beneath her ass as images of Fabian flashed through her mind. He'd been her life, heart, and soul. *He* was the one she loved.

She couldn't deny that truth either, as her love for him

remained. She also couldn't deny she'd come to care deeply for Brokk while here. It wasn't love, but she *did* have feelings for him.

Could those feelings ever become the soul-encompassing love she'd felt for Fabian? She didn't think so. No one could ever make her feel like that again, but Brokk had made her *alive* again, and she'd savored every second of their time together.

Great sex isn't love. No, but it had changed her.

And what of him?

Kaylia bit on her bottom lip as her gaze ran over Brokk. He was a dark fae, and while they could fall in love, his father and Cole certainly had, it was rare for the typically self-involved creatures to do so.

But he's also a vampire and... and vampires have consorts.

And when a vampire finds their consort, they love deeply.

You're getting way too far ahead of yourself here. He said some strange things while half asleep and after having been drained of his essence. It was probably all rambling nonsense.

But his and her ability to withstand those creatures was anything but nonsense. It was as real as her throbbing, bloody fingertips.

Shifting her attention away from Brokk, she spotted Allegra gliding across the clearing toward the river. She walked with her hands clasped behind her back and her head bowed.

Kaylia glanced at Brokk, who remained fast asleep. She rested her hand against his cheek and was dismayed to find his skin still clammy and cool, but his breathing was steady, and when she placed her hand on his chest, his heartbeat was strong.

Torn between staying with him and trying to find answers, Kaylia glanced back at the jungle as the shadows swallowed Allegra. The flickering flames from the torches illuminated some guards; if she went to speak with Allegra, Brokk would be safe for a bit.

She pressed her palm more firmly against his cheek. "I'll be right back."

He showed no sign of having heard her. Reluctantly, Kaylia rose and slipped out of the shelter. She strode after Allegra, nodding to the guards before following the woman into the night.

She spotted the witch standing near the edge of the river. Her hands were still clasped behind her back as she studied their surroundings.

The crackle of the torches barely reached this area as the endless chirp, screech, and shrieks of countless creatures created a sound that interwove with the night. The setting sun had brought some reprieve from the heat, but the cloying humidity remained.

By the time Kaylia arrived at Allegra's side, sweat cleaved her shirt and pants to her. She stopped beside the younger witch and looked out at the river as it lazily rippled around tree roots and rocks.

She contemplated what to say while watching the water; just asking the woman if she was in love with Leonidas was a bit too abrupt. But she had to start somewhere.

CHAPTER SEVENTY

"ARE YOU OKAY?" Kaylia inquired.

"I'm fine."

Allegra's words weren't clipped or irritated, and she didn't sound like she'd prefer not to have Kaylia here, but she looked sad and resigned.

"How's Brokk?" Allegra asked.

"He's still weaker than I would like, but he'll be better when he wakes."

Or at least she *really* hoped he would. He should look better than he did now, but it might take more time to heal from what that bitch did to him.

If he heals at all, not even the mandaru knew if it was possible.

Kaylia pushed the negative possibility deep down into the bowels of her mind where it belonged. There was no way to know what would happen, and she was determined not to dwell on the bad; they already had far too much of that in Doomed Valley.

If he wasn't better by the time they were ready to leave, then she would take him back to Dragonia, where he could heal in peace. He'd fight her on it, but she would win the battle.

"I'm sure he will be," Allegra murmured.

"Were any witches lost last night?"

"No, we were fortunate to escape unscathed this time."

"Good." Kaylia studied the river as she tried to figure out how to get the information she sought. She decided to dive right in since she wasn't good at subterfuge. "Why do you stay with them?"

Allegra didn't tear her attention away from the water, but a flash of sorrow crossed her face. "The amsirah pay us well, but we've also lost friends and family to this valley; retreating now would be a disservice to their memory. We owe it to them to see this through and ensure we kill the monsters who destroyed them."

There was more to it than that; Kaylia could tell by how carefully Allegra chose her words. It was as if she was trying to give enough of an answer without giving it all.

Kaylia wanted to push the witch for more but didn't think an aggressive technique would work with the younger woman. They'd worked together in Doomed Valley, and knew each other before meeting again here, but they didn't share the close bond Allegra had with the other witches here.

Kaylia couldn't blame Allegra for not revealing everything; they were acquaintances, not friends. And if she was in love with King Leonidas, then this was a sore subject for her, but Kaylia was hoping to learn more from her.

"I'm glad the mandarus are all dead. Not hearing the whispers is a relief," she said.

"Me too."

And then, knowing she couldn't put it off anymore, she had to prod on at least one thing. "I'm glad they didn't have the same effect on Brokk as they did on everyone else."

Well, not her either, but Allegra didn't have to know that. A subtle twitch near the corner of Allegra's eye told Kaylia she'd struck a nerve. She could tell Allegra they also hadn't affected her as much, but until she understood *why* better, she wasn't ready to share that information.

"It was very fortunate for everyone," Allegra murmured.

Kaylia waited for something more from her, but Allegra didn't speak again. After a while, Allegra turned to face her. "I'm sure Brokk will be okay. Dark fae and vampires are both extremely strong."

"They are," Kaylia agreed.

Plus, he'd withstood a dark fae sword through the heart. He could survive this too.

Allegra rested her hand on Kaylia's arm and squeezed it. "Good night, Kaylia. Try to get some rest before we move on tomorrow."

"You too."

Kaylia watched the young witch stroll away through the trees with her shoulders hunched forward as sadness emanated from her. Allegra hadn't said it, but Kaylia saw the truth; the woman was in love and suffering. She would recognize that fact anywhere; she'd lived it for centuries.

But that didn't mean Allegra had also withstood the effects of the mandarus. That didn't mean love… or, at the very least, having feelings for another made fighting off the mandarus' seductive powers possible.

There could be another perfectly reasonable explanation for it, and she hadn't considered it yet. Maybe, for a reason unknown, she, Brokk, and possibly Allegra had simply been able to fight the pull of the mandarus more than the others.

That is a possibility, which means you're driving yourself crazy over nothing.

She told herself this, hoping she might get some sleep tonight, but she didn't believe it was so simple.

CHAPTER SEVENTY-ONE

IT WAS STILL night when Brokk woke, and its blackness clung to him as he struggled from sleep. For a second, he was too disoriented to recall where he was and why he felt so weak.

His throat was dry, and the hunger twisting in his belly made it almost impossible to piece together the scattered fragments of his memory. *Why am I so hungry?*

He couldn't remember ever feeling this ravenous before. He'd always fed both his vampire and dark fae halves at regular intervals to ensure he didn't lose control, but now his veins burned for blood, and despite his weakness, his cock ached as it sought the sexual energy the dark fae required.

He tried lifting a hand to his pounding head, but it felt like someone had tied a thousand-pound weight to his arm. As fragmented memories spun through his head, a new sensation crept in to replace his hunger.

Something warm, supple, and oh-so-tempting pressed against his side. Saliva rushed into his mouth as an earthy scent filled his nostrils.

Kaylia.

Despite his exhaustion and the ravenous appetite clouding his judgment, he knew she was there. No one felt or smelled as amazing as her.

When he twisted his head to look at her, the pull of something on his neck caused a flood of memories to return. Those *monsters* had done this to him, and they'd paid for it, but he'd like to sink his fangs into their throat and shred their veins as he killed them all again.

He ignored the weakness in his body as he lifted his hand. He flexed his fingers while trying to comprehend they were his. They were there; he saw them moving, but they were weak and distant, like they belonged to someone else.

When he dropped his arm, it felt more like a rock falling to the earth than anything he could control. Brokk ignored the hammer beating on his head as he rolled to the side, planted his strange-feeling hands on the ground, and pushed himself up.

The movement made his head spin, and he nearly toppled backward. Determination was all that kept him from falling over again as acid burned up his throat.

He had no idea how long he'd slept, but he should feel *better* than this. Sleep should have healed him, not made him *worse*.

When his gaze fell to Kaylia, curled beside him with her hands under her head and sweeping lashes shadowing her cheeks, his anger faded. With fingers that felt at least three times their normal size, he awkwardly lifted them to stroke her cheek.

He traced the contours of her face while savoring her silken skin. She was beauty and life. Something about her captivated him so much that it pierced through the power of the mandarus and allowed him to evade their treacherous, seductive hold.

He'd managed to retain control of himself and kill that woman because of *her*. Things would have been a lot worse otherwise.

As he watched her, his heart swelled until it felt like it was twice its normal size. He swore it grew so big his ribs wouldn't be able to contain it anymore.

She'd pulled him back from the certain death of those creatures and taken care of him afterward. For months, she'd been a part of his life. Initially, she hated him, tolerated him, and finally came around to liking him, but he wanted more.

He wanted it *all*.

And that was something he never thought he'd seek from a woman, but he did from her.

As that realization settled into a knot in his chest, the memory of the ghost between them returned. Her fiancé, a man she was still in love with, haunted every aspect of her existence; she couldn't enjoy her life without guilt because of him.

She'd never allow herself to embrace a life of happiness with *him*, even if it's what the man would have wanted for her. If Fabian had loved her too, then her happiness would have been the most important thing to him, but Kaylia would never see it that way. To her, it was a betrayal to Fabian if she allowed herself to feel anything for *him*.

But if she somehow moves past her guilt, that doesn't mean she'll want you too. At least, not in the same way you want her.

Immortals only fell in love once. And while, until this moment, the idea of love had never crossed his mind, sitting there, watching her sleep, he knew it was there, growing inside him with every passing second.

This wasn't helping the pounding in his head as frustration over his weakness faded and fury rose to replace it. There was nothing he could do to chase away a ghost.

He could try to make her happy and ease her guilt over living her life. However, while she might come to love him too, it would never be in that head-over-heels way she'd experienced in the past.

It would never be as much as he loved her.

He loved her stubborn nature, her fierce protectiveness, the endless bravery she exhibited, and her giant heart. She was everything he'd never known he desired, and she was *his*, even if she couldn't ever *be* his.

Fuck!

His head understood why they would never be equal in this relationship, even if it ended now or bloomed into something more. Immortals were loyal creatures who rarely gave their hearts; once they did, it was for good.

His heart screamed against the injustice of it all. It would never be satisfied with anything less than *everything* from her because that's what he would give her.

And he would have to learn to accept less or say goodbye once their time in Doomed Valley ended.

CHAPTER SEVENTY-TWO

HIS HEART CONSTRICTED in his chest. It shrank at the idea of parting from her as the vampire half of him raged against such a thing.

He'd always considered his two halves equal, but now the vampire part of him was screaming to be heard and wouldn't be denied. His fingers curled into the bedding as his fangs lengthened, and it took all he had to resist marking her as his.

For his sanity, the best thing he could do was let her go and retreat somewhere far away from her, but the vampire part of him would never allow such a thing. He was certain of that as it threatened to break free and take control.

He'd never experienced such a thing before, but now the vampire sought to stake its claim while he struggled to control it. The fact he remained so weak was probably the only reason he didn't go to her now.

When her eyes fluttered open, some of his stress eased as she yawned before her gaze settled on him. Her sleepy smile sent his pulse into hyperdrive.

As she took him in, her smile faded, and she sat upright. "How are you feeling?"

He managed to retract his fangs before replying. "Don't worry about me."

"Of course I'm worried about you. We've never encountered anything like the mandarus before."

"I'll be fine, Kaylia. I already feel better."

It wasn't entirely a lie; he could stay awake now where he couldn't earlier. When his eyes fell to her neck, saliva filled his mouth as his earlier hunger roared back to the forefront.

The shocking realization of how much he'd come to care for her buried his hunger for a bit, but it was back. His fangs throbbed in rhythm with every beat of her heart.

Her eyes raked over him; she obviously didn't believe him. "We should return to Dragonia, check in, and take a better look at you. We're still not sure what the lasting effects of the mandarus might be."

"We're not leaving without the crudue vine."

"We can come back."

"No. You heard Ryker; the jungle changes around us. Locating this place again, and him, could prove impossible, and we can't leave a portal open because who knows what might go through it. Besides, Ryker and the witches have lost some of their own to help us with this; we *will* see it through with them."

"I'm not suggesting we abandon them."

"I know, but we can't leave."

He loved how the cleft in her chin became more noticeable when she set it in that stubborn way. She was adorable and would probably punch him for thinking so since she looked so determined to make him do what she wanted.

"You should get more rest in a safer place. You still look pale and"—she rested her fingers against his neck as she leaned over to inspect his wound—"that's not healing as fast as it should."

When she leaned closer, her scent engulfed him, and his dick jumped as the dark fae also sought to be sated. Memories of her moving against him, crying out his name, and unleashing her power nearly sent him spiraling out of control.

Part of why he wasn't healing as fast as he should was because of how desperately he needed to sate his appetites. The mandaru had drained his energy, and his body sought to replace it... with her.

She'd given herself willingly to him before, but that didn't mean she would do so again, and he'd never been a man to force himself on anyone. He'd die of starvation or kill himself before he did that to her.

Turning his head away, he closed his eyes and leashed the ravenous impulses battering him. His fingers dug into his palms.

"I have to feed." His voice was thick and distorted by the fangs he couldn't control. "I'll feel better after that."

Kaylia's fingers stilled on his neck, and her breath tickled his cheek as her scent intensified. Her pulse became a riotous crescendo in his ears, but he couldn't tell if it was his hunger making it sound so chaotic or if it *was* beating faster.

But then, it could be her apprehension propelling it to faster and faster levels. She'd let him feed from her before; that didn't mean she would again.

"I have to hunt," he choked out.

"No, you don't." Her hand moved beneath his injury to stroke his neck. "I'm right here."

Without warning, the memory of the taste of her blood and the rush of its power exploded in his mind. When an inhuman sound issued from him, Kaylia's heartbeat picked up a little, but she didn't shy away from him.

She had to sense how starved he was, yet she kept her fingers on his nape as she inched closer. All he could think about was sinking his fangs into her throat and fucking her until everything else ceased to exist.

His need for her was a physical ache that held him immobile

as her taste, scent, and feel bombarded his senses. But Brokk was afraid if he started, he wouldn't stop and, in the end, he'd leave her weaker than him... if not worse.

CHAPTER SEVENTY-THREE

"I can't," he grated out.

"Why not? I'm here, and you're not in any condition to hunt anything for its blood, especially out there."

When he met her gaze, the vivid red of his eyes reflected at him from hers. It was an effort to keep speaking, but he had to make her see. "Because I don't just thirst for your blood. I want *everything*."

Her eyebrows rose, and she stopped breathing. He didn't know if she understood exactly what he meant by that. This wasn't about sex or blood; it was about *them,* her heart... and the ghost haunting it.

Before he could make that clear to her, she leaned forward and kissed him. At first, it was only a brush of lips that held the promise of more to come, but it still shot blood straight to his cock.

For a second, his fear of hurting her and desire tore him in two, but he couldn't resist her allure. His fingers twitched as he struggled to lift his arms. He loathed the weakness still clinging to him but eventually got them around her.

Pulling her against his chest, he locked her there as he savored the taste of her while the kiss deepened. Tasting her again soothed some of his appetites, as touching her strengthened him.

Still feeling thick and awkward, his fingers moved a little easier as they threaded through her hair. He cursed the clothes between them when she melted into his embrace. *Every* part of her was exquisite, and she fit against him as if she were made for him.

Her hands tugged impatiently at his tunic, pulling it upward until she broke the kiss. Brokk somehow managed to get his fingers to release their hold on her and not fall limply to his sides while she pulled off his tunic.

When she tossed it aside, his arms fell to the ground. His fingers twitched as he eyed her tunic, and through strength of will, he managed to get them to rise.

Concern flickered through her eyes when she noticed his struggle, but she grasped the edge of her shirt and pulled it over her head. Every cell in his body fired at once as a loud ringing sounded in his ears, and her tunic fell to the ground.

She was magnificent, with a body made for fucking, and while his arms and fingers still felt rather useless, his dick did not. Her simple white bra followed her shirt, and when she came back to him, the sensation of her bare flesh against his sent him spiraling.

Somehow, he managed to get his arms around her waist, but he couldn't lift them any higher to lock her against him. When she turned her head to expose her neck, concern he might harm her flashed through him, but the temptation of her blood was too much to resist.

His lips skimmed back as his fangs elongated; her skin was warm beneath his mouth when he sank his fangs into her exposed vein. She gasped when he pierced her skin before releasing a low moan.

As quickly as she'd tensed against him, she relaxed and shifted to wind her legs around his waist. Her fingers threaded into his hair, pulling him closer as she moved in an erotic way that almost made him come in his pants.

The woman was a temptress whose sounds and movements told him she enjoyed this as much as him. Her pleasure heightened his own as her blood doused some of the fire raging through him.

Her power made him strong enough to move his hands up her back and flatten them against her shoulder blades. Relief filled him; that awful weakness created by the mandaru wasn't permanent.

He'd had to feed, and what a banquet he was receiving.

As one of his hungers ebbed, and he felt a little more in control, he retracted his fangs, licked away the beads of blood trickling from his bite, and kissed her. Now, another hunger had surged to the forefront, demanding to be sated.

With some maneuvering, he removed what remained of her clothes before tugging off his own. Planting her palms on his chest, Kaylia pushed him back and straddled him.

She settled over his shaft but didn't take it inside her as she held his gaze while leisurely rotating her hips in a tortuous dance. Feeling more in control of his limbs but still weaker than normal, Brokk seized her hips as she gave him a small, seductive smile and bent to kiss his chest.

When she started inching her way down him, he let her go and laid back to watch as she licked and teased her way down his body. He couldn't take his eyes off her as she clasped his erection and met his gaze.

With a teasing descent, she took his head into her mouth before sliding down the rest of his shaft. Brokk sucked in a breath as her mouth, tongue, and hands weaved magic over him, and he loved *every* second of it.

"If you don't stop, I'm going to come," he grated through his teeth.

She paused to give him a mischievous smile before continuing. Brokk dug his fingers into the bedding beneath him as his head tipped back, and he gave himself over to her. A tingle ran down his spine, and his hips arched off the ground as he came.

CHAPTER SEVENTY-FOUR

KAYLIA RELEASED Brokk's dick and licked her lips before kissing her way back up his body. The taste of him lingered in her mouth, and she thrilled at how alive and seductive he made her feel.

She held him in the palm of her hand, literally and figuratively, but then, he had the same effect on her. She was fully alive with him again as magic and energy crackled across all her nerves.

She'd do anything he asked of her to keep riding this high. It was *addicting*. *He* was addicting.

When she started to settle herself over his shaft so she could take him inside her, he grasped her hips, lifted her, and pulled her higher.

"My turn."

The sound of his throaty growl sent a shiver down her spine. But then he managed to lift his hands to grasp her and settle her over his face.

Her fingertips crackled, and the earth vibrated with life as his tongue found her clit. While he tasted her, her head fell back, and her legs trembled until she came apart with a cry probably heard throughout the clearing, and she didn't care.

She almost collapsed on him, but he lifted her again and settled her over his waist. "I'm not done fucking you."

His words made the hair on her body stand up in anticipation. If she had her way, he would never be done.

Despite having just spilled his seed, his cock was thick and rigid as he entered her, stretching her... *claiming* her. Her fingers dug into his chest while she rode him, and he feasted on the energy their union created.

She felt him gaining strength from her, which only spurred her on as she lost all control. Because of her, he was stronger and healthier. Because of him, she was *alive*.

This time, when they came, it was together. And like the last time, a burst of power radiated out from her before she collapsed onto his chest.

Gasping for breath, she lay on top of him, relishing his warmth and the beat of his heart as she tried to understand what this was between them, but she couldn't think straight as small waves of pleasure continued to race through her.

What does this mean for me?

Kaylia had no idea and wasn't in the mood to contemplate it when she still felt so high and content. She was safe in his arms, secure, and happy. That was all that mattered.

"I'm still not done with you," he said.

"Good."

With that, their mouths found each other's again.

CHAPTER SEVENTY-FIVE

GUILT AND UNCERTAINTY gnawed at Kaylia as she carved through the jungle behind Brokk, Ryker, and some of his men. Not only had she forgotten Fabian again for a bit, but she had *definitely* developed feelings for the dark fae prince.

She didn't know how it was possible when immortals didn't give their hearts twice. In all her many years, she'd never heard of it happening.

There was always a first time for everything, especially with immortals who lived such lengthy lives, but it wasn't something she ever saw happening to *her*. She'd loved Fabian so deeply; his death devastated and nearly destroyed her.

While she wouldn't call what she felt for Brokk love, or at least not the kind of love she once shared with her fiancé, feelings were there. After contemplating it more, she was certain those feelings were why she'd withstood the pull of the mandarus' allure.

Her feelings for him had helped her stand against those creatures. Her emotions were a barrier to the mandarus' powers, just as they had been for Brokk and, most likely, Allegra.

That was why the guilt was tearing at her this time, not

because she'd allowed herself to forget Fabian again, but because Brokk cared for *her* too. Considering what he was, she hadn't believed such a thing was possible, but Brokk withstood those mandarus because of *her*.

And she would most likely end up hurting him.

Brokk was a good man who deserved someone to love him with everything they were…. That could never be her. She cared for him; she enjoyed spending time with him, *really* enjoyed it, but it could never be the all-encompassing love she'd shared with Fabian, and Brokk *deserved* to have that in his life.

She could never open her heart up again like that. She was too aware of how it all ended and the devastation that would follow if she did.

Never again would she allow someone to tear her heart from her chest, which meant she could never give Brokk everything he deserved. Whatever this was between them, it had to end. No matter how amazing it made her feel, she couldn't allow it to continue.

A lump formed in her throat as sorrow pumped through her body. It was so new between them, and it should have been easy for her to end it before she broke his heart, but as she told herself this, her body craved more of him.

He continued to awaken and bring her back to life *every* time they were together. She'd never lost control of her power during sex like she did with him. He was an amazing rush.

She didn't know if her reaction to him was because she'd shut herself down for centuries and was experiencing a sexual reawakening or if it was because of *him* and everything she felt for him. Kaylia suspected it was the latter. Something about Brokk was different for her.

She didn't want it to be that way; it had somehow happened. But she couldn't deny the truth… after Brokk, she could sleep with a hundred other men, and *none* of them would make her feel like he did.

With a sigh, she focused on her surroundings as misery weighed heavily on her shoulders. The jungle wasn't as thick through here. Vines pulled and tugged at her, and she was sure some of them moved toward her as they tried to hinder her progress, but she pulled free or cut them away with her sword.

Kaylia wiped the sweat from her brow as Brokk came into view again. Since feeding on her multiple times last night, the color had returned to his face, he showed no signs of the sluggishness he exhibited upon first waking, and the wound on his neck had healed.

She'd looked for it many times today but didn't see any lingering effects from what those creatures did to him. Still, she kept an eye on him in case he showed signs of weakening; he'd never admit it if he was.

Sensing her attention, he looked at her and tilted his head to the side. The sun glinting off his aqua eyes caused them to twinkle.

His smile created a physical reaction inside her as she stopped to drink him in. Did the man have to be so damn irresistible? It was going to be *so* difficult to let him go.

Somehow, she managed to offer a tremulous smile before his attention shifted to the jungle. She admired the flow of his muscles as he continued through the trees. She knew exactly what it was like to grip that back, dig her fingers in, and cling to him while he unraveled her.

When one of Ryker's men nearly walked into her, Kaylia shook her head and continued. Separating herself from Brokk wouldn't be easy if she kept letting her mind wander down paths almost as treacherous as the one they traversed.

Although, this path wasn't dangerous. It had been a relatively quiet day in the jungle, which only made her nervous. Things were *never* quiet in Doomed Valley.

At this reminder, the hair on Kaylia's neck rose as she

glanced nervously around the jungle. It remained hushed, but that was probably because it hid something.

She lifted her sword and cut away the vines reaching for her while following Brokk down the path. Damp with sweat, her clothes cleaved to her, making movement in the green tunic and soft brown pants a little uncomfortable, but she'd grown used to the cloying sensation since arriving here.

She'd only made it another fifty feet when a shout from ahead stopped her again. "It's the crudue vine!"

Kaylia's heart leapt into her throat as her hand fell to her side. *Crudue vine!*

The *entire* reason they were here. It was everything they'd fought, suffered, and lost others for, and they *finally* almost had the key to saving Lexi in their hands.

They could leave this place and never look back—okay, maybe not never, as they still had to help Ryker, but they could escape for a bit, save Lexi, and regroup to destroy the monsters ruling this hell.

CHAPTER SEVENTY-SIX

BROKK GLANCED BACK at Kaylia as they hurried through the jungle toward the shout that had alerted them to the presence of crudue vine. She was *finally* smiling again. Throughout the morning, he'd sensed her distress but refused to let it dissuade him from his goal of having her.

He'd live with the ghost of her ex-fiancé, and if he could one day vanquish it, he would. He would *not* let it come between them or make her feel bad for choosing to embrace life again. She deserved happiness, and he would make sure she got it.

He didn't know what this was between them, but he wasn't going to let it go for the memory of a dead man. If she told him he didn't make her happy, he'd move on, but only then.

The idea of losing her made his fangs tingle. Possessive instincts he hadn't known he possessed roared to the forefront. He'd let her go to make her happy, but if anything else tried to come between them, he'd tear this jungle, the realms, and anything in his way apart to keep her.

He didn't understand his extreme reaction to the idea of losing her, or his increasing need for her, but he couldn't deny it. She was his.

Brokk wanted nothing less than *all* of her, and one day, if she let him, he'd make her understand it was okay to love again. With that set determinedly in his mind, he focused on the prize ahead.

They were so close to finally claiming what they'd come here for, and once he got his hands on the crudue vine, he'd get it to Dragonia. They'd have to come back here to help Ryker free his king, but first, they would save Lexi.

He wiped the sweat from his brow and adjusted the grip on his sword as he shoved aside some of the already chopped foliage. The broken leaves tickled his skin, leaving a wet trail across his arm.

A muttered curse from behind drew his attention back to Kaylia as she pulled a vine from her hair. It had entangled in her braid.

He returned to help her remove the vine entangled deeply. In the end, he cut it and tossed it aside.

Over her shoulder, he spotted the witch who had stopped behind them. Her forehead furrowed, and her lips pursed while she watched them. Sensing his attention, her gaze met his; her expression cleared before her eyes darted away.

Brokk scowled as he finished pulling the vine from Kaylia's hair. He didn't give a shit what the woman thought of him or his relationship with Kaylia. He'd take on all the witches too, if that was what it took to keep her… but that would only upset Kaylia more.

He released the vine. "You're free."

She offered a tremulous smile. "Thank you."

Unable to resist, he brushed her hand with his. When their fingers entwined, he squeezed hers before letting go as the rise and fall of excited voices carried back to them.

Lifting his sword, he hurried to catch up with the others. When he went around a turn in the makeshift path, he spotted a row of backs. Within a section where the trees were a lot thinner and the foliage wasn't so dense, Ryker and his men stood in a line before him.

Brokk made his way to the end of the row of amsirah and stopped at the edge of a clearing choked with thick, neon red vines. It grew up from the ground at the base of the trees, entwined around their trunks and limbs before climbing across to other branches.

The canopy of vines creeping from tree to tree was so thick it blocked the sun; only small rays of light pierced through to illuminate the jungle floor nearly devoid of vegetation. Thorns that could shred the flesh from any immortal covered the vines.

"There's so much of it," Kaylia breathed.

"It's in the trees this time," Ryker said. "The last time we encountered the vine, it covered the ground. Before that, it grew straight up from the middle of the clearing to wrap around the limbs. The vine is always changing."

"As is the jungle."

"It enjoys keeping us on our toes."

Brokk eyed the tree next to him and the vines as thick as his wrist encompassing it. Carefully placing his fingers between some of the vines, he rested his blade against it, but before he could start cutting, Kaylia rested her hand on his arm.

"If you cut it from there, it will kill all the vine. We don't need that much of it, and it will go to waste as we'll never get it all out of the trees," she said. "We can't have that. It's too precious and rare to waste."

Brokk released the vine. "How else are we going to get it?"

Kaylia looked around before pointing to a tree outside the clearing. A single vine had crept high into the tree to encircle the end of a branch. "I'll climb up there."

Because the trees' thick canopy blocked the sun, the lower branches had all died off. The first thirty feet of the tree was nothing but a trunk so wide he couldn't wrap his arms around it, but he wasn't about to stand and watch while she scaled the tree.

"I'll do it," he said.

"I can climb a tree," she replied.

"I know, but I'll do it."

She looked about to protest but stopped herself and nodded instead. Her hand fell away from his arm as she stroked the vine he'd been about to cut.

"We finally have it," she murmured.

Not yet. But he intended to remedy that soon.

CHAPTER SEVENTY-SEVEN

BROKK SHEATHED his sword and walked over to the tree with the thin strand of vine stretching into it. Clasping the trunk, his hands barely curled around the edge of the curve, but it was enough for him to get a grip on the massive tree.

He braced his boots against the trunk and used his hands and feet to inch toward the end of the vine. While he worked, movement from below drew his attention as the others wandered into the clearing.

He paused to watch Kaylia tip her head back, hold her arms wide, and smile while closing her eyes. Her joy emanated from her as she basked in the life force surrounding her.

Is there anything as beautiful as her? He didn't have to think about it; he already knew the answer.

No.

Grinning like an idiot over her joy, he started making his way back up the tree, but Ryker's words stopped him. "Cut some down for us too. We need it for the ophidians."

Brokk glanced at where the man stood near the edge of the clearing, gazing at him. "I will," Brokk assured him.

He didn't look down again as he scooted further up the tree.

He only made it another five feet before a startled shout, followed by screams of agony, erupted from the clearing.

Brokk's head jerked around, and his fingers bit into the bark. His gaze latched onto Kaylia as she stood, gawking at the jungle with her hands at her sides now. She'd drifted further beneath the trees but remained close to him.

With his sword drawn, Ryker sprinted past her, but before he made it five feet, something erupted from the earth and shot up to ensnare him inside it. Dirt and debris rained down from the silver netting, incasing Ryker as the man's face twisted in agony, but no sound issued from him.

Already caught in nets, some of the others dangled from the trees. Some of those traps held three of four immortals, while others had only snagged one.

Brokk looked for strings to indicate where the nets were placed or reveal how they dangled from the trees but didn't see anything. Some kind of magic must have put them in the ground and now hung them from the trees.

Body parts littered the ground beneath some of the nets. Brokk didn't know what had caused this disfigurement, but blood stained the dirt and rained into the clearing as the maimed immortals moaned.

When anyone trapped inside the netting moved, cries followed, and though the nets swayed in the trees, those inside them didn't move. Only a handful of immortals remained free; Kaylia was one of them.

Whoever set these traps would soon arrive to claim their reward.

Brokk dropped his feet and eased his grip on the tree. Jagged pieces of bark dug into his flesh as he slid down the fifteen feet he'd ascended and hit the ground.

He gripped the handle of his sword and pulled it free before sprinting toward the clearing and Kaylia. Movement from the corner of his eye drew his attention as ophidians slithered into view.

Brokk's heart hammered as Allegra edged away from the monsters approaching them. She was the closest one to them, but she could set off another trap if she moved too far. All the ophidians held long silver poles before them like knights charging into a battle.

Torn between running and possibly setting off another trap, one of Ryker's men stood his ground as he held his sword before him. The first ophidian managed to avoid the man's lethal swing, but the second lost part of its tail when it swung at the man.

Black blood sprayed over the amsirah and splattered the clearing as the end of the creature's tail flopped across the ground. When more creatures encircled the man, he took out another one before the ophidian behind him jabbed him with the pole.

The amsirah's choked shout cut off as his body spasmed and blood poured from his mouth. Brokk suspected the man had bitten off his tongue before collapsing on the ground.

When more ophidians closed in on Allegra, she edged further away and closer to Kaylia. He couldn't hear what the witches said, but their hands moved as they cast a protective spell.

Before they could complete the spell, one of the ophidians jabbed a metal pole at Allegra, and she jumped backward. When she did, the earth exploded as another net shot into the air, except Allegra wasn't entirely inside when it snapped shut.

The force of the net's closing sliced the witch in two. Half of her went into the air, while the other half hit the ground with a thud. She landed only feet away from Kaylia.

Kaylia slapped her hands over her mouth, muffling her scream as blood splattered her and the remaining free amsirah. Brokk willed himself to be beside her.

The familiar sensation of air pushing back against him filtered across his skin until he broke through the barrier. In a single step, he teleported from his location to standing beside Kaylia in the blink of an eye.

He caught her arm when her surprise over his sudden arrival caused her to stagger away from him while the ophidians continued toward them. Moving across this ground wasn't a good idea considering the traps surrounding them, but neither was remaining there to be trapped by them, and he couldn't teleport with her.

He only made it three feet before the ground erupted, and dirt, sticks, and stones pelted them as a net broke free and ripped them off their feet. His arms cinched around Kaylia, and pain tore through his body.

The silver netting encasing them felt like it sliced through his flesh, carved into his muscles, and embedded itself in his bones, but when he looked down, he didn't see any blood. The small movement of trying to explore injuries that didn't exist caused more agony to explode through him as the net swayed.

A scream echoed in his head, but he clenched his teeth against it and kept Kaylia nestled securely against him. He didn't know what the silver netting was made of or bespelled with, but everywhere it touched, it felt like it flayed off his skin.

Breathing through his nose in a useless attempt to calm the feeling of multiple knives shredding his flesh, he concentrated on opening a portal, but nothing happened.

He didn't try to teleport as he wouldn't leave Kaylia alone, but Brokk doubted he could do that either. Whatever this net was, it not only hurt like a motherfucker, but it also stopped him from using his abilities.

"Shit. Can… you… use… yo… yo… your… powers?" The words came from between his gritted teeth.

Kaylia's hands waved before her as she murmured some words. "No."

When she lowered her hands, she touched the silver netting.

"Don't," he warned.

But he was already too late. She hissed in a breath, and her hand trembled as she cradled it against her belly. "Oh, Hecate, Brokk. That's… that's… brutal. Are you okay?"

Tears choked her tremulous voice, and she tried to move again but stopped when the net dug deeper into his flesh and he sucked in a breath.

"Brokk?"

"I'm… fine."

When she stilled against him, the net swayed back and forth above the clearing. Below, the sounds of the fight from those who had remained free dwindled.

The hush that followed sounded louder than any battle as they helplessly waited to see what horror awaited them next.

CHAPTER SEVENTY-EIGHT

KAYLIA TRIED NOT to move as the net swayed back and forth while the ophidians carried it deeper into the jungle. Every time she shifted, Brokk sucked in a breath and his body spasmed against hers.

Tears clogged her eyes at the reminder of his suffering while he kept her away from the net. Everyone else suffered because of the magic used to weave this trap, but she remained protected by Brokk's arms.

She'd only touched the net once but could still feel the brutal shock of it all the way to her toes. If it wouldn't harm Brokk, she'd lift her hand to ensure her flesh wasn't flayed from her fingertips, but she couldn't move, and no blood marred her clothes.

No, her skin was still there; it just felt like someone had stripped it from her. She couldn't imagine how Brokk felt as this vile shit encompassed him.

Whatever or whoever weaved these nets, they'd used a fierce spell to keep them bound inside and their power leashed. Brokk was suffering because of it.

Closing her eyes, she tried to suppress the emotion rising

330 BRENDA K DAVIES

inside her. It wasn't love she felt for this man, but it was something so close it was nearly as painful and beautiful as love.

Her fingers found Brokk's, and she rested them against her belly. He squeezed her hand before a fresh tremor wracked him.

She craved more from him than this brief connection, but it was all they could experience while trapped inside this horrible thing. She'd give anything to be nestled against him, somewhere safe, but feared they might never get that chance again.

Moving only her eyes, she tried to see the ophidian behind them but could only see the one ahead. After the ophidians lowered them from the trees, they'd placed a pole through the netting, and the one in front of them held it propped on his shoulder.

His dark brown hair flowed nearly to his waist as he held on to the pole with both hands. The muscles in his bare back glistened in the sun while his tail slithered beneath them on the ground.

Kaylia swallowed the lump of apprehension lodged in her throat while watching the reptilian man. There was a reason these things had kept them alive, and it couldn't be good.

She didn't ask for that reason; they wouldn't tell her. The creatures didn't speak while slithering forward with easy grace through the realm they ruled.

The jungle that had clung to and restricted their movements seemed to part for these monsters. Either that or the ones ahead of them were carving a much better path through the foliage than they ever did.

Her back and legs ached from her cramped position, but she didn't try to ease the stress on them. If she did, it would only hurt Brokk. This discomfort was nothing compared to what Brokk endured to protect her.

He hadn't wavered in his determination to keep her sheltered from the net, which only made her feelings for him grow. This powerful man contained the DNA of the two species she'd always disliked the most, yet somehow, in him, they'd made for one of the kindest, most protective, and unwavering men she'd ever encountered.

If she hadn't met Fabian first, she could have fallen head over heels for Brokk.

What she wouldn't give to kiss him, probably one last time, but she wouldn't hurt him to fulfill her selfish needs. Instead, she remained still while inwardly weeping for everything they might have had if life were different.

Her fingers tightened on his when through the dense foliage a towering, silver pyramid came into view. It loomed over them, but still wasn't tall enough to pierce through the numerous trees surrounding it.

Tucked into the shade beneath the trees, it was hidden from view from any dragons that might come searching for them.

The few beams of sun that glinted off the silver structure cast reflections.

Kaylia recoiled when one hit her in the eye, blinding her before she could lower her gaze. She squinted her eyes closed before blinking until she could see again.

When her vision finally cleared, they were almost to the shadowy doorway on the side of the structure. Her heart sank as she realized that once they entered the pyramid, there might not be an escape for them.

She squeezed Brokk's hand as she fought to suppress the waves of panic crashing over her. Taking deep breaths, she did her best to calm her crushing anxiety as she resisted beating and kicking the net.

The only thing she'd succeed in doing was hurting her and Brokk, but every part of her screamed against remaining still and not doing anything to help free them. She didn't know what she could do, though.

Her magic didn't work inside this net, and neither did

Brokk's abilities. Touching the thing had rendered her nearly useless; she didn't know how to combat that.

So, while it went against everything she was, she remained motionless while these hateful monsters carried them toward certain doom.

Before they were taken inside the pyramid, she tipped her head back and spotted the single eye at the top of the structure. Like the ophidians surrounding them, the eye's iris was yellow, and the pupil was elliptical in shape.

The eye gazed over the land before blinking and shifting down to them. Kaylia's gaze clashed with that awful eye before darkness enveloped them, and they entered the pyramid.

The creatures slithered downward as they traveled deeper into the pyramid and further below the ground. As they moved lower, the stone walls of the pyramid gave way to compressed dirt and rocks along the twisting passageway.

About every fifty feet, lanterns hung from the walls, and small fires danced behind the glass. Their dim glow was the only illumination in the increasingly cool tunnels.

While in the jungle, heat and humidity were a constant companion. Down here, goose bumps covered her skin as the damp air chilled the sweat still on her from the jungle. She resisted rubbing her arms to get some warmth into them.

Her mind raced as she tried to formulate a plan to get away. The fact they were so deep into the pyramid didn't bode well for them, but they could find a way out; she was certain of it.

When they came to a stop, there was a chance they could break free of the nets. They would then have a chance of escaping through a portal or fighting their way free.

The creatures hadn't stripped them of their weapons; there'd been no reason to when they were all held immobile by the vicious webbing surrounding them. That had been a mistake on the ophidians' part, and she'd make them regret it.

Finally, after what seemed like hours and hundreds of feet of earth, they stopped. From up ahead, scuffling and shuffling sounds pierced the shadows; soft clinks and then the resounding crash of metal slamming against metal followed them.

Kaylia's heart thundered as the noises from ahead continued, and after each clanging bang, they inched their way forward. A lump clogged her throat while she waited to see what fate awaited them.

Are they slaughtering them? Throwing them into dungeons? What is going on up there?

The questions screamed through her mind as nausea coiled in her stomach. She wouldn't throw up all over Brokk, but it took everything she had not to vomit as saliva filled her mouth.

She glanced at the thick walls as she tried to formulate some plan, but her only hope was the ophidians would make some mistake and they could flee this place. No one would hear them scream down here. No one would find them this far beneath the earth. They did something, or they died.

CHAPTER SEVENTY-NINE

Closing her eyes, she resisted giving in to her terror. It wouldn't do her any good to break down now.

The line inched forward until they were at the front. Soon, Kaylia would have the answers to all her questions as the ophidians carried them from the tunnel into a long, thin room with more lanterns hanging on the wall.

Kaylia gulped when she spotted the cages lining the wall ten feet away. Some were already full and closed, but others had their doors open in anticipation of new occupants.

Brokk's breath hissed in when the ophidians plopped the net outside two empty cells. Kaylia gasped and shuddered as the silver metal folded over her, seeming to slice through her body, though it didn't leave a mark.

She tried to cringe away from it, but there was no evading it now that the ophidians had closed the net over her. Growling, Brokk held her closer as he tried to shelter her from the links pressing against her flesh, but it was impossible.

The warmth and strength of his body warmed the ice seeping into her. She melded against him as she uselessly sought to escape this nightmare.

"It. Will. Be. Okay," he bit out through his teeth.

But they both knew it wouldn't.

The creatures that had carried their net bent to pull on thick metal gloves that ran up to their elbows. When the gloves were in place, they lifted their hands, and the light glinted off the metal before they bent and started working with the net.

Kaylia cringed as they pulled some of the net back, and hands reached for her. She tried to wriggle away from them, but there was nowhere to go.

Brokk released an inhuman sound, and despite the agony of the net all around them, he lashed out at a hand, knocking it aside. He grabbed the other hand and jerked the creature forward.

It hissed as its fangs flashed. Its eyes swung toward them a second before it fell on the net and started screaming.

The others rushed forward in a wave of hissing sounds that drowned out all other noise as Brokk seized the fallen ophidian by his throat and jerked him forward. Kaylia closed her mouth against the hot wash of blood pouring over her while Brokk tossed the ophidian's ruined throat aside.

Despite the excruciating pain it had to cause him, Brokk tore at the netting as she kicked out to push it aside. Contact with the mesh caused her teeth to slam together while screams echoed through her head.

Her movements were nowhere near as fast as they should be, but one foot broke free, and the cool air brushing over her leg was a welcome relief.

So close! So close!

For a moment, she believed they might break free of this place, but then the ophidians produced one of those long, silver sticks. Kaylia eyed the thing as she tore at the netting, trying to break free before they arrived with it.

Before she could succeed, the creatures slid the stick through the netting and pressed it against Brokk's side. Whereas he hadn't screamed before, a shout erupted from him as his arms convulsed around her, involuntarily ripping her away from freedom.

His body jerked on the ground, his heels kicked against the earth, and his teeth clattered together with every spasm wracking him. Terror for him burst through her and out of her mouth.

"No!" she screamed.

She kicked and thrashed as the netting pulled apart, and two ophidians seized her. When Brokk's arms remained locked around her, they pushed the stick into him again, but this time, they kept it there until he let go.

Pulled free of the netting, Kaylia shrieked as she swung at them. Her fingers hooked into claws, and she threw herself against the creature holding her while going for his eyes. She'd tear them from the creature's head and shove them down his throat for harming Brokk.

The creature screamed when her fingers gouged into his eyes, tearing into the sensitive organs. Before she ripped the orbs free, one of the snakes pressed the metal stick against her side.

It was like a bolt of lightning had hit her as her entire body bowed to the point where she believed her spine might snap. She clamped down on her tongue so hard blood filled her mouth and spilled from her lips; her fingers and toes twitched while her head jerked repeatedly to the side.

Their hands felt over her, tearing away her weapons. Dimly, over the clattering of her teeth, she heard the clink of metal against metal as they threw her weapons onto a growing pile of them.

Her eyes rolled in her head, making it impossible for her to focus on anything as they kept the stick against her side while carrying her over the earth. She tried to get her feet to work enough to kick them, but she had no control over them as they continued to spasm uselessly.

She didn't realize she was in one of the cages until her back hit the ground and the metal door clanged shut. Unable to move, her body twitched as she breathed in the dirt while the cool earth calmed her tortured nerves.

Unable to rise, she got her rolling eyes under control in time to see the creatures carrying Brokk into the cell next to her. They dumped him on the ground.

Her fingers and feet continued to twitch, and her head occasionally jerked to the side as the ophidians retreated before slamming his cell door shut. They were all still wearing those thick, metal gloves, and she suspected the silver bars surrounding them were either made of the same material as the netting or bespelled to keep them in here.

She didn't know how much time had passed while she lay there, unable to move as she listened to them stripping away more weapons and doors closing. Eventually, the snakelike creatures retreated with the nets and their sticks in hand.

Once they were gone, the only sound in the dungeon was the crackling flames from the torches lining the walls. No one else moved or spoke.

They were all too shocked and battered to express what she already knew… they were trapped here, and if the bars of these cages were anything like those nets, there was no way out.

From a few cells down, an amsirah bellowed and charged at the bars. He hit them with a bang and screeched as they flung him back. He hit the back wall with a sickening thud as his head crashed against it.

Kaylia suppressed a sob as everything went silent again. The bars weren't big enough for Brokk to stretch his hand through them, but she could slip hers through if she turned it sideways.

When she slid her hand into his cage, his fingers found hers and gripped them. She held tight to him.

He was her only saving grace and hope in a place of misery and death.

~

Read on for an excerpt from *Secrets of Ruin,* book 11 in the
series, or download now and continue reading:
brendakdavies.com/SRwb

Stay in touch on updates, sales, and new releases by joining
to the mailing list: brendakdavies.com/ESBKDNews

Visit the Erica Stevens/Brenda K. Davies Book Club on
Facebook for exclusive giveaways and all things book related.
Come join the fun: brendakdavies.com/ESBKDBookClub

SNEAK PEEK

SECRETS OF RUIN, THE SHADOW REALMS
BOOK 11

LIGHT DIDN'T OFTEN COME to the bowels of the pyramid; when it did, it never brought relief or joy. In this dark pit of misery, light meant the return of their captors and pain.

After their arrival, when the first torches lining the walls burnt out, they remained that way until the ophidians returned to relight them. And when they did that, it meant only one thing... they'd returned to have fun... or at least it was fun for *them*.

For the prisoners trapped in this endless loop of suffering, filth, and sorrow, it meant only agony.

Everything here brought hurt and discomfort from the captors who so loved to torture them to the hard, dirt floor that dug into Kaylia's increasingly protruding bones when she tried to sleep. The bucket in the corner, holding her waste, cast a foul smell, but this whole place consisted of awful smells that she'd somehow adjusted to, but it was adapt or go insane in this place.

They were in Hell, but instead of burning in that fiery place, a chill encompassed the damp air of the dungeon. It had crept into her bones until she was permanently cold, and the ophidians didn't provide blankets or warmer clothes to ease the ice inside her.

Kaylia had no idea how much time had passed since the ophidians confined them—time meant nothing here. It was endless but steady as it ebbed and flowed like the waves of the ocean she feared she'd never see again.

Without the sun or moon to mark the passing days, there was no way to track them, and she wouldn't even if she could. Why did she want to know how much of her life had been wasted here?

The only thing that gave her hope, and kept her sane, was holding Brokk's hand. Lying on her side and through the bars of their cell, she could stretch her hand far enough into his cage to clasp his.

Night after night, and day after day, she sought Brokk's solid presence in this Hell that reeked of waste, fear, sweat, and death. And *so much* death had occurred since their arrival; far too many of their group had perished in this pit.

More would soon follow; she did not doubt that as the ophidians enjoyed their demise. They loved their torment too, so they drew out their deaths, but it was only a matter of time before those monsters destroyed them all.

As time passed, Brokk became a shell of the man he used to be. The ophidians brought them shitty food and gave him blood, but it had been....

Well, she had no idea how long it had been since they were last together, and he'd nourished the dark fae part of himself. It could have been a month or a year.

Now, in the dim light of the glowing torches the ophidians left behind after their last visit, she studied Brokk as he lay, staring at her, his hand encasing hers. They were all weakening in this place, but the toll of their inadequate nourishment had been hardest on him.

Dirt marred his cheekbones, which were far more prominent than before he had entered this place. His once lively, aqua-blue eyes were duller, and their twinkle had vanished.

The ophidians sometimes brought in buckets of water and soap for them to wash, probably when they could no longer stand the smell of them, but it had been a while, and grime had turned his dark blond hair brown. A thick, brown beard obscured his handsome features and grew an inch or two past his chin.

Sometimes, the twinkle in his eyes would return when he looked at her, but not today. It hadn't been there since they watched the ophidians torture and kill another amsirah.

That man's death wasn't that long ago, as the torches remained lit. They'd soon go out and plunge them back into darkness. Until then, she planned to relish being able to see Brokk again.

Kaylia turned her hand over and lifted her wrist toward Brokk. He shook his head as his thumb traced the two puncture marks there. A matching set marked her other wrist.

Sometimes, he'd feed on her, but he never took enough. Her blood helped keep the vampire part of him nourished. However, the dark fae part of him was starving as, without sex, he grew weaker.

At first, dozens filled the dungeon cells; now, only a fraction of that number remained. Hopelessness swelled amongst the survivors; it permeated the air and came out in muffled sobs or terrified whimpers.

No one looked at those who broke down in tears; they all needed their moments in this place. So far, no one had completely cracked and slipped into madness, but Kaylia suspected it was only a matter of time… if any of them lived that long.

Eventually, the ophidians would destroy what remained of them. Until then, the hideous monsters would continue torturing them until their spirits broke.

To her right, Ryker shifted in his cell. His movement drew her attention from Brokk to the large man standing in the center of his small cell.

Before coming here, he'd been bulkier with thickly corded muscle on his arms and chest, but he'd shriveled in size. He hadn't lost as much as Brokk, but he was barely recognizable as the man he once was.

Fresh marks from a whip marred his chest and back, but though the ophidians had flayed him open, he hadn't made a sound. He'd stood there and took it as they tore away his skin.

Beneath the fresh marks lay faded white scars. Some of those scars had come from his time at war, but judging by the shape and size of them, Kaylia suspected many of his scars came from other beatings. Those beatings must have been brutal if he still bore their marks.

Ryker stared relentlessly ahead; his beard-covered jaw moved back and forth as he ground his teeth together. His hands fisted at his sides while he glowered at the locked door where the ophidians entered and exited.

He'd barely moved since the ophidians left after killing another amsirah. During their time here, his dark brown hair had grown past his shoulders, and his silver eyes shone with a hardness that wasn't present before his imprisonment.

Beyond him, more of Ryker's men remained in the other cells that stretched into the shadows until Kaylia couldn't see the ones at the end. Most of those cells used to be full, but not anymore.

Only two witches who'd helped the amsirah in Doomed Valley remained. The others had succumbed to the ophidian's endless torture. Kaylia shuddered as she recalled what it was like to suffer at the hands of those monsters.

~

SENSING HER DISTRESS, Brokk squeezed her hand. A smile curved his mouth when she shifted her attention back to him.

That smile didn't reach his eyes but did reveal the tips of his retracted fangs.

Despite his weight loss and the dirt and blood marring him, he was still gorgeous. Kaylia's heart beat faster, and her breath caught as she basked in his smile.

Before being tossed into this dungeon, her feelings for him had grown to the point where guilt and uncertainty over her emotions battered her daily. She'd pledged to spend the rest of her life with Fabian, a man taken from her by the senseless act of a vampire; she shouldn't be experiencing anything for another man… but she was.

To deal with Fabian's loss, she'd locked herself away in the crone realm as she tried to come to terms with losing the only man she'd ever loved. Free of that realm, and in Doomed Valley, she'd discovered a sexual reawakening with Brokk, but more than that, she'd developed feelings for him… something she'd believed impossible.

Immortals only ever loved once; it was just the way of things. They didn't give their hearts easily, but when they did, they never gave them again.

However, over their time in Doomed Valley and inside these bars, she couldn't deny that she'd come to care deeply for Brokk. If she ever got the chance to get free of this place and destroy these monsters, she'd gladly make the ophidians pay for what they'd done to Brokk.

Never had she enjoyed taking a life; she killed when it was necessary, but she would *relish* slaughtering these reptile pricks who'd stolen the twinkle from Brokk's and their freedom.

"Everything okay, beautiful?" Brokk inquired.

His voice was far raspier than before they entered here, but it still made her heart beat faster. A small shiver ran down her spine as her hand tightened on his.

She doubted she looked beautiful right now, but when he said it, she *felt* it and believed he meant it. No matter how she looked, he found her beautiful.

"Just another day in paradise," she whispered.

He smiled as he adjusted his hand to stroke his thumb across her palm. The bars were so close together that he couldn't fit his hand through them, but she could get hers through without touching the ensorcelled metal.

If they accidentally touched the bars, the metal created intense pain that could shoot an immortal across a cell. She'd made the mistake of touching one once; she wouldn't make it again.

"What's your idea of paradise?" Brokk asked.

They'd spent countless hours discussing different things, asking each other random questions, and learning more about one another. They often lay silently, just holding each other, but she enjoyed learning random facts about him.

"I'm not sure," she answered.

At one time, her answer would have been easy. Paradise was anywhere with Fabian.

However, that answer didn't come to her now. And neither did the guilt that once accompanied the realization that her dead fiancé, the man she'd loved more than any other, was slowly becoming less of a once-in-a-lifetime love to her.

She should have remained in love with Fabian and loyal to him until the end of her days, but Brokk changed that. She still loved Fabian and always would, but he'd ceased being her idea of paradise.

Someone else was steadily replacing him as that man. Guilt momentarily flared and faded when she met Brokk's eyes again.

"Anywhere outside of here and..." her words trailed off as they lodged in her throat.

His thumb stroked hers before he kissed the tips of her fingers. "And?"

"Somewhere warm, but *not* humid."

He chuckled as his smile widened. After their time in Doomed Valley, neither wanted to experience the oppressive humidity of the jungle again.

"Somewhere with friends who have become family." Her fingers tightened on his while speaking; her words came out more broken as a sob lodged in her throat. "Somewhere... outside of... here."

He rested his forehead against her palm. She shouldn't say it, but he deserved to know how much he meant to her; they might never leave this place, and she couldn't hold the words back.

"Somewhere with *you*."

Brokk lifted his head, and when their gazes locked, the steely gleam in his eyes shook her. *Did I say something wrong?*

"I'm going to get you out of here," he growled. "I don't know how I'll do it, but I promise you will *not* die here, Kaylia.

Kaylia closed her eyes. "You can't die here either."

Her heart couldn't take the loss of another man she loved.

"I won't let these fuckers kill me," he said.

And she believed him. She didn't know how they'd escape this place when they'd failed to do so already, and it seemed impossible, but he'd find a way.

"What's your idea of paradise?" she asked.

"Being back in Dragonia with my family, friends, and *you*. It sounds so simple, but it's all I want."

"It's all I want too. I wonder if my familiar will finally find me when we return."

"I've never seen your familiar."

"Her name is Ursula; she was a white cat in her last incarnation. She passed before you and Sahira found me in the crone realm. I've been waiting for her to return, but she hasn't yet... or maybe she has, and I've been trapped here."

"Could she find you here?"

"Maybe, but I doubt it. Our familiars are attracted to our energy; it's how they find us throughout their different incarnations. I doubt I'm giving off much energy this far below the earth." And this emaciated, but she kept that to herself; it would only upset him.

"You'll find her again."

"I know."

Before they could say anything more, the scrape of a key turning in a lock alerted them that the ophidians had returned. Things were about to get a *lot* worse.

∾

Download *Secrets of Ruin* and continue reading:
brendakdavies.com/SRwb

∾

Stay in touch on updates, sales, and new releases by joining
to the mailing list: brendakdavies.com/ESBKDNews

Visit the Erica Stevens/Brenda K. Davies Book Club on
Facebook for exclusive giveaways and all things book related.
Come join the fun: brendakdavies.com/ESBKDBookClub

FIND THE AUTHOR

Brenda K. Davies Mailing List:
brendakdavies.com/News

Facebook: brendakdavies.com/BKDfb

Brenda K. Davies Book Club:
brendakdavies.com/BKDBooks

Instagram: brendakdavies.com/BKDInsta
Twitter: brendakdavies.com/BKDTweet
Website: www.brendakdavies.com

ALSO FROM THE AUTHOR

Books written under the pen name
Brenda K. Davies

The Vampire Awakenings Series

Awakened (Book 1)

Destined (Book 2)

Untamed (Book 3)

Enraptured (Book 4)

Undone (Book 5)

Fractured (Book 6)

Ravaged (Book 7)

Consumed (Book 8)

Unforeseen (Book 9)

Forsaken (Book 10)

Relentless (Book 11)

Legacy (Book 12)

The Alliance Series

Eternally Bound (Book 1)

Bound by Vengeance (Book 2)

Bound by Darkness (Book 3)

Bound by Passion (Book 4)

Bound by Torment (Book 5)

Bound by Danger (Book 6)

Bound by Deception (Book 7)

Bound by Fate (Book 8)

Bound by Blood (Book 9)

Bound by Love (Book 10)

The Road to Hell Series

Good Intentions (Book 1)

Carved (Book 2)

The Road (Book 3)

Into Hell (Book 4)

Hell on Earth (Book 5)

Into the Abyss (Book 6)

Kiss of Death (Book 7)

Edge of the Darkness (Book 8)

The Shadow Realms

Shadows of Fire (Book 1)

Shadows of Discovery (Book 2)

Shadows of Betrayal (Book 3)

Shadows of Fury (Book 4)

Shadows of Destiny (Book 5)

Shadows of Light (Book 6)

Wicked Curses (Book 7)

Sinful Curses (Book 8)

Gilded Curses (Book 9)

Whispers of Ruin (Book 10)

Secrets of Ruin (Book 11)

Tempest of Shadows

A Tempest of Shadows (Book 1)

A Tempest of Thieves (Book 2)

A Tempest of Revelations (Book 3)

A Tempest of Intrigue (Book 4)

A Tempest of Chaos (Book 5)

Historical Romance

A Stolen Heart

Books written under the pen name
Erica Stevens

The Coven Series

Nightmares (Book 1)

The Maze (Book 2)

Dream Walker (Book 3)

The Captive Series

Captured (Book 1)

Renegade (Book 2)

Refugee (Book 3)

Salvation (Book 4)

Redemption (Book 5)

Vengeance (Book 6)

Unbound (Book 7)

Broken (Book 8 - Prequel)

The Kindred Series

Kindred (Book 1)

Ashes (Book 2)

Kindled (Book 3)

Inferno (Book 4)

Phoenix Rising (Book 5)

The Fire & Ice Series

Frost Burn (Book 1)

Arctic Fire (Book 2)

Scorched Ice (Book 3)

The Ravening Series

The Ravening (Book 1)

Taken Over (Book 2)

Reclamation (Book 3)

The Survivor Chronicles

The Upheaval (Book 1)

The Divide (Book 2)

The Forsaken (Book 3)

The Risen (Book 4)

ABOUT THE AUTHOR

Brenda K. Davies is the USA Today Bestselling author of the Vampire Awakening Series, Alliance Series, Road to Hell Series, Hell on Earth Series, The Shadow Realms Series, A Tempest of Shadows Series, and historical romantic fiction. She also writes under the pen name, Erica Stevens. When not out with friends and family, she can be found at home with her husband, son, and pets.

9 798873 358151